SCAFFOLDING

SCAFFOLDING

A NOVEL

Lauren Elkin

Farrar, Straus and Giroux
New York

Farrar, Straus and Giroux
120 Broadway, New York 10271

Copyright © 2024 by Lauren Elkin
All rights reserved
Printed in the United States of America
Originally published in 2024 by Chatto & Windus, Great Britain
Published in the United States by Farrar, Straus and Giroux
First American edition, 2024

All emojis designed by OpenMoji—the open-source emoji and icon project.
License: CC BY-SA 4.0.

Library of Congress Cataloging-in-Publication Data
Names: Elkin, Lauren, author.
Title: Scaffolding / Lauren Elkin.
Description: First American edition. | New York : Farrar, Straus and
   Giroux, 2024.
Identifiers: LCCN 2024008318 | ISBN 9780374615291 (hardcover)
Subjects: LCSH: Paris (France)—Fiction. | LCGFT: Novels.
Classification: LCC PS3605.L3975 S33 2024 | DDC 813/.6—dc23/
   eng/20240304
LC record available at https://lccn.loc.gov/2024008318

Our books may be purchased in bulk for promotional, educational, or business
use. Please contact your local bookseller or the Macmillan Corporate and
Premium Sales Department at 1-800-221-7945, extension 5442, or by email at
MacmillanSpecialMarkets@macmillan.com.

www.fsgbooks.com
Follow us on social media at @fsgbooks

1   3   5   7   9   10   8   6   4   2

For B. H.

אני לדודי ודודי לי

When the previous occupant has left, others will take his place, moving around the furniture, getting rid of a fireplace, the one with the mantelpiece that supported the pendulum, the shells, the knick-knacks, or changing the purpose of the room by adding a partition. They will repaint, change the wallpaper.

   – Michelle Perrot, *The Bedroom*

The other must remain absolutely strange within the greatest possible proximity.

   – Hélène Cixous, 'Extreme Fidelity'

With time things emerge!

   – Jacques Lacan, transcription of *Seminar XX*

I

Listen. Someone is playing the piano.

What does it bring back?

A hectic street, rising uphill.
A green door in a stone building.
A place where you used to live.
A place you've never seen before.

The day I met Clémentine was the day after she moved in. She was standing outside the bottle-green door to our building, punching different combinations into the keypad protecting the entryway. Bulging plastic bags dangled from the crooks of her elbows. I was dripping with sweat from my morning run: the August heat was intense.

21B12, I say twice before she hears me.

The door clicks open. I was afraid I'd have to wait for hours out here for someone to come out! Clémentine says, with a nervous laugh. She is tall, but somehow delicate. Small nose. Blonde hair.

The gardienne would have let you in, if you had buzzed her, I say. Madame Vasquez, she lives right there. I gesture at the concierge's home on the ground floor. In case it happens again.

Oh, I thought I might remember it sooner or later. I have a funny memory like that. Things disappear until I happen to bump up against the right drawer in my brain and then it pops open and – there it is! The thing I was looking for.

Clémentine had just moved in with her boyfriend Jonathan, she tells me, as we stand in front of the mailboxes. They live in building B. My husband and I live in building A. We speak for a few moments about moving, and movers, learn each other's names. I look at my watch. I'm sorry, but I have an appointment soon, and I have to jump in the shower. Why don't you come over for tea sometime this week?

Clémentine comes on Thursday afternoon. What a lovely home, she says, and goes straight to look out the window. From our spot up on the hill we have an unobstructed view south, to the hodgepodge of Paris, rounded slate rooftops in jigsaw formations as far as you can see, with modern housing estates immediately below, the middle finger of the Tour Montparnasse in the distance, and the pastry-like dome of the Panthéon to the left.

Thanks, I say. We just redid this room.

The enormous windows take up most of two walls, one side overlooking a calm side street, the other the rue de Belleville. David had restored them by hand, ripping down the layers and layers of old wallpaper and paint which had accrued over the years, repainting their frames, keeping the original single-paned glass. It's noisy, but we don't like the look of the new double-glazed windows with their PVC frames. We fetishise, of course, originality. The builders are scheduled to start at the rentrée: the kitchen is up next, then, at some hazy future point when we have a bit more cash, the bathroom.

Outside the building as well, the work is about to begin. Every ten years or so, Parisian buildings must be refaced, and it is our bad luck to have caught the ravalement so soon after moving in. It is going to be expensive and immensely disruptive. We voted against it at the owners' meeting but you can't outrun it forever; into every Parisian life a little refacing must fall, expensive and inconvenient.

With the travaux inside and out, I say, it feels as though our actual inhabiting of this space keeps being deferred. When will we really start *living* here?

Our apartment is still a complete mess, Clémentine says. It's nice to get out for a bit, and not to have those boxes staring me down, waiting to be unpacked. She takes in the neat predictability of our living room. It isn't very big – that morning I had done some yoga by the window and knocked over a vase on a table with my foot – but it's cosy and I am house-proud. Chevroned hardwood floors, solid square coffee table bordered by an L-shaped sofa, in a corner by the window the elliptical poise of a Saarinen tulip table (where once there had stood a vase). A nubby throw sprawled across the sofa from my morning nap. A red lacquered table behind the sofa, and on it a mid-century ceramic lamp, red-banded, East German. David's plants, some delicate and tendrilly, others wild and aggressive, in varying states of thirst, since I am the only one watering them, and I often forget. Here and there, the things we've acquired from our trips – David loves to travel – artfully arranged on bookshelves, a little red London bus the latest addition. The shells I can't resist picking up on beaches, stones from random places, their location carefully inscribed on them with a fine-tipped black pen. The ink has smudged over the years; I know some of them are from Vermont while others are from Brittany, but they look the same to me. There are some paintings on the floor I haven't yet been able to hang; they face the wall.

I like your lamp, she says.

Oh thanks. We've been planning to go back to the flea market where we got it and buy a set of beat-up art deco mirrors we saw there, but we never get the chance. When David comes to visit, we don't want to waste what little time we have on shopping. Someone else has probably bought them.

They probably have, she agrees.

Do you ever think about the people who moved into the

apartments you didn't? she asks. Like if you'd taken the place, they'd be living somewhere else. Your decision has had an immediate impact on the lives of total strangers.

Or the people who move in after you move out, I say, thinking of our last apartment, and the couple who'd come to visit who'd ended up taking it, the woman heavily pregnant. Where would they be living if we hadn't decided to move out at just that moment? Sometimes I pass by their windows, further down the hill, and think about them, and their baby, who must be almost a year old now. It feels a bit like they're living our lives for us, and we are living someone else's still.

We sit in the sunniest part of the living room, the windows open to the balcony, a breeze, finally, after all that hot air. She immediately seems at home in my home, perched on the arm of my sofa. We drink tea and smoke her pack of Lucky Strikes. As she holds the cigarette to her lips, I notice the tattoos on her right hand, long elegant arrows, with double chevrons. I look reflexively to her left hand. On the ring finger there is a tiny double-headed arrow. She catches me looking, and I look away. The groan of a garbage truck sends its exhaust up to the fifth floor, which mingles with the smoke.

The air quality is so bad these days, isn't it? I say as I get up to shut the window. David's mother sends me articles about it once a week, trying to convince us to move out to the country, where they have a house; it would be easier on me once we have a baby, they say, they can help with the babysitting . . .

You know, the pollution is so bad lately that if you walk half an hour in the city it's the equivalent of smoking a pack of cigarettes, Clémentine says.

Is that true?

Yes! Do you use face pads to clean your face at night? Haven't you ever noticed how black they are?

Yes, I guess, but I thought it was just dirt or oil.

Where do you think it comes from! And the buildings too, you see it on the buildings. No sooner are they refaced but they're dirty again. Anyway I figure if the air is slowly killing me, I may as well smoke as much as I want.

I inhale deeply. The tobacco is heavy in my bloodstream, and calming.

What does your husband do? Clémentine asks.

He's a lawyer. He's working on a project in London right now. Something to do with Brexit, I don't really know.

London's not far, she says.

Two hours on the Eurostar.

So I guess you're going a lot.

No, I haven't been yet. I don't really like London.

She picks up our wedding album from the coffee table, carefully turning the onionskin front pages. I once knew a David. Back in high school. How did you two meet? Sorry, am I asking too many questions?

It's all right, I say. We met through friends. A jackhammer in the road downstairs drowns out my voice, and we both make gestures that say it's too loud to talk, and I stub out my cigarette, and we sip our tea.

My boyfriend works late these days, Clémentine says. But I guess I should be glad he's in Paris, at least.

What does he do?

He's a lawyer too. They've just given him a pretty big case, so he's working a lot more than usual, trying to stay ahead of it. I hate it! she says, with a nervous laugh. I wish he could stay home with me all day, and we could go and watch old movies in those run-down cinemas near the Sorbonne, and make lunch together, or just, I don't know, stay in bed all day long . . . My father used to work all the time. My mother too. I guess I'm used to it. But I still hate it.

What do your parents do?

University professors. Philosophy and math.

She tells me she grew up in the 5th, in a large apartment on the rue Claude Bernard. That would explain her messy student look, as if she'd spent her teenage years handing out fliers for Amnesty International and marching in protests. The thick cotton scarf, intricately woven around her neck, in spite of the heat; the oversized V-neck sweater; the army trousers; the scuffed Chuck Taylors which seem, at one point, to have been off-white. A lacy camisole is visible under her sweater where it looks like it's about to slip off her shoulder.

My dad's a teacher too. Lycée. He's American.

Oh really? What does he teach, English?

Biology. He wanted to be a doctor but didn't have the test scores for it. He met my mom when she was an exchange student in high school and they decided to move to France together. He went to university here.

Clémentine seems to be thinking of something else. She lights another cigarette, gets up, goes to my bookshelves. She scans them as if looking for something familiar. A finger across the spines of the collected works of Freud. You have a lot of stuff about psychoanalysis, she says.

I'm a psychoanalyst, I say.

Another one! she says. It seems like half the people in Paris are shrinks. The other half are in therapy, she jokes. I thought about studying psychology, was it very difficult? It seemed very difficult. Too much science. I guess your father helped you. She takes down a volume of Lacan, opens it, makes as if to close it, then looks at it more closely. *Seminar Sixteen, D'un Autre à l'autre.* From an Other to the other. Homophobe, she says, and puts it back on the shelf.

He was the one who got me really interested in science, though honestly I didn't have to do much of it after my undergraduate degree. He would take me on nature walks to this pond near our house, and tell me all about ecosystems, how delicate the balance is in any natural environment – if there is any disturbance, the whole structure is affected. Like, for example we had this dog once, and when he was a puppy he liked to go and trap the frogs who lived there – really, we should have kept him away, but it was so funny to see the dog with the frogs jumping around under his nose! As the dog got older, he started actually killing them. And with all the frogs disappearing there were too many fish in the pond and not enough food for them all, and they started going belly-up by fall. My dad had to go in and skim them out.

Wasn't he disturbing the ecosystem too, in a way? Why didn't he just let the fish decompose? She pulls out another book, Janet Malcolm's *Psychoanalysis: The Impossible Profession*, and sits down with it.

I think it was to prevent further disruptions. I don't really remember.

It makes me think of this art piece I saw a while back, at Documenta, in Germany? I shrug. It's an art show, happens every five years. My parents started taking me to it when I was a kid. Anyway the one I'm thinking of was when they had Pierre Huyghe, he's a French artist? Anyway he made this woodland, it was very beautiful, it was like a rarefied garden like the Jardin des Plantes and a compost heap all at once, and you had to walk through it looking for a dog with a pink leg that lived there or something, I don't know whose dog it was but it was all very Surrealist. But like if the Surrealists gave a shit about the environment. There was a sculpture of a woman reclining, and her head was made of a beehive.

Oh, that guy. I think I saw his bees at Beaubourg.

Yes they were there soon after Documenta. Anyway it was very much about the tension between the natural world and the man-made one – like the dog with the painted leg, I think the artist was trying to say that we can't help leaving an imprint on the world – the Anthropocene and all that – but we have to make our interventions beautiful and surprising rather than destructive.

You know so much about art, I say. I know hardly anything!

Oh, I'm studying art history, Clémentine says, the book open against her chest. I just finished my masters. Can't decide if I should keep going with a doctorate, or stop, or what. I'm taking some time off to make up my mind.

This surprises me. She has a way about her that suggests experience, confidence won by doing. How could she still be a student? Where does this confidence come from? Is it innate? Is it money? How old *are* you? I ask, trying not to sound rude.

Twenty-four, she says, and smiles. I know, people always say I look older than I am. I have a feeling I'm going to get tired of it soon.

Oh no, I say. I didn't mean.

Maybe I want to be a curator, she goes on, or just . . . do something else entirely.

I try to take in the novelty of someone not knowing what they're going to be when they grow up. So – how do you spend your days?

They're pretty open, Clémentine says. It's nice to have a bit of free time. I mean I do a lot of volunteering with some local women, some organising, some protesting. But in terms of a career, I don't know . . . I write poetry, and I take some pictures, but I don't commit myself to anything. Oh and there's the modelling. That brings in a bit. I nod as if I know all about the extra money from modelling.

As we talk I learn all kinds of things about Clémentine, from the name of the first boy she slept with (Thibault) to the name of the first girl (Céline). She's mostly dated girls, she tells me. She says she identifies as queer, she says the word in English. But she doesn't know if she really likes girls or if she desires them because all the pornography is from heterosexual male perspectives so she's been taught to desire women. What would our sexuality look like without the male gaze, she asks. I learn that when she was little she wanted to be a puppeteer on *Les Guignols*. We discover a shared interest in yoga, tarot, astrology. (Her: Pisces; me: Scorpio.) I tell her how I speak English with my dad, how I grew up spending summers in Vermont with my American grandparents, how my parents raised me with a sense of being Franco-American, how when we spent vacations with our family on the coast of Brittany and I complained about the smell of the seaweed drying on the beach my French cousins made fun of me, called me the dumb American, and how I had gone to university in the States (Bennington, to be close to my grandparents) to explore that side of my identity, leaving me feeling like even more of a hybrid than I had felt as a child. I do not talk about my miscarriage, or the fact that I have been put on medical leave from work. I watch as she lights the last cigarette in her pack, the sun fading in the sky behind her, turning the walls of the buildings across the way their early-evening shades of pink, orange and, finally, deep blue. The dregs of the tea have long since gone cold in the bottom of the pot. I offer Clémentine some wine, but she says she doesn't drink. I have to go, she says, we're going to try that Laotian restaurant. Will you be OK?

Me? Of course. I have some reading I should do.

There's some good stuff on tonight, she says, what's it called, *The Grass is Always Greener*? We discuss the comforting unreality of reality television as I walk her to the door. She makes to leave, then remembers Janet Malcolm, still on the table. Can I borrow this? she asks. Of course, I say, I trust you to return it. Oh I will, she promises. I'll read it right away.

As I close the door behind her I lean against it for a while, listening to the sound of my new friend's sneakers padding down the wooden steps. When the sound fades, I go into the narrow kitchen to pour myself a glass of wine. Refill the Brita while I'm at it. I look around the stale, dim room. There's so much to be done in here, it's a minefield of other people's choices, I feel like I'm fighting with the past. It has to be entirely stripped and rebuilt – starting with the wallpaper in rotting shades of orange and brown. Here and there it peels away from the wall. Then the brown tiles over the stove with the owls on them. Owls, for god's sake! Hit them with a hammer, crack them into pieces, scrape off the mortar. Replace with metro tiles, bevelled white, pristine for now, yet to meet the splashes of oil and sauce. Install butcher's-block countertop, never to run with the blood of animals; we are vegetarians and our children will be too. Then there are the cabinets, on which we are forever hitting our heads when they're open. Tear them out (how joyful that day will be). Honest exposed shelving running along the walls. Nothing to hide. Here are our glasses. Here are our plates. David's mother made little sceptical noises when we mentioned the open shelving. That's how dust accumulates in your glasses, she said, you'll be rinsing them out all the time. Not if we use them regularly, we answered, and we had every intention of doing so, but now it's just me, and I use the same two drinking glasses and the same two wine glasses, one's in service and the other's in the sink. The rest of our glasses are safe in the Formica cupboards that were there when we bought the place and by the time we have our open shelving I hope, I hope, David will be back.

I often think of the woman who lived there before us. She died, right there in the apartment. Which room, I didn't ask. Pulmonary embolism. She was also a psychoanalyst, her son told us, when he sold us the place. Lacanian, he said, at the closing. She did her training analysis with him, he said, with a hint of pride. Ah, I said, so did my training analyst. Quite a lineage.

Yes, he said. She had taught at Yale for many years, I recognised her name when he told me what it was, she was a fairly well-known French feminist theorist in American academia, she had brought the great man – the maestro, the son called him – to the US for a lecture tour, had in some way contributed to his being taken up there as he had. She had retired home to France not long ago, and then—

What was the son called again, I try to remember. Isaac something, a different surname to his mother, something unpronounceable. He had such a strange air about him. Bereft, but as if he had been that way for a long time. He had been so relieved to sell the place; we had been so relieved to buy it. As for the apartment itself, it had a weird feeling of gratitude, like a dog who has finally been adopted by owners it has a good feeling about.

But there's something else too, some presence. Maybe hers. At least that's how it feels as long as the owls are still hanging out in our kitchen. She's a kindly spirit, I think, but she has to go. There are too many people living in our apartment.

I pick up the wedding album from the place on the couch where Clémentine left it, and leaf through it, pausing over the obligatory photo of us kissing while our friends and family cheer us on. David, dark-haired in his light-grey suit; me standing on tip-toes in my red high heels. Our courtship was brief but intense, and after six months or so, we married at the town hall, with a small reception at a château we rented outside of the city, where the symmetrical gardens could be glimpsed from the salon through the glass windows, the kind that with age begin to look as if they're melting, or who knows, maybe they looked like that three hundred years ago when they were installed. The weather that day was cool but bright, and my mother had grasped David to her side with pride. My handsome son! Look at my handsome son, she said to her guests. The album had been a present from her, for our first anniversary.

And then a couple of years after that we had moved into this apartment on the rue de Belleville, high up the hill, past l'Égyptien, as everyone in the neighbourhood calls the guy who runs the spice shop, past the Chinese greengrocer, past the Algerian locksmith who knows all the local gossip, past the bookshop and the organic supermarket, the posh wine bar and the posh cocktail bar, high enough on the hill to see all the nearby rooftops and beyond. It's the Parisian apartment I had always dreamed of living in. I pictured it when I was a little girl, when my mother brought me to Paris once a year to see the Christmas windows at the Galeries Lafayette, and then for hot chocolate at Angelina's, where I would try very hard not to get the thick, pudding-like treat on whatever pristine outfit my mother had picked out for the day. I pictured it when I was at university in snowy New England, studying late into the night. And I pictured it when I was living on the other side of the river, in a tiny maid's room that looked directly into the tiny maid's room across the street.

It's not large, just under seventy square metres, but it's bigger than any place I've ever lived as an adult. Our previous flat was fifty at the most. That one, the one we yielded to the couple and the baby, was downhill a little bit, a tiny two-bedroom with a laminate floor, and all the original features taken out. The new apartment has all the indispensable Haussmannian details: a fire-place in each room, over which hang oversized gilded mirrors covered in age spots; white-on-white mouldings, ornate wrought-iron window grilles; a balcony running along the windows in the living room; original parquet floor. When we bought the place I saw myself growing flowers in window boxes and herbs in the kitchen, throwing dinner parties for friends and lighting candles in the fireplace, and sitting up nights collaborating on bottles of wine and planning our future. Not my future or our respective futures but *our* future, as if we only had one between us, our *we* a flotation device with which to survive whatever rough waters we might encounter. All of that had yet to begin. I have my office in a tiny room that had once been an independent studio or a maid's room – it has its own entrance from the landing – but at some point it was integrated into our apartment. It was going to be the baby's room, and I was going to look for a small studio to rent in which to receive patients, but then the baby didn't come.

It's a small room, with calming light-blue floral wallpaper. Chintz, I guess they call it. I had positioned my chair and the patients' couch so that they both angled toward the window, facing out over the rooftops, in the hope that my patients would find the view as therapeutic as I do. There is a primary school nearby, and every day at four thirty the hyperactive voices of childhood drift up from five flights down, the shrieks and stamping of feet running on the sidewalk pinballing up the side of the buildings. At such moments I stop what I'm doing and look up from my desk to the window, to where the rooftops of the buildings across the street align, impeccably uniform in their slate armature, their sloping curves, their chimney pots, their only variation the peeling of the paint or the stain of a graffiti tag. And beyond, Paris. Looking at Paris, I lose track of time. What day is it? What year is it? But then there was always a knock on the door, and a client to let in, and I could give myself over to their problems. Now I take refuge from my own in the view from the window.

The daily normalcy of marriage only lasted so long before slivers of the past resurfaced, like razor blades washing up on the banks of a once placid, now polluted river. In the years before David, I wasn't sure what was wrong. Why I seemed built to be unhappy. I had no real reason to be, no particular trauma, nothing like what I see in my part-time work at the childhood and adolescent unit at Sainte-Anne. Maybe that's part of why I wanted to study psychoanalysis, to try to understand sadness. When I started my training, I had to begin a course of psychoanalysis, where I worked through all my relationships, assessing how each one had formed or wounded me. My mother. My father. My boyfriends. All the encounters and conversations and feelings that combine and recombine, producing the variations you find within a psyche, bumps and ridges and valleys. But there was nothing serious or tricky in any of it. My past was formed of an entirely ordinary topography of discontent, disappointment, the standard feelings of insufficiency and fears of abandonment. In the beginning, I went three times a week, and over time, as my studies advanced, I stopped. I became a therapist myself, a listener. My patients had all kinds of things happen to them, from the banal to the unthinkable. Problems at work or divorce, bereavements sustained recently or long ago. One little girl I saw at Sainte-Anne had lost her mother at the Bataclan. Some I helped process; some I helped make connections or just manage to talk through a narrative of what was happening. I saw it as my job to piece things together, and to shine a light on repetitions, preoccupations, slips of memory.

So that was my life – working on myself, working on my patients, my apartment. Until we lost the baby and everything stopped except the therapy, which intensified. I went to see Esther, my old psychoanalyst, for what they call a control – a kind of checking-in that is also a cleansing, a means of verifying that the therapist has not completely lost her shit and can go on seeing patients. But it was clear to Esther that everything was far from under control. She extended my medical leave, I stopped being a therapist, and once again became a patient. I've been going four times a week, dutiful.

Esther told me to keep a journal, to write every morning. She told me to think about things like *subjectivity* and *objectivity*. But mostly she doesn't say very much. Is the remodelling perhaps an attempt to try to control something ultimately uncontrollable? I asked her one morning. She didn't answer. It's good that I'm throwing myself into a project, I said, as I looked out the ground-floor window at the doorway of the building across the street, missing my own view of Paris. But I feel like I need to get clear on the reasons why I'm so single-minded about it. I looked back at her soft-blonde highlights that did not, nor were they meant to, cover her grey, the camel cashmere cardigan around her thin shoulders, the skin gone soft and relaxed above her décolleté, like a piece of silk someone had crumpled up into a ball and then spread back out again. When I first started seeing her I was so eager to please, to show what a good therapist I could be by being a good analysand. There was no terrain too painful to charge into barefoot. I went everywhere. Over time it started to feel a bit – mechanical.

Still, I tried; I pressed my ear against the wall of my unconscious, listening hard for an echo of what was happening on the other side. Another morning I tried to figure out how I felt about David working in a different city. He hadn't wanted to go; I told him to. I'm a little afraid of losing him, I said. I didn't know if it was true, but it sounded plausible, so maybe it was, what do I know. I don't think he would ever leave me, I would have to, I would have to – I tried to think of something that might push David away, but couldn't. Even if I were unfaithful, or something like that, I don't believe he would leave me. She waited. But I'm afraid he'll stop loving me the way he did before we lost the baby. I want to make him happy, and I don't know if he is. He's not, I mean. We're not. I don't know. And you hear about this kind of thing driving couples apart, like they can't deal with their unhappiness if they're constantly faced with the other's uncontainable sadness. Is it possible that I'm leaving him somehow, by sending him to London? I asked. So he doesn't have to face my feelings? But it's not like something truly bad happened to us. We lost a pregnancy. I don't know how upset I'm allowed to be, what's appropriate.

What *is* appropriate? she'd replied, inscrutable as ever, a mirror, an echo.

But when I wake up alone every morning, when I climb into bed by myself; when I prepare dinner for one and eat in front of my laptop, binge-watching whatever Netflix series is getting me through the week, I know that all I want is for us to get back to normal. To go to Fontainebleau Forest on a Sunday and stay too long and then try to find the car in the dark. To drop in on my parents for dinner and take the TGV home the next day. To have David's brother over to watch the football. To complain about whatever irritating thing David's doing now and withdraw to my office.

I wish there were still something to withdraw from.

I've been running every morning, despite the heat. Over to the Buttes-Chaumont, once around the park, and back home. It takes about an hour. It's one of the vaguest hours of my day and I like it. I'm my body and that's all.   That's all.   That's all.

A strange thing happened the first time I went out. I left before breakfast, and forgot to take my wallet. On my way home, forgetting that I had forgotten my wallet, I stopped at the bakery to pick something up. I was taking out my headphones, lost, still, in the music. I stepped forward at my turn and asked the owner for what I wanted, and went to pay for it, and had nothing to give. I was already saying, oh don't worry about it, when the man queuing behind me said, if you please, I will pay for the young lady's bread.

I turned to look at him. He seemed trustworthy enough. Tall, with clipped grey hair. Thick black glasses. Handsome in that well-looked-after older male way, skin perfectly moisturised. He didn't smile, but he didn't not smile. I tried to refuse but he insisted. Mais je vous en prie, madame. I walked a little ways down the hill, made sure he wasn't following me, and ravenously tore off the top bit of the baguette to eat as I went, as if my hunger were something to hide from him.

What does it mean when an older man pays for your bread? It was a gesture at once chivalrous and unnecessary, and it made me a little uncomfortable. But it established some kind of rapport between us, and now, whenever we run into each other, we exchange niceties, and he always buys my bread, no matter how much I protest. He doesn't want to talk, he doesn't want to get to know me; on the contrary, he behaves as if he already does. One of these days I think I'll go and give the owner some money and say: this is for my next ten baguettes, and his as well.

But money is getting tight, so I don't.

Because I'm always in my workout clothing when we have our run-ins, he often commends me on my devotion to health. Some days he just nods and says to me bonne continuation, as if every day were a new repetition in a lifelong exercise session. As indeed it is: I have been jogging, or going to the gym, or doing step aerobics or hot yoga or Zumba or whatever's come into fashion since I was in my early teens. First I went with my mother. Then I went on my own. My bakery friend looks pretty fit. He probably plays tennis. Twice a week, at the club. Doubles. Or maybe squash, with an old friend from school who knows his ex-wife and all his ex-girlfriends.

David does hardly anything, he eats whatever he wants and doesn't exercise and stays pretty thin. Personal upkeep is not his thing. One time I watched him while he got ready for work. He takes a shower; that lasts ten minutes at the absolute most. Some days he shaves. Five, maybe ten minutes. He brushes his teeth. He uses the bathroom. He selects a shirt, a sweater and a pair of trousers. He puts on a pair of socks and a pair of shoes. He is ready.

It takes me considerably longer to get ready in the morning, or to go to sleep at night. Leaving aside the complicated network of decisions involved in putting clothes on, there are a nearly infinite number of products which must be employed in the ongoing campaign to appear young, thin, well rested, and, if I'm lucky, and all the potions have worked, pretty. Glossing cream (my hair tends to be dry). Some powdery stuff to give it texture (it is too straight, too fine). Micellar water, with a stack of cotton rounds and a cup full of Q-tips. Eye make-up remover, oil-free. Evian in a spray can. Two different kinds of serum. Day cream, night cream (premières rides d'expression). Sun cream, to mix into day cream, SPF 50, I am very fair-skinned, when I was little my mother always protected me from the sun, big hats, big umbrellas, because her mother didn't, she said, and now she's paying the price. Eye cream. Thigh cream. Body lotion. Foot cream. One bottle of perfume, used daily. (Three bottles gathering dust.) Two kinds of eyeliner (charcoal and black liquid). Concealer. Pressed power. Several shades of eyeshadow. Lipsticks, several. Lip gloss, several (none new). Liquid blush. Solid blush. Assorted brushes, nail files, bobby pins, barrettes, tweezers, samples of other potions which I might eventually use, thrown into my little shopping bag by a shop assistant when I paid for the potions I do use, in the hope no doubt I would return to buy full-sized versions of the potions.

These are the tools that make me a human giving a performance of a certain kind of femininity, instead of a conglomerate of organs, bones, flesh, a former baby-house, now a neutral organism with no particular purpose except its own continuation. The elements of my daily refacing, and the first lines of defence against the inevitable. It started with an old lipstick that my mother gave me when I was twelve, and it will go on, I imagine, until I die and the mortuary assistant makes me up for the funeral, and into the ground or the fire I go.

I have patients whose sole reason for being in my office is that they are ageing. The mind frays like the body, sometimes with alarm. After they leave, I spend time looking outside, thinking of how long the window and all it holds has been there before me, and how long it will be there after, wondering if the view will change very much, as it hasn't seemed to for at least a century, with few exceptions. Every building with its history. That one en face, old for this neighbourhood, eighteenth century. That one over there, nineteenth, Haussmann. That one over there, recent, 1980s maybe. Will it be bombs or age or flood or fire that will change the view?

In August we were going to go on vacation, to get away from what had happened, from the city, the heat, the tourist throngs, the shopfronts with their corrugated-iron curtains down, CONGÉS D'ÉTÉ REOUVERTURE FIN AOUT. Then David got the job in London and had to start immediately. They don't take the whole month of August off in London. And really they don't here either; Belleville is bustling. The wealthy half of the city go on and on about their *vacances* to make the rest of us feel bad for not having the time or the money to go. And to give civil servants an excuse not to answer emails. Still: everyone acts as though everyone else is away.

To be fair, a lot of the people I know are indeed on vacation. My friends left for their country houses or their summer rentals one by one. My therapist went to the south, as she does every summer, available for emergency phone calls only. And then David went too.

Right up until he left, the plan was for me to go with him. We were going to rent out our place, he found a flat in East London, it was all settled. New city, new life. I would see patients there. A real French psychoanalyst, they'll love it, he said. And you speak English! You'll be perfect. In the end I couldn't bring myself to go. I don't want to leave you alone, he said. I said I won't be alone, look at all the other people out there. He said that doesn't mean you won't be alone. I said OK then don't leave me alone. He said I'll come back on weekends. And he has, mostly.

The worst part about Paris in August is not the tourists, but the other Parisians who've stayed and think they have the city to themselves, so they have big parties at all hours. One night the neighbours across the road partied till five in the morning. They kept me awake with their laughing and hooting, their yelling and singing, their Rihanna and their Madonna. Then, in a nice surprise, they played Céline Dion's 'On ne change pas', trop ringard, but that song was important to me a million years ago, when I'd first moved to Paris and knew basically no one, it was on the radio a lot then, and it had something to do with helping me decide the way I wanted to shape my life. Sometimes I wish I could reach out to the girl I used to be, and tell her something, though I have no idea what.

And the song ends and some other crap begins and I think about calling the neighbourhood complaint line. Why am I not with my husband in London, I ask myself in those moments. What is wrong with me.

The smells of Paris are more intense in August, bodies and perfumes, warm rubber rising from the subway grates, the damp exhale of the buildings from their basement windows, synthetic scent of baking bread from second-rate boulangeries, hops and wood varnish from the Irish pubs, cigarettes, always, everywhere. It's going to be 34 today. (The summer temperatures now reach numbers you never used to hear in my childhood, 34, 35, 36.) At night I sit alone in my office, looking out the window until late into the evening. Rimmed with the red sunset the earth looks infected at the horizon line.

Alone in the apartment is my preferred state. I can eat what I want, when I want. Watch what I want, while I eat what I want. Clean up the next day. No longer having to organise my day around other people, David, patients. And there's something more physical about the aloneness, as well. I feel the space around me differently. It's not that it's quieter; it is a bodily experience of quiet. I am in the air differently.

Looking out the kitchen window, across the street, there is a light on in the chambre de bonne. As I stare at it, in the building dark but distinct against the sky, it seems to me that I am suddenly seeing the light on in that room as others have seen the light on in that room for a hundred years. The light itself no doubt changed from candlelight, to gaslight, to electricity. The change would have been subtle, the movement of the candlelit shadows giving way to the fixity of electric shadow. I feel unmoored from time.

I mirror this feeling of drift in my habits. I avoid my phone. I watch television on the TV instead of my laptop. It's a real psychological shift, to give myself over to the unpredictability of programming after the specificity of the series (Let's watch *The Wire*. I've never seen *The Sopranos*. Is it time to watch *Breaking Bad*?). It feels like wandering through a crowd, or some kind of county fair, people getting up to things I didn't know they were doing (and all this time that I've been living my life in these apartments, they've been out there doing these things. At the very same time!). I click through people gardening, people making jazz music, experts in space travel speculating about what the Americans will do next, a documentary about the TGV, an old film about Vincent Van Gogh that has a very young and very beautiful Elsa Zylberstein in it as a prostitute in some kind of riverbank bordello. I land on a talk show in which women talk about the tribulations of new motherhood. About the way our society has transformed motherhood into a capitalist institution, how it is both competitive and possible to outsource. The guests talk about alienation from their labour and lament the loss of their jobs, their bodies, their identities. I change back to Elsa Zylberstein.

Some days I lie on the bed immobilised for hours, as if a large sheet of cling film were pinning me in place.

Or I stand at the window as the sky does its daily thing.

In the shower, I turn down the hot and turn up the cold, and it feels good and alarming at the same time.

One day, on my way home from my run, I pass a sign which has been affixed to the wall of the building next door:

TU N'ES PAS SEULE

I don't have long to puzzle it over because I run into Clémentine in the courtyard. She thanks me for the Janet Malcolm, says she's almost done and will bring it back soon. Says she wants to talk to me about transference, which she's never understood. Malcolm, she says, says something like transference is the explanation for why we can never really know the people we live with – because we invent them for ourselves, instead of seeing them as they are. *We cannot see each other plain*, she says meaningfully. That's exactly what I've been trying to write about, Clémentine says. Can we discuss?

Come whenever you like, I say.

On my way upstairs the old woman from the sixth floor is just ahead of me. We climb in tandem, very slowly. I don't want to rush her. I'm not in a hurry. I sometimes hear her radio. It's been a while since I've heard it though and I was worried that something had happened to her. Maybe she went away, to visit one of her children perhaps? We've never introduced ourselves and now it's too late, we just say bonjour and make our way slowly up the stairs, one after the other.

I wake in the middle of the night from a bad dream that was actually a good dream. In my dream I was pregnant. It was before and I was still pregnant. I was so relieved to find out I hadn't lost the baby after all. And then when I wake up I am devastated all over again.

I go into my office, switch on the desk lamp, pull out my journal. I've been trying to track each of the turns we've made together, David and I, to see why I'm reacting (overreacting?) the way I am to losing this pregnancy. My husband is living in a different country, maybe it's as simple as that, but nothing's that simple. They were simple once, though. Weren't they? We're both calm people, willing to talk things through. We disagree on what this means about us. David thinks it means we're meant to be. The person you marry, you love more than the others, or you would have married one of them instead, David said. It was sweet of him to say, and maybe he believed it, but he was wrong. Everyone I had loved, I had loved as much as him. And those I had lost, perhaps, although I would never admit it to him, I might even have loved more, because they were lost, because I had known I would lose them. But maybe that's a different kind of love, the doomed kind, whereas we had the enduring kind, the don't-have-to-work-too-hard kind.

The problem with being the last person a person will ever love is just that: you're last. You come after a long list of desires and longings and carnal fits and temporary satiations. I found this fact almost unbearable. Not that I'd have traded places with anyone from David's past. But the thought of his desire concentrated on someone else made me shake with a fury I didn't understand. I could never forgive David for having wanted other women. Perhaps that's because I thought he would never forgive me if he knew how much I'd wanted other men.

I once checked an old boyfriend's email, wondering if he was still in touch with his exes. I found exactly what I was looking for, of course. An email he had written not long after we got together. Her name was Aude. He told her he was with someone new, but that he still thought of her. He said that he longed for the *strange beauty* of their connection. Reading that phrase made me recoil from the computer. Was I upset that he was capable of saying such things to women, or because he'd never said anything like that to me? I googled the girl but found nothing. Or rather, I found too much; her last name was too common, her first name as well, there were too many hits. The search dissolved in uncertainty. Our relationship too.

With another boyfriend, rooting through a shoebox jammed at the back of his closet, I found the reason why some of the people I met through him seemed convinced they had met me before. Inside were photographs of my boyfriend with a girl who looked just like me. It was eerie. Some people just have types, a friend said. Skinny white girl with brown hair – you're not that unique, you know. But this resemblance was too close to chalk up to having a type. I wondered if I was an echo of the other girl, or if the other girl was a placeholder for me.

Maybe it's better not to know anything about the past. One time, getting to know someone new, I steadfastly refused to tell him anything about my past relationships, or to hear anything about his. When things didn't work out I wondered afterward if I should have been more open. But there was too much I didn't want to face just yet, or trust him with.

With David I have been calmer; he knows the broad outlines

29

of where I've been and vice versa. I have never checked his email. Once, in his old apartment, I opened a desk drawer looking for a pen or something and found a pile of notes, photos, postcards from women. The paraphernalia of romantic history. I shut the drawer and when we moved in together, I wondered if these ephemera had come with him. I did not look to see if they had. I wanted us to come to each other new. What other shapes had I taken as I lay next to him, was I shorter, taller, thinner, fatter, darker, lighter than the girls he'd been with? Smarter, dumber, funnier, quieter? I didn't want to have another set of measurements to compare myself to. I wanted to keep the ghosts out of the bedroom.

To come to each other new. How impossible that is.

I tell Esther about all this, next time I see her, about the shoebox and the girl who looked just like me, about the jealousy.

Maybe, she says, the key thing is that you've never been with your partners when you haven't been there, and other girls have. Jealousy is about wanting to know more about the people we love, and knowing we'll never be able to. Who is he when you're not there?

Clémentine comes over to bring back the Janet Malcolm book, but also to escape from the boxes at her place. I don't know why I can't unpack them, she says, it's not like I don't have time. I just feel like Jonathan should help. But he doesn't. He's perfectly happy living his life among the boxes.

Men, I shake my head.

He works so much, she says. I just sit around the house writing poetry and masturbating.

That doesn't sound terrible, I say.

She sits on the sofa, wearing a rumpled little sundress. When I ask him to unpack a few of them he says it's August, we're going away soon, we'll deal with them when we come back.

Where are you going for your holiday?

To my family's home in Normandy. He's never been out there. We'll swim. Are you going anywhere?

No, I thought about going to see my parents but I'm not sure I really feel like it. Maybe I'll go to London. Maybe not.

She looks at me for a while, and I think she's about to say something, but she stops. There is a moment of silence. I hold it with her.

So the Malcolm, she segues. You know, I'm not a big fan of psychoanalysis, obviously I'm sceptical of the whole Mommy–Daddy–Me structure, like there's no one else in the world who affects who we become, or the binary take on gender, you know what I mean? It's, like, patriarchy, bottled and distilled.

I know what you mean.

I meet a lot of shrinks, and none of them can ever tell me how psychoanalysis can be really socially transformative. But the Malcolm! I loved it. I mean it's a little dated, the homophobia is frankly chilling, but it was more coming from the other guy, the psychoanalyst, than her? I loved her scepticism, too, about the cult of psychoanalysis. Even while she's writing a book about it.

But do you really believe in the talking cure? she goes on. Like, if I have a problem, and I come and talk to you about it for a few years, and talk about my parents, and all of that, that I will feel better? I mean I've been in therapy, and I never found it helped me very much.

Well, I say, it's a little more complicated than that. The kind of psychoanalysis I subscribe to is more Lacanian, it's less about your coming up with a narrative that explains and cures your symptoms and more about what might be suggested during the therapeutic process, how the way we talk about our lives encodes the way we think about them, the things we want, our desires, how we might learn to live with them instead of being led by them. You'll never be cured, so to speak. There's no cure for being human.

Mm, she says, unconvinced.

Have you read Deleuze and Guattari? she asks, and I have to hide a smile; she hasn't acquired the defensive veneer that would prevent her from asking open-ended questions like that. There is something so earnest about her, a yearning for connection on some other plane than the everyday, or that she's not getting on an everyday basis. I take a wild guess that her partner has not read Deleuze and Guattari, and that she wishes he did.

I think they make a very strong critique of Freud, she goes on. They reject this idea that we are one thing, one entity, with one past, that affects us in a particular way. They have this very multiple idea of the self, and of desire. I think that's so important. Fluid. Revolutionary.

I suddenly have a flashback to grad school, sitting in the BNF, grappling with *Anti-Oedipus*. I make to agree, but she's already on to another subject.

When's the first time you had an orgasm? she asks.

Um. I don't remember? Let me think. When did *you*?

Oh god I was young. I used to do gymnastics, she says. And one day I was on the balance beam sitting and watching one of the other girls do her floorwork and I was kind of idly rocking forward and back and forward and back, I think I was bored, but I started to feel this blurry starriness between my legs and I just kind of went with it, back and forth, back and forth, and I closed my eyes and kept going till it popped.

I take this in. Slightly embarrassed, but wanting to be as open with Clémentine as she has been with me, I tell her I didn't have one until I was in college. I didn't do gymnastics.

So was it with a guy? asks Clémentine. Or a girl?

It was alone. A friend told me what to do, so I went home and fiddled around until I figured it out. No one had ever told me about the clitoris! I thought I had to just jam a hairbrush up there and move it in and out and it would eventually happen.

She laughs, then stops. Oh, that's not actually funny, is it.

We smoke in silence, watching a tabby cat prowl across a roof below, then miraculously dart inside an open window.

Anyway, she says, gesturing at the Malcolm. Thank you for this. Her sentences! It made me want to be a writer.

But you are a writer, I say. You're a poet.

Oh but I'm not, she says. Nothing I write is any good.

I used to write poetry, I say, when I was in high school. I wanted to be a poet and write about the body but all I could come up with were lines like *toenails are extremely annoying*, so I gave it up.

Toenails are extremely annoying is not a bad line, she says.

In bed that night, I try to touch myself, but there's no response. I don't know what to do with this thing, my body.

From the window in my office I can see into the neighbours' apartment. They have a little girl who likes to dance. Lately it's been to a Taylor Swift song that she blasts from an iPad, which echoes across the street and into my window, shake shake shake shake, she sings though she doesn't understand the lyrics, what is being shaken out and off. In their kitchen I can see they have an electric-blue bowl and it is often filled with lemons, and the contrast of the yellow against the blue gives me such longings. And it is also because of these longings that I tell myself I am turning into one of those people on Instagram consumed mainly with thoughts of my own home and how it appears. But it feels deeper than that, and more existential, as if I will only survive through my environment and my belongings, my be-longings. I think of a blue bowl I had that was not the same colour, it had a Moroccan pattern, I bought it in a shop in the Marais, long since closed and turned, I think, into a Uniqlo – I can't remember exactly where it was on the rue des Rosiers but I know it was in a courtyard and it was immense and had a kind of low mezzanine level when you first walked in and that's where I found my blue Moroccan bowl, and I used it to keep oranges in until it was broken by some Airbnb people to whom I sublet my tiny studio one summer. I could buy a blue bowl now but it wouldn't be the same; I have to wait for one to come back into my life. And here one is, but it isn't mine.

Some days are cling-filmed in the morning but by afternoon my self-loathing has transformed into energy and it propels me into my trainers, and out the door. By the time I go for my run it's after five, and the man isn't at the bakery at that hour.

It has crossed my mind that one of these days I might proposition him, bring him home. There's no one else here. Maybe it would be nice to have his hands on me. David and I have not been intimate since I lost the pregnancy. This is beginning to alarm me; I am thirty-nine now, and I am all too aware that the window in which to get pregnant, and stay pregnant, is closing. When we try, my body tightens and there is no entering it. It's outside my control; I very much want to have sex with my husband, but my body does not. At first it seemed like a perfectly understandable response to trauma, but it's been a few months now, and I'm wondering if it would work with someone new. David would never know. But just as I've somewhat, sort-of decided to give the man my number, he stops coming to the bakery – I guess he's gone off wherever he goes in the summer – and soon it's the dead of August and the bakery is closed too.

Fans full blast, shutters closed. Lying on the couch the smell of cat wee wafts over from some unidentifiable source.

The light in August brings the street together. When the sky goes deep blue, earlier than it has been, you can either turn on the light, and decide it's evening, or sit a while longer, watching everyone else turn on theirs, creating orange pools in the dusk spill. The light recedes from the street, replaced, slowly, by windows like beacons. You can stand at your window and not be surprised to see your neighbours standing at their windows too, pausing to watch the conversion from day to night.

And when you have sat long enough with the night, you can go into the hall and turn on the light. The separation has been observed.

A long time ago, I was in love with a boy called Jonathan. He and his family were varying degrees of Jewish. He and his dad were atheists, but his aunt and uncle observed Shabbat, and we would often go to visit them. I loved the candle-lighting and the prayers, but what left the deepest impression on me was the ritual performed on Saturday evening, when Shabbat was over, to mark the end of the day of rest and the beginning of the new week. Blessed art thou, our lord, who distinguishes light from dark. They said the prayer, lit a candle with several wicks, and passed around a bowl of spices. I inhaled the cloves as they were passed to me. Havdalah. Separation.

It is good to separate, to recognise the passage of time, to sanctify one part of time above another. One time has ended and another has begun. This has stayed with me, years after I lost touch with Jonathan. But even in separation, even as we move on to whatever comes next, the thing from before is still there, in the past. We sanctified it through our observance, and we let go of it. We separate, but it still exists. That's why I told myself never to fight a separation.

Separation is one of the two things we fear most.

The other thing is coming together.

Another sign on the street today. Thick, capital letters, deliberately spaced like a ransom note.

PAPA,
IL A
TUÉ
MAMAN

Clémentine comes over and somehow in conversation I tell her how long it's been since I actually saw a patient, and I tell her why. She nods, and smokes.

After a while she says: the reason I got my undergraduate degree so late is because I was in the hospital for a year.

I nod, and smoke. Surreptitiously I look for scars on her arms, and find none. She says no more about it, and neither do I.

One day, with nothing else to do, I go back to my old journals, rows and rows of black leather notebooks I filled up for years, the neat graph paper covered with my tight, uniform writing. All the things I wrote about Jonathan, all the pages he took up until, eventually, his name stopped appearing.

We met soon after I started grad school. I was twenty-five; he was twenty-two. He quickly took over the journals. Rereading them, I remember how intense it was between us, no one had ever looked at *me* that way before, the word I put to it was *smoulder*, and it felt like over-writing, something from a romance novel, but that was the only word that captured it. I was addicted to the way he looked at me, and, though I was wary at the outset – he was younger, unsure of himself – I let myself be drawn in. Why are you here, why are you with me, I remember asking, and he said, I fell for you, I keep falling for you. Thinking back to the restaurant we had been sitting in when he first smouldered at me, I can recall with great precision the look in his eyes, and it occurs to me that there was more in it than burning, that there was also, and maybe this is just with the benefit of hindsight, but I think I knew it then too, his own wariness, a sense that he was trying to figure something out. How do you burn for someone and look askance at them at the same time?

At the start what I wrote most about was his family. Jonathan's father was a prominent psychoanalyst, the kind who writes books for an impressive publishing house alongside well-known philosophers and sociologists. No one I knew growing up wrote books. I was dazzled by this provenance, Jonathan's proximity to greatness, to a real intellectual life. I knew his father's work before I met him, had read his books and some of his articles. Max Weisz was born in Budapest but when they passed the racial laws in 1938 the whole family, aunts, uncles, cousins, the whole lot, had emigrated to France along with little Max, who was about five then. Everyone settled in for the long haul, except for Max's parents; they felt something in the air and decided to chance it in Mexico. It was a decision that saved their lives, though most of the rest of the family weren't as lucky. Max returned to France for university, stayed to do his doctorate, went on to teach. He had been married several times, I knew. Jonathan's mother, his second wife, had been English. I never met her; she died of cancer when Jonathan was a toddler. Max remarried a Frenchwoman, a shiksa, when Jonathan was sixteen, not long before we met. He was hostile toward his step-mother, and generally had as little to do with her as possible, difficult when he still lived at home.

It was Max Weisz who made me a Lacanian. One of his books, a classic, the one everyone has to read in grad school, was about sex, desire and infidelity. *L'Indisponible*, it was called. *The Unavailable.* He published it in the 80s, when Jonathan was a little boy. In fact he shares some adorable anecdotes about his son in the introduction, as a way of laying out his ideas about wanting what we can't have. Like Freud describing his little grandson's fort/da game, in which he hid his toys (*gone!*) so that he could find them again (*there!*), putting himself in control of the trauma of loss and the pleasure of rediscovery, Max describes Jonathan's replication of Max's parental authority, his echoing of the particular tone of voice when his father says *no* as a searching for a means of controlling his own disappointment when things are denied him, and turning his father's authority against him. *My son is affectionate but domineering,* Max writes, *claiming all of his mother's attention, and eager to assume the role of the father, dictating who can do what in our small kingdom. Desire*, he says, *can only exist by virtue of its alienation.* Drawing on Freud, but also on theories of love going back to Plato, Kierkegaard and Goethe, Max describes the way that the loved one becomes an object of desire only when it is lost.

The book focuses on Lacan's twentieth seminar, *Encore*, the one where he says sexual relations don't exist, women don't exist. He's caught a lot of flak for saying those things from people who don't understand that he didn't mean them, not literally. Lacan liked to get a rise out of people, he was a showman. He meant they are constructions, that we can't apprehend them directly, purely, except through the fog of language, even when we touch someone we desire, our desire is filtered through everything we have ever thought and heard and encountered, everything the culture has taught us about desire. Language isn't innocent; the body isn't innocent. I go to my shelves, look for it in the confusion, I haven't had a chance to organise them yet, they are in general sections but not given any order within them. After a while I finally put my finger on the spine of the thin paperback I bought so long ago, with Bernini's *Ecstasy of Saint Teresa* on the cover. I flip through its pages, noticing where I have placed neat little crosses in the margins to indicate a significant point. Heady stuff. *To speak of love is in itself to experience pleasure.* And then quickly thereafter – a tiny bomb going off amid so many other pyrotechnics – the part where he says that the female orgasm is proof that God still exists. Lacan, forever trying to reconcile his religion with his hedonism. Ah this is where he talks about History with its big hache, with its big axe. And that final line – *the real, I would say, is the mystery of the speaking body, it's the mystery of the unconscious.* That line is why I became an analyst. We say and say but can never convey any kind of whole truth, only half say it. What we think we know we understand unconsciously, or with our bodies. For me, Lacan is a philosopher of desire.

In the summer of 1973, after the *Encore* seminar, he wasn't invited to the big psychoanalysis conference in Paris. There is something about Lacanian psychoanalysis that the profession has always had trouble with, some underlying unresolvable ambiguity. It's not like he was Wilhelm Reich or something, fucking his patients and rationalising it into a philosophy. Lacan was a Catholic, thought about becoming a priest (in founding his own cult, he succeeded, somewhat, in his early aspirations). He was deeply moralistic – but alive to the mysteries.

Near the Lacan books I spot Max's and take it down, remembering vividly the nights I spent underlining it, copying out passages to get them into my body. His book changed so much for me, it helped me understand Lacan to begin with, and I don't think it's an overstatement to say that it saved my life after Jonathan left me. In it Max wrote something about desire and original loss, and it stayed in my mind, le fait de jouir n'étanche pas le désir original, the act of coming does not quench the initial desire. Desire stems from foundational loss, the moment of separation from our mothers, from being cast out of that oceanic dyad into our own distinct individuality. Mother becomes other and we are from that point on forever adrift; but it is that loss that triggers desire, all our desires forever after. In those early days after the break-up, it was consoling to think that it wasn't just him that I missed, and that if he were to return to me, the void would remain. Jonathan was the malady, and Max's book, Lacanian psychoanalysis more generally, the remedy – though not an absolute cure.

I think I was a little in love with Jonathan's father, and with his family, their culture, their story. We used to talk about going to Budapest together, or Mexico City to see his elderly grandparents. But we never did. We went to Brittany, Cornwall, and even once to Prague, but never Budapest, and never Mexico. I thought about him in terms of places that were a part of him and places that were a part of us, places we went and places that without him would be forever impossible to access, even if I were to visit them myself. I found a journal entry from the January after he left me:

> I mourn summer, England, St Malo, even Budapest, with Jonathan. Things I love like the heat of the sun on my hair and in my eyes and buzzing cicadas and an expanse of grey river are all tied up in wanting him. And not being able to have him – not being able to so much as talk to him – is like not being able to have summer.

These connections we feel to places we've never been through the people we love.

He was jealous, I remembered, looking through the notebooks. If I spoke to another guy at a party he would instantly be at my side. He'd ask if I remembered our first date, and I'd pretend to confuse him with someone else. More wariness, I can see now. I don't know what I thought I was doing at the time. He would wax romantic and I would wisecrack, ill at ease with his intensity. We were often on the same frequency but when we weren't, we weren't. I was jealous too, of course, but it was easier to let go of my jealous tendencies with him; he was so young; he hadn't had any meaningful relationships yet. A girl at lycée. A few girls in Cameroon where he'd gone to volunteer with a youth group on some kind of environmental protection programme. Nothing serious. I was older, had already lived with a boyfriend, was living on my own, while he still lived with his parents; I'm not surprised he felt like there were things about my life he didn't know and couldn't understand.

There were things about his life, too, that he had trouble grasping. His mother's absent presence in his life, we talked about that a lot. His struggle to understand his father's womanising.

Jonathan hated him for doing it and he hated his stepmother for coming into the picture and stopping his doing it; she destroyed the patterns through which he understood his father. He refused to go to therapy; to go would have been to acquiesce to his father's wishes, Max's way of seeing the world. Instead, there was me. Not his father's student but someone who knew his work; I was, I thought, perhaps some kind of go-between for Jonathan, a way of working through all these difficulties without confronting them head on. I didn't mind; I could be whatever he needed me to be. But then he eventually placed what I thought was an arbitrary limit on my role in his life, as well.

A few pages on I notice that I wrote down something else he once said: *Jonathan said today that he could never be with a French girl.* I remembered the conversation. I told him I'm only half French but it didn't matter. People who'd lost people were told they had died *for France*, but it was the French who'd rounded them up and delivered them to the Germans.

Who deported our parents? he'd repeat from time to time, like a litany, like it was something he'd overheard. No one, actually, had deported his parents. But he spoke for an entire people. *The French. Who drove the buses? The French. Who drove the trains? The French. Who ran the camps at Drancy, Beaune-la-Rolande, Pithiviers, Gurs? French police. Who came to arrest our parents at dawn? French police.*

He felt an intractable sense of betrayal, and I agonised over the fact that he had condemned me along with the country of my birth. What can you say to someone who rejects you for a fault you didn't commit? But he had nightmares, he ground his teeth when he slept, he was as traumatised as if those things had actually happened to him. I thought it was more likely that his mother's death, his father's infidelities, his difficulty forming a protective shell of capable masculinity were the cause of his teeth-grinding, but no, he said, it was History, avec sa grande hache.

One day, he told me we had no future because of our different religions. I never found out what had shifted in him. We were in completely different stages of our lives, I told myself. I never heard from him again.

David appears infrequently in those journals. We met, we fell in love, that was that. There was nothing to worry over or analyse. He was a fact, whereas the journals were full of speculation. Sometimes I think about throwing them away – I honestly don't know what purpose they serve.

My mother calls and wants to know why I'm not at their house for the summer holidays. Everyone is away, she says, David is away, your patients are away, you should be here with us, we can go to the sea? And I tell her I can't get away, I'm working on the kitchen, and when we hang up I pin some photos to my Pinterest page, and get distracted by something I see on Twitter, and end up reading a story by the *New Yorker*'s television critic, which leads me back to Netflix, and I forget entirely that I even have a kitchen, or a family, or a body.

It really ought to have rained, no? When was the last time we had rain?

It's Friday afternoon and the key is turning in the lock. David? I'm on the sofa, doom-scrolling Twitter, and then there he is. I scramble up to greet him, and he takes me in his arms, tight squeeze, kissing sounds on my neck. What are you doing here? I ask, my voice hingeing around the lump in my throat. He wears the same leather jacket he wore on our first date. I inhale its familiar smell, calf's leather mixed with aftershave and the slightest suggestion of cigarette smoke.

I thought you might like a surprise, he says. You sounded so sad on the phone this morning that I threw my things in a bag and hopped on a train. Come on, get dressed, I haven't eaten – I'm starving! I let myself be swept up, as I always am, by David's energy.

We go to the Italian restaurant near the métro, small and warm with its washed-out yellow walls and cherrywood panelling. They are juillettistes; they take their holidays early and serve all through the month of August. The young owner and chef opened the restaurant in homage to her nonna, and the pasta she produces from the tiny kitchen behind the dining room is infused with some maniacal Tuscan genius. I always order the same thing. David likes to try different things every time. On the few occasions I've branched out, I have always been disappointed. Not that the new dish hasn't been good, but it hasn't been *my* dish. Ordering something else always seems like a missed opportunity to get exactly what I need.

He holds my hand across the table. So what have you been up to this week?

Not a lot. How about you?

David helps himself to some of my dinner. You know. The usual. A bunch of us went out the other night, some guys we're working with took us to that Japanese place I told you about. We had a lot to drink and we had ourselves a bit of a man chat. One of them broke up with his girlfriend a while back, was really devastated, just devastated, and last time we saw him he was barely holding it together. He had lost all this weight, was talking about ghosts, he was really far gone. But then we saw him again this week, he looked much healthier, maybe a little too healthy – he was telling us how he's sexing his way through Hackney, which is impressive, but kind of worrying. I mean, the guy's thirty-five years old and he's hooking up with these really young girls, like twenty-one, twenty-two. He met this one girl who he really fancied but she was just too much for him. Too good for him, I mean. She was pretty upset when he let her down and he felt really bad. I don't get this guy, because all he says he wants to do is to start a family. And who did he go home with that night? A twenty-one-year-old.

Over dessert, he asks how therapy is going.

All right. Esther is away now, so I'm not really going.

Is that OK?

I think so.

He pushes his grilled peaches around on his plate.

Do you ever talk about me?

Not really, I say. Sometimes. You're not the main thing.

A beat.

Does that disappoint you?

I guess. Or – no, I guess it means we're OK. That, or you don't think I'm worth talking about. He laughs, and inside his laugh I hear the real question he's asking. I move the remnants of dessert aside, and take his hand again.

I talked about you more when you first went to London. I was wondering if that was your way of dealing with – not dealing with – losing the – with everything, I finish. But now I don't think that now.

It was bad timing, he says.

We don't need to talk about it any more.

Don't we?

Rue Piat, on the way home:

NOUS SOMMES TOUTES
DES HÉROÏNES

Look, I show David. They've been cropping up all over Paris.
Aren't they incredible?

But what does it mean? he asks.

That night, as David sleeps beside me, I come in my sleep and the vibrations shake me awake. I touch myself to prolong them, but whatever or whoever it was in my dream that made me come has left.

And August sweats on into September.

It's the rentrée. Everything's reopened and everyone has a renewed energy, like an appetite for life. My bakery friend is back at the bakery, buying my bread. On the street outside the little girls are all wearing Elsa dresses, pretending everything they touch turns to ice, like in the Disney film. The builders are due to start in the kitchen any day now. I'm supposed to call them to confirm. Esther has returned from the south; she smokes e-cigarettes while I sit across the room from her. Before the summer she smoked actual cigarettes. Maybe she's trying to be healthier. She changes the cartridge while I'm talking, and I wonder if she's timed it to subtly disrupt my train of thought, reroute it. Lacan said that to be a psychoanalyst is to say the right phrase at the right moment. Esther doesn't say very much, but perhaps she's trying to make the right sounds at the right time.

David went back to London this morning.

Mm?

All day the apartment's felt so empty. I went into the kitchen, ran my hand along a countertop, and I had this sense of claustrophobia. And I realised it didn't have to be that way, that we could create our own space.

Mm.

All we'd need to do is take out some of the ancient cabinetry that's, like, encrusted on to one of the walls, and we can knock it down. We really don't need it. Then we could put a big table there, to divide up the space a bit. I'm picturing a bare-wood, stripped-down, farmhouse kind of table, preferably one from an actual farmhouse. I can see us sitting down to eat at that table, over a meal I've cooked. It's been months since I've cooked anything more complex than pasta, or warmed-up frozen dinners.

Mm.

Well, maybe we won't knock down the wall. It's probably really expensive. And who knows how long it would take. I guess I could go stay with David in London while they did it.

Esther doesn't even bother making her *I'm listening* sound. Is she tired of me going on about the kitchen? (Am I tired of going on about the kitchen?) There are times when I think I will put my pen through my eye if my patients don't change it up a bit. Why am I so preoccupied with it, anyway? It not like I miscarried while I was cooking. It happened when I wasn't doing much of anything. I was at home, I was checking my email, I was doing my hair, I was cleaning the bathroom, I had just come in, I was just going out. One minute I was reading the paper and the next I was doubled over.

The blood was excessive. There could have been a bit less blood and the whole thing would have felt less melodramatic and possibly more real, more personal. So much blood, like a B movie. I lay for hours, instead of sleeping, wishing for a more dignified end for our future baby. I didn't dress, I didn't bathe, I didn't eat. I didn't rise from bed to pee, but kept a pot beside the bed. I didn't shit for a week.

I didn't go through the painful, but healing, stage of calling myself into question, asking myself what I had done to lose the pregnancy. David said it wasn't my fault. I hadn't replied. I didn't have an opinion on the question of fault. If there was a foetus in my uterus or not, I didn't see what it had to do with my will or intentions. Apart from having had unprotected sex with my husband, I had not put it there, and I did not take it out. It just started bleeding. Avortement spontané, they call it. Spontaneous abortion. A better term than the English *miscarriage*, as

55

though I had carried it badly, or wrongly, though the association with abortion seems misleading, given the weightiness of *that* term. *Fausse couche* isn't great either, false childbirth. A nineteenth-century term – I looked it up, curious about the way the words moved around – for slandering a certain kind of man, for calling him a failure, a coward, lacking in virtue and talent. No better way to say it than nineteen weeks along, out of the first trimester, starting to show, already telling people.

After the surgery, and all that followed, the hospital where I practised had put me on an arrêt maladie psychologique until Esther cleared me to go back to work. The kids at Sainte-Anne wouldn't miss me too badly; they were well supported by the rest of the staff. As for my private patients, none were in extreme situations. They were ordinary people, with ordinary troubles. But dropping my patients was almost as awful an experience as the miscarriage itself. You can't just stop seeing patients, these people are in the middle of, hopefully, deep psychological work; it's a major disruption to abruptly disappear. And besides, no one wants to hear that their shrink has gone off the deep end.

Worse, I had ceased to value what I did. Why look in other people's narratives for the metaphors, the gaps, the gaffes, the subtexts, that point you toward what they themselves may or may not realise? Maybe the words merely point to themselves, my patients are only using language the way everyone else does, a common vernacular that has nothing individual about it, just a whole culture and its shorthand for experience coming at me day in and day out. What if none of it actually meant anything? It wasn't that I couldn't go back to work. It was that I couldn't go back to work *if that was what work was.*

I couldn't tell if David was affected by what had happened. He was so busy looking after me, and then he threw himself into his new thing in London, and left me to mull it all over. Or at least that's what I accused him of. I knew it was his coping mechanism, but what about me? What was my coping mechanism? He had offered to turn down the job in London. I told him to go. If he stayed, I would have felt guilty for keeping him here, and there is only so much one person can hold inside. It was the kind of thing I would have said to one of my own patients, but now I was learning first-hand the limits of what our bodies can physically contain. And where I had been emptied out, a sense of my own failure leaked in.

Where was I.

Frozen dinners, she says, inhaling her nicotine steam.

When was the last time you were happy? she asks.

What do you mean, happy? I was happy when David came home this weekend.

I don't mean happy like a mood. I mean happy like a state of being. A more or less continual state of contentment.

Genuinely happy? Not just happy enough?

What do you mean by genuinely happy?

I guess I meant – unafraid. Open. Is that what you mean by happy?

She gives a little shrug, as if to say: it's your definition that matters, not mine.

I know it well. I used to shrug like that at least once a day.

On the métro home, there are the mothers getting on and off with their kids, the students leaning against the poles, earbuds stuffed in their ears, the Chinese women sitting with their shopping bags between their legs, the braying warning as the doors are about to close, the soft rubber chunk-chunking of the train on the tracks, the lean-to as we round corners in the tunnels, and someone's head occasionally jostling against mine in the backwards-facing seats behind me, and in amid the texture and noise and contact of an average day in Paris, I think about Esther's question. The last time I was happy, genuinely happy? Who's happy, these days? I catch a glimpse of someone reading that morning's *Metro* across the way. On the cover is Emmanuel Macron, looking beleaguered; two members of his party have quit, citing the way the government is using the ongoing state of emergency to deprive people of their civil rights.

Jonathan used to be on constant watch for the government's abuses of power. I guess he must be saying things like that even more loudly now, after the attacks. I thought of him when they took the hostages in the Hyper Cacher; he had relatives who lived over there, who were very observant, who probably shopped there. But I didn't recognise any of the names they listed in the paper. I didn't want to think about Jonathan then, and I don't want to think about him now. Jonathan was the demarcation line, the divider between me as I evolved from my upbringing and my education, cared for by the family I was born into, and the me I became once I was out in the world. Jonathan was the first person to interfere with me, as they used to say. I sometimes wonder who I would have been if I hadn't met him. I feel very sure I'd be happier.

I think of him less since I moved out of the 5th, where we spent so much time together. I lived in the rue Claude Bernard; he in the rue Monge. In time he lived more at my place than at his father's, but he was only ever a guest at my place; he wouldn't leave so much as a toothbrush. He was aching for independence. In our neighbourhood there was a building that was covered with scaffolding, that we would sometimes pass by. One day he said: see that building over there? The one with the scaffolding up? My cousins own an apartment in it. I may rent it from them when I finish law school so I don't have to live with my dad. After we broke up, I used to walk past that building all the time, even years later, long after they had taken the scaffolding down, hoping I would run into him, or his cousins. But as time went on I forgot which building it had been. And as even more time went by, I stopped thinking about him every time I walked down the rue Monge. I eventually stopped thinking of him altogether. I'd occasionally trip on a bit of the debris he left behind, like when I was cleaning out my hard drive and found this picture of us together, in St Malo, one of the rare times when we had asked a stranger to photograph us. It was of the two of us standing on the ramparts at St Malo, the wind blowing my hair straight across my face. His curls went the same way. We looked so alive in the wind.

The night we met, we were in a bar, and he had his hand on the back of my chair. Our friends had left us alone together. It was noisy in the bar, and he had to lean in to ask me questions right in my ear, so I had nearly to rest my forehead on his shoulder to hear him. Some guy came along and asked if he could put his coat down on an empty chair at our table. He held a camera in his hand. Give me that, I'll take a picture of you, I told him, drunk and playful. In the light of the flash, he looked awful. He would probably delete it. Then he said, now let me take one of you, les amoureux. We hadn't even kissed yet. I wondered if he would keep that image of the two strangers who watched his coat for him, or if he would ask himself, in the sober light of day, who are these people? and delete our picture without a second thought.

Jonathan must have had hundreds of pictures of us together on his computer. He took his camera with him everywhere. Those were the days of the digital camera, before the rise of the smartphone. I hardly ever remembered to take mine. One night when we were away together in St Malo, as we were making out back in our hotel room after dinner, I realised only one of his hands was on me, while the other was off to the side, holding up the camera, turned to the video function. I made him watch it with me after. I tried to realise the girl in the video was me but I couldn't, even though I had just done what she was doing, what she would always be doing, caught in that moment, for as long as her pixels existed. After he left me I wondered if he kept that video. I hoped he had. I hoped he had kept all the photographs of us, as I was left with these images of him. I have missed him for far longer than the time we actually spent together, not more than a year.

Jonathan tore himself out of my life, leaving the edges ragged. For years, they had stayed that way. If he had called, if I had seen him again, perhaps I would have snipped them off, cut him loose. I couldn't bear not seeing him again. I told myself I needed *closure*, but I knew it was a dumb idea, there is no such thing, we are always open. I just wanted to see him again. I ran into his friend Thomas at a gig, who told me Jonathan had become a lawyer and married some girl from Israel.

Once, not all that long ago, I passed him on the boulevard de Courcelles, god knows why I was way over there but I was, and there he was too. He crossed the street, wearing an expensive-looking navy suit, and he stopped, and he looked right through me. I couldn't tell if he saw me and didn't want to say hello, or if I didn't even register on the sidewalk. I emailed him afterward: *was that you, what a small world, I hope all is well.* He didn't reply.

I ran into his father at a conference once. He made a point of saying hello – he has always been very generous with young analysts. I didn't ask how Jonathan was. Max was on a panel with a psychoanalyst who'd done a lot of work on the children of survivors, Nathalie Zajde. I bought her book, and read it attentively, feeling ashamed for not having known about it earlier, when I was with Jonathan. But I'm glad to know about it anyway, even after Jonathan; it's helped me understand how trauma can function within a family, down the generations, how it may have been more than his mother's death and his father's remarriage that made him grind his teeth at night, that it could very well have been, in fact, History. It helped me come to terms with our break-up. I hope his Israeli wife understands him the way he thought I never could. I hope, wherever he is, that he's happy.

As I open the door to our building I see Clémentine putting the trash out in the courtyard. We wave. She mimes holding a phone to her ear and I mime one back.

Happy, I say to myself, walking up the stairs, scooting to the side to allow the old woman from upstairs to get past with her cane. I think how absurd the word is in English. Say it often enough and it sounds like a child babbling at its dolls. Haaaa-peeeee. Infantile. No one is happy. My clients are – were, I guess – inconsolable, divorcing, panicking, despairing, angry. At the café up the hill I sometimes go to, the owner complains and the workers drink their eleven a.m. Kronenbourgs and the students knit their brows and smoke. David used to come home from work and couldn't believe the shit his colleagues got away with, and needed a cigarette in my office to calm down at the end of the day. No one's happy. And what's with this thing about everyone having to be happy, anyway? An American import. Who needs it. I put the keys in their place and shut the door behind me.

I remember the last time I was happy, I say aloud to my empty apartment. It was when I knew he was going to be a father.

It still hasn't rained. The air, usually humid, is dry. I wake up with my nose blocked most mornings. They're asking people to limit how much water they use. Not wanting to waste any by flushing, I pee over and over into our toilet, all day and all night, until the smell gets acrid, like the underside of a bridge down by the Seine. Then, and only then, do I permit myself a flush.

I run into my bakery friend coming out of l'Égyptien. He accompanies me uphill as we talk about the tahini he has just bought, he opens his *New Yorker* tote bag (he reads the *New Yorker*?) to show me several jars of it. He has recently discovered its existence and is in ecstasies, he can't get enough, he slathers it on everything, crudités, chicken, bread, tomato salad. I'm crossing here, I say, not sure if I should let on where I live, I still don't entirely know if he's creepy or friendly or just has a baguette kink. He's always studiously polite; I am beginning to trust him. Ah you live over there, he says, I used to live over there. You're a long-time Bellevillois, then, I say, as we wait for the light to change. Oh not originally, he says, but I suppose I am now. It's my shtetl. Too late to go somewhere else. The light changes, and I cross, and I know he's watching me, but I key in the code to my building and go inside, having accepted that I have given him this information about myself. It's his shtetl, I think; he'll find out where I live anyway, one of these days.

Since the rentrée the letters have been appearing with increased urgency. As if the walls of Paris were speaking – or like the spirits of abused and murdered women had taken up residence in the buildings themselves, like urban naiads.

On the avenue Simon Bolivar near the Buttes-Chaumont:

À QUOI ÇA SERT
D'ÊTRE SUR
LA TERRE
SI C'EST POUR
FAIRE NOS VIES
À GENOUX?

On a wall near the rue des Pyrénées:

ELLE LE QUITTE
IL LA TUE

The buildings are being resurfaced with care for women's bodies, their consent, their right to exist. Some of the slogans confide in us, others chastise us, others yell for us to listen. I look around but no one else seems to be noticing the astonishing things the walls are saying.

My mother visits. The last time she came was after it happened, and she stayed with me for a week to help me recover. We nearly killed each other. I think she's forgiven me for staying in Paris this summer. She's trying to give me my space.

She doesn't like that David's not here. I head her off when I sense she's about to ask when he'll be back, get her to change the subject, shift her focus from me to the world. She wants to go to a café down the hill, which is usually populated by excellently dressed young people, really stellar examples of people being young, beside whom I feel old, as old as a mother, but not a mother. An acoustic cover of 'Chasing Cars' plays on the radio, it makes me cringe but also involuntarily summons the image of young lovers sheltering in bed, am I thinking of a scene from a film or did I once hear it played on the radio as I lay in some-one's arms, I can't remember. I'm not sure when other people's arms stopped being comforting, perhaps it was when the private world of sex opened up into the public world of pregnancy, medicine, surgery.

When we go out to the bakery to get a baguette for our dinner, we run into my friend. He holds the door for us, nods politely, wishes us a good day. He stands in the street for a minute after we've gone in and then moves on.

Who was that? she asks me, always protective, trying not to pry.

Nobody, I say.

One of those dreams where I find a whole other wing to my apartment that I was previously unaware of. Great joy to find there is new space in which to be. Followed by anxiety: what am I going to do with it?

Ten a.m. I'm just out of the shower when Clémentine shows up at my door with wet hair and a loaf of sourdough. Anna! she says, heading toward the kitchen. Why didn't you tell me there's a really nice pool in this neighbourhood? Because I don't swim, I say. But if I did I don't think I'd go to that pool. Whyever not? she asks. Because it's in the rue Denoyez, and I'm superstitious.

Drowned People Street, she says. The most Belleville thing ever to put a pool on Drowned People Street. Anyway this bread is from the bakery opposite, it cost a fortune, you have to eat it with me.

In the tiny kitchen we brush past each other as we gather plates, knives, butter, jam. She notices the Brita is empty and fills it for me.

Today Clémentine is wearing blue eyeliner today she's wearing pink lipstick today her nails are painted today they're not today she's wearing lace tomorrow leather and then a massive hooded sweatshirt. I can't pin her down, she is simply, and thoroughly, herself. I see her pretty much every day now. She knows what time I get tired of being alone, and turns up. Sometimes she's on her way out to meet a friend, and just wants to check in. Clémentine goes places. The theatre, the cinema. Out for drinks. Once: bowling. I just run in my circles around the Buttes-Chaumont. She's taken the place of all the friends I don't see any more. The ones with kids (can't bear it). The ones who are pregnant (fuck them). The ones who are trying to get pregnant (don't want to hear about it). I figure she's too young to know what she wants kid-wise so it's perfect. One night we take a selfie with her Polaroid, she kisses my cheek, my smile makes my eyes squish shut.

After she leaves one evening, I google my exes. One, who used to be a classical pianist, now works at a software company. Another, a guy who drove a Vespa and used to do really filthy things in bed with me, is now the principal of a Catholic primary school in the provinces. Then I search for *Jonathan Weisz*. I have tried this before, without much luck; there is next to no trace of him on the internet. I have come across a LinkedIn profile detailing all the law firms he's worked for, and what he's specialised in. Civil responsibility law, it turns out; claims department. He has uploaded a picture since I last looked at his profile. He looks good. Round tortoiseshell glasses. Clipped facial hair. Bit of grey speckles in. Same smile. Same hair. Fuck.

One evening Clémentine shows up with an uncooked quiche and borrows my oven, theirs is on the fritz, she says. While she's there I try to ask her about redoing the kitchen, what does she think we should do, should we knock down the wall? She refuses to be drawn in on a practical level, has things she wants to say about the whole *idea* of home renovation. Redoing your house is a way to feel special, she muses. Where I live matters, I am not like all of you. Look at the things I choose, the care I put into it. See my specialness.

I'm learning enough about Clémentine's way of being in the world not to be offended. I think that's probably right, I say.

I am lying in bed late this morning when I hear singing coming up through the window. An accordion playing. Curious enough that I get up to see what's happening. A group of people, dressed in old-timey clothes, singing an old-timey song. *Tant que tu m'aimes bien j'ai besoin de rien.* Men in fedoras and flat caps, women in cloche hats. I think I may be hallucinating, or I've skipped back a century. Then I see the cameras. They are filming something, there in the streets of Belleville. I ask the gardienne when I go out what it is, as they're packing up their equipment. They're remaking *Sous les toits de Paris*, she says, you know, the René Clair film? Ah, I say, vaguely, I think I saw it a long time ago. All the old stories being retold, she says, and I can't tell if she's nostalgic for the old stories or impatient with the lack of new ones.

A number flashes on my phone, and the name of the contractor I was meant to have called by now. I don't answer.

The WhatsApp notifications are piling up: David, my mother, *his* mother. I leave them unread.

Climbing the stairs to see Esther it always smells of incense and there's a machine hum, like a vacuum cleaner, but who runs their vacuum for so long and every time I'm there? Is someone operating a sweatshop behind one of these cheap wooden doors? There's a power cord that snakes up the stairs, the baseboard of which is crumbling and entirely gone in some places.

Her office is at Bastille. I have to get the métro there, it's the only time I take it these days. I ride the line 11 to République, then change to the line 5. You see more interesting people on the line 5, I don't know why. Today: a second soprano with highlighted score, some choral music by Liszt. A girl in a red T-shirt who is alone until Richard Lenoir when her boyfriend gets on. The way they lace themselves through each other is delicate and fragile. Someone standing near me smells like they've been fucking then slid their pants back on and ran for the train.

A man comes through begging for money in a nasal voice, madame monsieur, madame monsieur, long pauses between supplications, like the voice of conscience in our minds. We all half-smile to say sorry. My skin turns yellow as I grip the central bar.

Today Esther says something.

You talk about remodelling, and this wallpaper in your kitchen, and I'm wondering what's underneath it.

Underneath the wallpaper?

She sucks on her e-cigarette and I might be imagining it but I think she's glaring at me. Yet the answer is so obvious I don't feel like supplying it. You have a failed pregnancy, a breakdown, you reach the point where you figure that if you're going insane there's a good chance it's because of the wallpaper. At least it's not yellow.

Well, I say, I think I just really need a change. A fresh start. A new setting.

You talk about renovation every time you come in here, but nothing is being renovated, everything is as it was.

Is it?

Stasis, she says. You are enjoying the fixation of your desire. You're afraid to get it moving again. There is nothing you actually need, except to go back to work. You have a kitchen.

She takes a sheet of paper from her folder, signs it, and shows it to me. Her consent to let me begin seeing patients again. The days of sitting doing nothing but staring at my laptop, or out the window, are finished. My breathing constricts. It's been months, what if my patients have started seeing new therapists, whom they prefer? What if I'm not ready to hear their stories again? What if I don't know what to say to them any more? You can start next Monday, she says with a smile. I think it will help break the stasis. I think it will be good for you.

Good for me, I repeat to myself on the métro ride home.

Walking downhill from the métro I encounter two more signs:

STOP FÉMINICIDE

NOUS SOMMES
LA VOIX DE
CELLES QUI N'EN ONT PLUS

I realise I have recently seen someone on the métro reading a copy of *Le Parisien*, with a headline about how many women have been murdered this past year, and how many more it is than last year. All of a sudden the signs begin to make sense.

When Clémentine comes over I ask her if she's seen them. Seen them! she says. I was out there a few nights ago pasting them up.

You should come with us next time, she says.

Another morning coming back from my run I see the sun glinting off a heap of metal on the sidewalk beside our building. As I get closer I see what it is: a pile of ladders, poles and fittings stacked like the bones of anonymous skeletons in the Catacombs, waiting to be joined up into their temporary structure, flush against the exterior of the building.

I go to my office and open the windows to air the place out. It's just starting to feel like autumn, the hint of a chill in the air. I've always liked the fall. Soon the clocks will go back.

The paper Esther signed is on my desk, slipped into my notebook. I'm going to have to go back to work. But it's not feeling possible. I still have too many cling-filmed days, when I can't get out of bed. No run, just the hours moving across the sky.

I am not ready to have anyone else join me in here.

Saturday morning and something has been pushed under my door. I take a closer look: it is a newspaper article, taken from *Le Monde*. *Aux femmes assassinées, la patrie indifférente: les «colleuses» d'affiches veulent rendre visibles les victimes de féminicides*. A picture of a blonde woman, who could be Clémentine, but isn't, is it? painting block letters on to A4 sheets of paper. Above her, pasted on a wall:

CÉLINE
DÉFENESTRÉE
PAR SON MARI
19e FÉMINICIDE

Across the bottom of the article, in red ink, Clémentine has written:

COME OUT WITH US

Saturday afternoon. Clémentine at the door.

Did you get my article? she asks.

It's very impressive, I say.

I think you should come out with us, she says. It's no commitment. We just need help.

Late Sunday afternoon, Clémentine knocks at the door, cheeks flushed, smelling of black pepper and something musky.

What is that smell?

I don't want to marry Jonathan, she says, but he wants to marry me.

Did he ask you?

It's just a perfume I got in the mail. Do you like it? She lights a cigarette. No he didn't ask me, it's just something I know. But I don't want to marry him. I don't want to get married at all.

Why did you do it?

For my family, I think. Yeah, I do. What is it?

I don't know. I can bring it next time. You can try it.

We move into the living room. Are your parents still married?

Yes, to each other.

Ah.

A pause.

I just don't think it's necessary to get married. It's a form of discipline developed to keep society moving along like a big normative machine. And I don't think married people should have special privileges unmarried people don't have.

Right, but then that means you and Jonathan, if you spend your lives together, won't have any of those privileges either.

I don't want those benefits if everyone can't have them, she declares.

That's very noble, I say, but what if you have children together? I think being married gives you more rights if it doesn't work out. I am losing the thread, vague on the very rights I'm supposed to be defending.

I don't want to have children, Clémentine says, and I try to absorb this and process, at top speed, the feelings it is making me feel.

I envy you that clarity, I say. I just – don't understand what the point of it all would be if you're not going to have a kid – I mean. I stop talking, afraid I sound like an idiot, like an old idiot.

What do you mean? she blinks at me. What is the point of anything?

I can't imagine what it would be like to be together without having children in front of you, it just sounds like a big blank. What are you going to do, travel? To see what? What would you be moving toward? What else would you be living for? Sex? Companionship? Being? Without the forward straining what is there to give you urgency? Just an inevitable end to everything? I'm talking too much, I don't know why it's irking me the way it is that she doesn't want children, who cares, what is it to me? Plenty of my friends and patients don't want them and it doesn't put me in this state.

It occurs to me that maybe I'm the one who doesn't want them.

Love isn't about straining toward something, she says. Other people try to move you forward. And then I never think I love anyone enough to want to tie myself to them for all eternity, Clémentine says. It never feels like enough. But at the same time once I commit I have trouble leaving. Or at least I've had trouble in the past. I worry I might marry the wrong person merely because I couldn't leave them.

Clémentine lights two more cigarettes, her hands shaking. I've got to stop smoking with her.

Hey is everything all right? You seem really worked up about this.

I just had lunch with my mother, is all, she says.

Sunday night and I'm in the kitchen, washing the dishes that have piled up for far too many days. The wine glasses have reached the point where it looks like I've had a party. The biggest items are the last to do, the heavy pot I made pasta in, the wooden cutting board I sliced the cherry tomatoes on. No more room left in the drying rack so I leave things on the counter. The Brita's empty again. All I do with my days, it seems, is drink water, piss, and refill the fucking Brita. I'm still thinking about my conversation with Clémentine. About the point of love, where we want it to take us, what we want from it. Everyone I've loved, I've loved with obsessive focus. I need an object, any object. If they resist, or try to leave me, I dazzle them with the power, the never-before-encountered power of my love. They have never seen love like that before, been loved like that before. It is irresistible to them to be loved in such a way. I point everything I've got at them, I shoot it all, until, one day, it's over. I can't stand to be around them.

It feels like Clémentine is helping me confront these things more than Esther.

In the bowl that is not my blue bowl are some late-season apricots, which the fruit flies are enjoying. I've been letting the wine bottles accumulate along with the dishes and they're breeding in them. I try to kill them but they are too fast for me. Someone is singing in the courtyard. Earnest tenor; wobbly vibrato. The guy who coughs coughs. Someone flushes a toilet.

I think back to the other times I'd been in love, when I was not the one who left. They were perfectly nice guys, who loved me, but loved me like their hearts were wearing condoms. My rush of love couldn't get through their protective barriers.

David doesn't fit either category. There is something exciting about him, but not threatening. I have sometimes wondered if finding him and being happy with him was just a question of calming down, of maturing. There are times when I wonder if I will remain this calm forever.

For a minute I have the strangest feeling like I can see through the wall to the living room, where a man sits, reading.

And I shake it off, and go refill the Brita.

Monday comes and goes, and I do not go in to work. I do not look at my emails. I do not answer my phone. OK Bartleby, I think, what's all this about? I slip the article Clémentine left me into my journal, along with my back-to-work paperwork.

While we wait in a long queue, my bakery friend gestures at the walls. Des petites annonces, he says, thoughtfully. That's what's missing. You used to have loads of little notes tacked up on the walls of the bakery, people selling things, or offering their services. Tutors, he says. Learn Spanish! Learn Greek! I wonder when they stopped having notes like that on the walls of bakeries. It's probably the internet's fault.

But on the internet you can learn Greek, I say, because I can see the line is going to take a while longer. They have apps for that.

Oh, apps! I don't want to learn Greek from a bot. That owl! I want to learn it from a young Greek student who's trying to make ends meet while he does his masters. Or an old Greek woman who's lost her husband. A real person, with a story. Maybe I will just move to Greece.

Walking downhill from the bakery I pass an elderly woman being pushed in a wheelchair. From under the red fleece blanket on her lap escapes one bare gnarled foot.

I think about my bakery friend that afternoon, as I tidy up the house. How quickly he's become a fixture in my life, a part of the day I look forward to, though I don't even know his name, and now that we've established this familiarity it feels weird to acknowledge we don't know something as fundamental as each other's names. I don't know if he has a family, children, what he does for a living, who he eats all that tahini with. He emerged from the city, is of the city. I don't even know where he lives.

His friendship, and Clémentine's, are experiments. I need to live more in the present, to take things as they come instead of asking what they are, what is their nature, what is their name.

I move very quickly at the beginnings of things. I can't stand the beginnings of things. Their eyes looking at me, the thoughts behind these eyes that I don't know yet, the uncrossable distance, how they move unfamiliarly through my personal space. Whenever I started sleeping with someone new, I coped with this by converting them very quickly from a stranger into a beloved. This is where things tended to get complicated. Because they're strange and foreign. And in the mad rush to cover that up, I formed attachments to people who weren't going to stick around. I have to learn to tolerate the time when they're a stranger. When they leave the house and I don't know where they're going or what they're doing. It's terrifying to accept the essential otherness of the people we care for.

But what is even more terrifying is admitting to yourself that in spite of the bridge you think you've crossed – in spite of the fact that time, and you, and their commitment to you, have converted them from a stranger into the person you know the best in the world – in spite of all that – they are still irrevocably Other.

With my bakery friend and with Clémentine it is different, there is something inarticulable about them, an ambiguity in our friendship that I'm not eager to iron out with information, which would only be an illusion of information, anyway. What do I need to know about my bakery friend beyond what I learn in our interactions? What kind of words do I need to put to Clémentine?

Wildfires burning in the south-west and Corsica, for lack of rain. The reservoirs are low, the rivers and lakes too. On France Inter they're talking about the way this will impact the wildlife that live there, and the knock-on effect, up the chain, on human life, on our lives, here in the cities.

Clémentine, sitting on the kitchen counter while I try to do the dishes that have been getting away from me again. Because her days are spent trying to figure out what she can do for a job (Anna, what am I going to do for a *job*?), she's trying to figure out my relationship to my own job. How it works, what exactly I'm doing these days and what it means.

So you were depressed.

Yes.

And they put you on leave.

Yes.

And now that leave is over and you're not going to work.

No.

She sits with this for a moment.

So you're on strike!

I don't know what I'm on.

A beat.

Are you going to come out with us tonight?

Oh, I say, trying to think of a reason why I can't. Oh I think I'm supposed to speak with David tonight.

OK, she says, and I know she sees through me. That's OK, maybe another night.

Phone call from my mother asking if I've gone back to work yet.

You know, I was thinking of buying a piano, I tell her, to change the subject.

Oh, she says. I used to love it when you played.

By the end of the week I finally get around to checking my email. Messages from my boss at Sainte-Anne, at first gentle, understanding, I was meant to come in was I not, and then gradually more frustrated, the last one, Thursday evening, saying we're going to have to explore our options at this point, they can't keep me on staff if I'm not coming in, and then Friday morning remorseful, I must be going through a difficult time, take it, take my time. Delete, delete, delete. I highlight my entire inbox, every email I've ever received, take a deep breath, pause for a minute and then hit *delete*.

Esther hasn't asked why I haven't started work again, though I'm sure she knows, I'm sure they've said something, but David, David asks. I avoid his phone calls. He calls in the morning and before bed but when I don't answer he texts to say that he loves me and he's here if I want to talk but that we're going to have to have a conversation about money. I don't want to talk about money but I know he's right so I keep on ignoring his phone calls.

I see a woman on the métro with longish hair that she lets rest peacefully on her shoulders — it falls so freely. I am always tying mine back, twisting it up, forcing it out of my face, why even have it, it does nothing for me, it's a nod to convention, it takes time and water and shampoo and plastic and chemicals to maintain it on my head like an exotic plant, why not shave it all off and be done with hair, femininity, the big beauty show?

The brown in the kitchen is getting to me and it's way too small in there and I'm starting to feel even more claustrophobic.

The piece of paper Esther signed is still slipped inside my journal. I haven't had the courage to call anyone, let them know I'm coming back. I can't check my voicemail. They're going to fire me if I don't get in touch. And there won't be any more money coming in if I don't start seeing patients. But I can't help them if I don't want to be there, listening to them. I feel like I'm being counterproductive to the universe, like I'm blocking some kind of essential flow. I'm not on strike, like Clémentine said, because I'm not serving anyone but myself. There's no greater cause, I just can't do it.

Soon, I tell myself. Take another week.

And Clémentine, and her friends with the collages. And the kitchen. When will I call about the kitchen?

That horrible wallpaper. Brown and yellow and orange vines, twisting down the wall, imprisoning each other, lush and prickly. I locate one of the spots where it's starting to peel away, lift my hand up to it, peel it away, a bit more, then a bit more, until I take a big swathe off in one massive go. Underneath, white wall, mottled with glue and age. I find some Blu-Tack and place the Polaroid of me and Clémentine there.

Eventually the email I was expecting, I've been fired, I'm not unhappy about it, on the contrary, now I can stop feeling bad about my patients.

I finally call the contractor. I'd given up on you, he says. You have missed the window, he says. But they can fit me in when they're done with the current job, the one they bumped up when they didn't hear from me. It serves me right.

David comes to visit. He seems mildly alarmed by the state of the place. He helps me empty the dishwasher, which I ran several days ago. Our ancient decrepit dishwasher is reliably bad and something of a joke. It came with the apartment and must have been one of the first dishwashers in Paris. It, too, is brown. Things that come out of it are also brown. David hands me a spatula I had put back in the drawer without looking at it. There's something still on there, he says. It is brown of course, gelatinous, and also feathered, as if a bird had flown into our apartment, then into the dishwasher, where it perished clinging to the metal spatula.

He takes me out for a walk, down all our familiar streets, the rue Denoyez covered in graffiti, up the rue Ramponeau where we once passed the famous Marxist historian who lives there, up into the Parc de Belleville which is the only place where I ever saw David get angry, when he saw someone had spray-painted tiny swastikas on to the Brutalist columns supporting the canopy over the section with the view of Paris and the telescopes. He was in the middle of reminiscing about his favourite writer Georges Perec and how he used to live here with his family until the war came and his dad died fighting and his mom died in Auschwitz and how years later in the 70s they tore the whole neighbourhood down to put in this park and that's when he saw the swastikas, and he utterly lost his shit. It's a weird park, the architecture reminds me of something you'd find in a 1990s-era Miami mall, except here the fountain references the water that used to flow beneath the hills of Belleville, probably still does, into the centre of the city. Les sources de Belleville, first built by the Romans, then restored by medieval monks. I don't know if the Miami fountains are references too but I tend to think not. They destroyed Perec's house to build this park, David said that day, and those of so many other Jews who were no longer here to defend their homes, at least they could have some respect. David's read *Life a User's Manual* half a dozen times, it's one of the reasons I gave him a second look, this self-assured law student I met at a friend's party. That and his love for Romain Gary.

On the rue Denoyez I tell David about how Clémentine goes swimming at the pool there and that she clearly isn't superstitious but he doesn't laugh.

Morning at the bakery, after my run. My friend is there, he tries to pay for my baguette, I try to pay for my own, for once he lets me. I notice for the first time the small gold Star of David around his neck, lying in a nest of grey hair. As we walk out the door together, I feel a few raindrops. By the time I get into my flat, it is pouring rain.

I wake up and it is dark outside. I am discombobulated; it must be the middle of the night yet it feels like I have slept for hours and hours. I look at my phone. It is 7:15 a.m. I forget, year after year, how dark it is in the morning by this time in October.

Walking up the rue de Belleville the man a few yards in front of me stops and embraces a person who is heading the other way, like chummy fleecy teddy bears, and then they each go their own ways, mushy with love. A woman walks by me, beautiful curly hair and a tote bag that reads: I ♥ Bratislava. There's been another flurry of signs today, Clémentine and her friends have been busy. Everyone's talking about les colleuses, I'm not surprised they're going all out, there's even an Instagram account now. Clémentine shows it to me.

MON UTÉRUS
MON CHOIX

NON C'EST NON

ON ARRÊTERA DE COLLER
QUAND VOUS ARRÊTEZ DE VIOLER

If I make it through my life without being murdered by some guy, she says, I will be astonished.

I have a new approach to the fruit flies. I take a pad of paper and crush them to the wall with it. It never fails; they can't get away quickly enough. Now my kitchen walls are spotted with pink splatters, though you can hardly see them on top of the muddy brown wallpaper.

One day Clémentine comes over and complains of having a stiff neck from posing. Posing? I ask. One of the artists I sit for, she sighs; he is very particular about how he likes me to sit, and today he sketched me looking back at him over my shoulder. She moans a little moan.

Oh *that's* the kind of modelling you do?

What did you think, that I was some kind of high-fashion model? She finds this hilarious.

I don't know! You said modelling brought in some money! But this makes so much more sense! You're an art model! I am delighted, I feel like I finally understand Clémentine. Shifted from fashion-adjacent rich girl more completely to earnest artsy student, she comes into focus, as if I have been the one painting her in my mind all this time. She is still beautiful, but with the kind of beauty that you try to look further into, not the kind they use to sell things.

I saw some more signs the other day, I say. They're very good. How do you decide what you're going to write?

We keep an eye on the news, she says, we alert people in the group when there's been another one, every time we go out we write a woman's name, along with the other slogans. Or if we feel like we're gaining momentum, like we are now.

Are you going out again soon?

Soon, she says. I'll let you know.

Another day Clémentine comes over and wants to talk about a television series she's been watching, based on an Irish novel, which I have also been watching. It's kind of annoying, says Clémentine. Like, sleep together, don't sleep together, do your thing. It must be because it's still a Catholic country. I keep waiting for someone to do something really shocking for TV, like, I don't know, fisting! nipple clamps! throuples! revolution! Instead it's just this *who cares* dialectic.

But dramatically necessary, I say. Keeps you watching. Gives people something to project themselves into, narcissistically. Introductory film theory. Or Aristotle.

Clémentine sighs. The most interesting part of infidelity isn't will they or won't they, it's everything else around it. What if it's *all fine*? she says, making a dramatic hand gesture.

Then no more conflict!

But there's still life, people leading lives! And the whole thing about needing to confess to the wife! She makes a little sound of exasperation. Fidelity is a container for sex, to keep it from being too threatening. I have no idea what Jonathan gets up to, she says, and I don't think it's my business to know. *I don't want to know anything about it.* It has nothing to do with what we have together. Don't you think? What about you and David? Do you only plan to ever have sex with him, only him, for the rest of your life? Or maybe you already have sex with other people, she says, her face properly glowing now.

I think about it.

I guess I'm sort of relieved not to have to worry about going out to find someone to sleep with any more.

Clémentine snorts. A ringing endorsement of marriage!

I think David is more committed to fidelity than I am, I say, in terms of the ideal of it; I'm more of a realist, but I'm also a pragmatist. People are unfaithful and that's human nature. I spend a lot of time with my patients trying to help them see how they can accommodate it, without letting it destroy them, whichever role they play. But I'd personally rather not bother with the drama of it in my own life. Leave that to the Irish novelists.

Have you ever cheated on David? she asks.

No, I say. Have you? On Jonathan?

No, she says. Then a second later: Well I did make out with a girl at a bar one time. I was out with a friend who was up from Marseille and we got very very drunk and we were talking to these people at the bar and you know, it's very easy to kiss someone –

Is it?

One minute you're talking and the next you're touching tongues.

Huh.

But I didn't, like, run home and tell him. Whatever disruption may come, in that sense, it has to be absorbed back into the relationship, and I think it was, I really think it was.

She pauses.

So David is being faithful to you in London?

I think so. I don't know. I don't mind if he kisses someone at a bar. No sooner have I said it than I know it's not true; I would be incensed, to think David's desire had moved toward someone else like that. But I don't take it back.

There's nothing actually that intimate about touching some-one else's tongue with your tongue, is there? she says. We just don't do it very often. We're confusing rarity with intimacy.

Surely the same definition extends to, like, genital sex? I say. That's generally also a pretty rare thing to do with someone new, someone who isn't your partner, I mean. Unless that's something you're specifically into, then I guess it isn't that rare. Which – no judgement.

No judgement, she says.

She thinks for a minute. You're always saying that Lacan says that as individuals we are constituted through lack, right? So I was thinking – she widens her eyes wider – that it's like an orgasm. So amazing as you're moving towards it and cresting over but even as you get there it's imperfect, you're flooded with memories of better ones, like it must feel to do a triple Lutz, even as you soar into the air you know you have done it better, and you want to do it again, better, right then immediately, and you want more, and you want it to go on and it's over too soon. You push against each other, fucking it out, trying to get there, trying to get back what you lost or never had.

That's love, I say. Lacan says something like our sex organs leave us after sex, or we shed them, I can't remember, and all that remains to us are memories quickly dissolving.

Yes! she says. So being in love, having sex, whatever, it's like we're dissolving as we're doing it and we keep doing it to keep ourselves together.

And I wonder what keeps her together with her boyfriend, what keeps them from dissolving. She's so – free-spirited, politically committed, young, and queer. Is she one of those girls who needs an older man to feel safe and looked after? It doesn't make sense. But then, I have found, people often don't.

That night I dream about Jonathan. Of all the relationships I had before and since, why is he the one I dream about? I can't remember the specifics, they were involved, plotty, I'm just left with the feeling of having spent some time with him.

David is in town, and since I haven't stopped thinking about my conversation with Clémentine, I decide to mention it to him.

All the girls in London are vulgar, he says.

You used to say that about me. You thought I talked too loudly. *American girls are vulgar*, you said.

That was before I moved to London. I've spent entire Eurostar journeys listening to two girls talk about their spray-tans, best techniques, how long it lasts. The other day I was walking down the street and this woman was approaching with some impossibly small dog wearing a jacket on a leash and she calls out, BABE. Like bellows it. And some woman in the doorway several houses down goes, YES BABE. And the first one with the dog goes, YOU'RE NEVER GOING TO BELIEVE WHAT JUST HAPPENED. Like it's totally normal to carry on a private conversation at top volume in the middle of the street. He shakes his head. I try not to laugh at him.

They sound amazing. How nice to be in a place where nobody gives a fuck.

He grunts.

So you're not cheating on me in London.

If I were, would you want to know?

We fight, briefly, about my going to London. I don't want to. He warns me the window is closing, Brexit is happening, soon it won't be as easy for me to move there with him. He's worried about money, still, who wouldn't be. He wants to sublet the Paris apartment, says it's too much to pay for his flat there and this place here. I know what he's getting at but I let him say it.

Well, as long as you're going to stay, do you think you might be ready to start seeing patients again soon? he asks, trying to be tactful. You don't have to go back to Sainte-Anne, but would it be so terrible to resume your private practice? Work from home? Make your own hours? Sounds like a dream to me.

My period is due, and the insomnia is upon me. David sleeps like the dead. I get up and pour myself a glass of milk. Coming back to bed I walk across the creaky floor and wonder who else has walked gingerly across it, trying not to wake someone up, a lover, a partner, a baby. Was the floor always creaky? Was there a time when it was true? When the wood hadn't warped but was laid so perfectly the floorer could go home feeling he'd done a good day's work, before time worked against him and loosened the joints and the fittings? There is a piece of packing tape across the crack between a couple of boards near the doorway. I noticed it when we moved in, thought that was a crappy way to fix whatever needed fixing, but elected not to peel it up. Who knew what it was holding together.

I run into Clémentine by the front door again today. She's standing outside of it, without moving. Did you forget the code again? I ask. She just looks at me.

What? Oh, no. No, I know the code, she says, and she keys it in.

Is everything OK? I ask.

Yes, she says. Everything's OK.

I go upstairs to my apartment, and she goes upstairs to hers. A little while later, there's a knock at my door. It's Clémentine, holding out a small metal container.

It's tea, she says. I brought some tea. Shall we make a pot? Mine's still packed away.

You still haven't unpacked? I'm incredulous. You've been there for two months!

She shrugs. We've reached an impasse about who's going to open the boxes. It's amazing how little you actually need to get by from day to day. Obviously my own clothes and things are put away, but not the kitchen stuff, not Jonathan's stuff. Cardboard boxes as home décor, what do we think. Very Demna.

As I pour the boiled water into my own teapot, and we settle down on the couch, she tells me what had happened to make her stop that way outside our front door. It was David, she says, and for a moment I'm confused. Where was David?

I saw my friend David, from high school. The one I told you about.

I can't remember her mentioning a David, from high school or elsewhere, but I nod.

I ran into him at the shop. Buying this tea. Well I wasn't there to buy the tea. I didn't mean to go into that shop. But I was passing by and I saw him and I had to go in. Want a cigarette? I shake my head, resolute today.

He was a bit older than me, when I said he was from high school I mean I met him when I was in high school, but he was already at university. He hung out with my best friend's older brother, they were artists, they were studying at the Beaux-Arts. We used to go to parties with them, gigs, whatever. I smoked pot with him for the first time. We spent so much time together. I think I was a little in love with him. He was so funny, and so talented. You could see it in his drawings, in his lines, he just had this very specific line, the way it moved across the page, I loved to watch his hands. Anyway. He got involved with this girl and it got really serious and they moved to Marseille together, and he didn't hang out with my friend's brother so much any more. I guess. All I knew was that he drifted out of the group and I never saw him again, until today, in that shop.

So what did he say?

Nothing really interesting, he's still living down there, just comes to Paris to visit sometimes. He married that girl. He shows his work in Marseille a bit. I couldn't tell if he has another job or if he makes money from it or what. She holds the cigarette off the table with her long fingers, which shake slightly. It was just very strange to see him. I have a different life now, I'm not a kid any more, and I have often thought that it was David who made me want to study art. I couldn't make it, but I could study it. Like if I understood it, I could understand him a little better.

Have you ever tried to draw or paint?

Sure, yes, of course. I used to try to imitate his line! He showed me one time with some charcoal, but I was like a little kid with a crayon, I had no control over my hand.

We sit, while she smokes, and I think of her hand, and how little control she has over it. So you weren't ever involved with him?

No, we were never *involved*. But there was this one night when we were all drinking and we went into the bedroom together, and we lay down on the bed, and he held me. We were all jumbled up together, our legs I mean, and it was like we were going to start kissing, but we didn't. I don't know why we didn't. I wanted him so badly. I saw him a few more times after that but really I think that was the end. We got too close. I wanted to go further, go closer, and he knew it, and he kept me on the edge with him. When I saw him today I saw that he remembered that night, I saw he was thinking about it. I saw he was thinking of taking me home with him. He was going to tell me the name of his hotel and then he stopped, and paid for his tea, and left.

That night, I dream about Jonathan again. I'm on the rue d'Ulm, I'm crossing the street, and so is he, and he doesn't see me. And I call out his name, and he stops and looks at me but still doesn't see me. And I don't know if I'm a ghost or if he is but one of us is there and one of us definitely isn't. The dream is so strong that for the rest of the next day, I feel so heavy.

They haven't turned the heat on yet; the mornings are cold. Cold air outside the duvet and the smell of someone's cigarette. Blue light leaks in around the curtains and the métro rumbles deep below ground. The guy who coughs is coughing a lot more.

My period has come, and the water in the shower runs red.

One evening there's a pretty young woman standing at one of the windows across the way talking selfies, dark hair, full lips, silk wrap, the one who, earlier this past summer, hung up a string of red peppers across the garde-fou.

Her next-door neighbour is a woman who keeps all her perishables in a wooden box suspended from her own guardrail. Her other windows are obscured by an ironing board and some other crap. She's putting some milk outside, and jars of things. She and her neighbour pretend not to see one another.

The next day there's a man howling nearby; the sound carries across the courtyard and we all go to our windows to see if it's someone who needs our help, or needs his privacy. Deciding it's the latter, we slowly close our windows, thinking of how close loss has come.

That day the cranking and thundering begin, as the scaffold-ing is screwed into place. The metallic grinding and drilling of something into something – into what? building? I always thought of scaffolding as something supportive that goes around or next to something else, but there is always at least one point of damage, they can't just pile it up free-standing. The clanging, the echo of metal being screwed into metal. The unidentifiable thrummings and clackings and clangings, things being hauled up, sawed, arranged, set. The deep deep sound of metal pene-trating metal. Metallic violence has taken over our windows, the sonic area of our home. The sawing sounds like an engine revving. Throughout the day the level rises, the noise comes and goes, and soon the top of a yellow hard-hat is peeking through the window. I feel like I should say hello, but I don't, I am too shy. I can see their shadows on the curtains, the hand with the hammer, striking, like the murderer with a knife in some slasher film. I wonder how many scaffolds he will build in his lifetime.

Scaffolding. Has the ring of the gallows to it.

What will it do to the view from my office? I wonder stupidly if my clients will mind when they return. There are no restaurants or shops in our building, no one to hang a sign saying OPEN DURING THE BUILDING WORKS! on the scaffolding. Just me, in my upstairs window, worried about the view, slowly being blocked off.

Saturday night, it's very late, and I'm already in bed with my computer and my glasses on when there's a knock at the door. Under her big wool coat Clémentine is wearing a thin white jersey dress, the top few buttons are undone, I can see the ribs in her chest, and the place where her small breasts swell and part. She has been drinking. She comes in, and tells me she fucked someone in a bar. A woman. Upstairs from the bar, she says, to be more specific, she lived there, above the bar she says, breathless, her eyes shining. I don't know how to feel. I don't think I should go home to Jonathan like this, she says. Can I stay here? And she does, she strips down to her panties and borrows a T-shirt and in the morning after she's gone the place in the bed where she's slept smells like cigarette smoke and something I can't quite identify. The T-shirt is folded on the pillow and there is a neatly sectioned grapefruit in a bowl on the kitchen counter.

Then one day the scaffolding's finished, clinging to the outside of the building like a metal exoskeleton. We have disappeared behind it. The light too. When they began the refacing it made a noise that got inside my head like a trip to the dentist, that feeling of being drilled in a place so interior, so private, no ordinary person can ever reach. But it's the smaller sounds that are going to drive me mad. Flint flint flint flint. They're getting in. Flint flint flint flint. There is no way to escape it, short of leaving the house. Every day they work in small areas from top to bottom, chipping the building's enamel down to its nerves. The hammer on the chisel. You can hear the rubble trickle off like marbles down a stairway. Eventually they'll reapply a thick coating of stucco. I look forward to that, to the caking, the smoothing. It will be so soothing after all this. And the building does need a fresh coat of paint.

At any hour of the day there are men crawling up the outside of the building, like oversized beetles, showing up through the window, walking on the balcony. I've been leaving the shutters closed, seeking shelter in the bedroom. But everywhere, even on the courtyard side of the apartment, the noise is oppressive. The flinting. And then the scraping. Back and forth. Back and forth. Beneath the scaffolding the ground has filled up with crumpled cigarette packets.

Clémentine comes for tea. She's smoking Marlboro Reds today. They're not ravaler-ing her building. Just ours, the side that faces the street. Really I should go to hers but she says it's still too messy. What does she do all day? I don't ask. I'm not one to talk. Sitting in the living room, we can hear the workmen talking on the other side of the outside wall, their voices muffled. Clémentine tells me about a poem she is writing. I try to follow what she was saying, though the men's voices are distracting. I'm trying to figure out if they're speaking French or something else. I can't put a name around the sounds they're making.

I'm very interested in catachresis, Clémentine is saying.

I'm not sure I've heard her correctly.

You know, like a euphemism, or a misnaming, or things that there are no names for. Mixed metaphors. Language is an imperfect tool, no matter what Flaubert thought. The mot juste is always an approximation. The word you think is the most right may in fact be the most wrong. We force words into place and they don't want to stay there. I love you, we say to someone, when we mean don't leave me. Don't leave me, we say to another person, when we mean to say I want to leave you but I'm a little worried you'll throw yourself in the Seine. Don't throw yourself in the Seine, we say, when we want to push them in. We can't stand each other but we love each other too much to leave. She sips her tea.

Is everything OK with you and Jonathan? I ask.

What? Oh. Yes! Yes of course. Things are great! Clémentine says, folding her long legs beneath her. This is just – you know. Stuff I think about.

It's interesting, I say. The kind of stuff I used to mull over a lot when I was in grad school. You know I started out studying literature? I love words, slippery words. I guess that's why I was drawn to Lacan. If the unconscious is structured like a language, maybe catachresis is the essence of the unconscious.

It's the essence of love, Clémentine says, earnest again. Love is always misplaced. It's always a misfire, or a misreading of the person we can't live without. How can we know them, really? We only know what we know to know. We can only recognise what we've already seen.

I worry that's one of my limitations, as a therapist. That I can only respond to what a patient is saying on the basis of my own narrow understanding of the world. I spend so much time read-ing, and watching these trashy television shows, trying to get a wider view. I feel like what I can see or understand is blocked somehow.

I'm sure it's true for all therapists, Clémentine says. How could it be otherwise?

My biggest problem is with mothers. I've read all there is to read about mothers, from Freud to Klein to Winnicott, and still don't feel I have any understanding of how anyone else's mother could be. My own looms so large that she stands in for all the others. I had hoped that becoming a mother myself it would help me in my practice.

Are you going to try again?

Yes but not now. You know? I'm just enjoying the, like, safe enclosure of my body. With David away, no one touches me, and I touch no one. There's no more early life dependent on my own. No alien second heart forming, with its second brain, second stomach, to compete with my own heart, brain, stomach. No more sickness and fatigue. Just my own body, closed off, singular. Anyway we don't have sex any more.

You don't?

Not since the surgery. My body doesn't seem to want to.

Clémentine says huh.

Clémentine abruptly stands up, goes over to my laptop, opens it. Password?

Oh – it's embarrassing. I'll do it. I type it in. Why?

She opens a tab in my browser, searches for something. Someone beating a tom-tom and playing a jangly guitar, and then a woman's voice singing 'Lola' by the Kinks, but this is not the Kinks.

Do you know the Raincoats? she asks. She doesn't wait for an answer, just pulls me out into the area behind the couch, starts doing a leggy swinging dance to the beat of the drum, makes me do it with her. She puts her hands on my hips and starts doing this knee-bending thing. She is the worst dancer I've ever seen. The music speeds up and so do we, because now the music is in my body too and the drum's making my head go double time and my arms are going to shake right off of my body and it's absolutely brilliant and mad and I'm singing and she's singing, looooh-la la la la la loooooh-la. When it's over she plays me all the rest of the album and we order in sushi and when I go to sleep that night it's Clémentine I see leaning over me, Clem with her fingers in me, Clem with her tongue on me, Clem with her cunt on mine, like wanting mouths.

The noise! The noise is everywhere. I live in the noise and it lives in me, around me, on my skin, in my skull. It braces me, pierces me, goes through me every way it can. Every day, from eight in the morning until eight at night, with only a break for lunch. What are they on, shifts? It can't be the same workers morning till night, hanging off the side of the building, chipping away. It gets so bad that week that I ask Clémentine to come over with a little bag of weed. We smoke in the living room, where the sweet smell dissolves into the fibres of the sofa, throw, rug, jeans, sweater, hair. I stroke my hair. My own hair. I used to love my name, I say, thinking of hair, and fibres; saturation, and bestowing. Because it's a palindrome. I thought it indicated that there was something deeply moral about me, that I was the same backwards and forwards, coming and going. They named me after Anna Karina. My mother loved her films.

I like my name, says Clémentine.

My grandfather called me Nana. I was shocked when I read Zola in high school, finding out this was a prostitute's name. I was furious, like why would my family do that to me? It was no longer the same back and forth. It said one thing one way, and something quite different back the other way.

Back and forth, says Clémentine. Her leg is on my leg. Her shirt is riding up a little bit; I can see an inch of pale skin above the waist of her jeans. I think for a minute of sliding my hand into the gap, but I don't. Instead it feels necessary to articulate something about Anna Karina, something that's always felt important about her. When I watch her films I think about how she ended up in the movies. She was at the Deux Magots when some scouts saw her and got her started as a model. That led to a meeting with Godard. She married him and starred in his movies. All because one day she was in the right café. I used to think of that when I went to cafés. That maybe it would be the right day to be in the right café. Not that I was pretty enough to be a model or a movie star. But I thought maybe something would happen if I made myself available to it. So I went out as much as possible, putting myself in public, putting myself out where I could be found.

Found, says Clémentine.

Oh shit! I jump up from the couch. David's plants! I haven't watered them in a week. The pot made me remember. David loves plants, I tell Clémentine, he has the greenest thumb, and I am terrible with them. I open the windows to the balcony. He tried all summer to coax wisteria to climb up these wooden lattice panels he bought for it and I keep not watering it enough.

Plants, she says, are how you know people in Paris have been there for a while and intend to stay – the thick foliage around their windows, trellising their balconies. Something as impermanent as plants suggesting human permanence, or the will to it anyway.

Well plants are definitely impermanent with me, I say. I bought a succulent a few years ago and that's the only one I can manage to take care of. I show it to her, a thick gouty one. I couldn't bear to lose it. It would be the proof that I can keep nothing alive.

I come back to Clémentine on the couch, and lie down with my head in her lap. She combs my hair with her fingers. I close my eyes and allow myself to ask her why she sleeps with men, if she so clearly wants to be with women.

It isn't so clear, she says, that's the problem, I want to sleep with men too, I wouldn't be with Jonathan if I didn't want him.

Did you start with men? I ask, testing the limits of our intimacy.

I fooled around with a boy in my high school and let him put himself inside me, but I wouldn't exactly call that sex, she says, though I guess that was technically how I lost my virginity. No, for me sex started with a girl, Céline, I think I told you about her. We met at a protest our parents took us to when we were twelve. It was the university protests, my parents were on strike and so was her mom. Her parents were divorced. We were friends, and then we were more than friends. She didn't go to my school, she lived in the 16th, she was like a secret life for me, away from home and the kids I saw every day. We would lie around kissing each other, we told each other it was because we were practising for boys, but then we started doing other things and suddenly we weren't practising for anyone else, we were really in it, with each other. Anyway it was the summer after we finished lycée and I went away with her family for the summer holidays, and her dad was there, staying at the house with us, and he swam with us, and drank with us, and smoked with us, and one day when I was washing my swimsuit in the laundry room he came up behind me and put his hand between my legs. And I liked it, Clémentine says, and I started sleeping with him, and I liked that too, I liked the hair on his chest, I liked how big he was, I liked hearing him talk about when he was young and having it be such a different time, he worked in cinema and he had loads of friends and I was so flattered that he would pay attention to me. When we got back to Paris I broke up with Céline and kept seeing Marc. I was so unused to seeing someone who had money, he paid for these splashy dinners and bought me the art books I wanted and anything else I wanted too. I started university and was still living with my parents but I stayed at Marc's place most nights. We had a big fight when they found out. They ordered me to leave him and I said I wouldn't.

Céline refused to see her father and I felt terrible, fighting with my parents I could handle but not causing a rift between Céline and Marc, I could understand why she didn't want to see me but I didn't want to drive *them* apart. Still, something in me couldn't leave him. I know it doesn't make sense because he was so much older and it might look like he was taking advantage of me, but he needed me, I swear, I was the one taking care of him. Her voice cracks a little.

Anyway, she says. That was a long time ago and I didn't really know what I was doing or what I wanted, I guess I still don't know, but it's good with Jonathan for now, it really is.

For now, I say.

For now, she says.

Flint flint flint flint. Flint flint flint flint. Flint.   Flint.
Flint flint.

   Flint flint flint flint flint   flint flint.

      Flint.

flint flint in bed, in bed at four in the afternoon, in bed hours before going to bed, I let my necklace dangle from a finger, in front of my face, self-hypnotising. flint flint flint. Back and forth. Back and forth. I try to reach David and can't get through. I think the worst. Not that he's lying in a ditch somewhere. flint flint flint. That he's lying in some other girl's bed. I remember how he broke up with his partner before me. They had been together for a few years, and then he suddenly got this urge to travel, he took time off from his job and he went travelling on his own in Australia and New Zealand for four months. He didn't invite her to come. She wanted to, he said, she wanted it to be something they did together, but he needed to do it alone. They tried to keep up the relationship long distance, but as soon as he got to Melbourne he was talking about staying on there, and he ended it. Is this what he's doing to me, now, in turn? I cry with frustration, and my nose gets stuffed from crying, and I can't sleep, and I start to cry some more. flint flint flint. I try to practise mindfulness, to watch my thoughts, an exercise I used to recommend to my clients when they got like this. You have control over your own thoughts. Watch them, see where they go, and you can reroute them. Make new pathways. flint flint flint. Flint.

This is what I tell myself, still lying in bed at three in the morning, still far from sleep, a sticky, teary mess. You can cry, or not cry. That's the choice. Not crying is so much more comfortable than crying.

The morning light sneers at eight a.m., too early to wake up, and yet there I am. Awake. And crying already. And already the *flinting*.

I don't see Clémentine for a few days after we smoke together; I expect her every afternoon but she doesn't come. Then, without warning, she does. She apologises for her absence, she says they've finally been unpacking the boxes, and it's been more stressful than she thought it would be. She is distant in a way she hasn't been previously, even the first few times we met. I am caught off-guard, it feels like she is a stranger, after we've spent so much time together I have this feeling like I hardly know her at all.

Are you OK Clémentine?

I'm OK, are you OK?

Are you OK? she asks.

It's been a strange day, I say. I saw the most fucked-up thing when I was coming home from my run. I was walking downhill and spotted one of the Chinese prostitutes walking a little ways ahead of me—

Sex workers, Clémentine interrupts, les marcheuses, they call them—

A marcheuse, OK, she was being followed by this guy who looked like he'd seen better days, a little grizzled, with a kind of limp. If you weren't from the neighbourhood and didn't know what the woman did for a living, you wouldn't have realised they were together. Then these three cops came out of nowhere and tackled the guy to the wall, accusing him of being a threat to the public welfare. They hauled this fragile-looking man into a police car and sped off, siren blaring. The woman herself took off at top speed. I saw her a little later, smoking a cigarette and arguing with someone, understandably pissed about missing out on this bit of cash. This paternalistic government that purported to protect her had essentially robbed her instead. I must have been looking at her too long because she yelled at me. What the fuck are you looking at! She got up really close to my face, and said it again, really quietly, what, the fuck, are you looking at.

And I felt such shame! That I was just watching all of this, at being just that – a watcher, a white woman, part of the wave of gentrifiers in this previously working-class part of Paris. Well, David was born in Belleville, his parents live on rue Piat. But still this shame, I can't shift it.

Why is that, do you think? she asks.

I don't know. I just felt shame at being able to watch, and go on with my day.

Don't you ever feel that way in your sessions? Isn't a shrink a kind of voyeur? Or, you know, they pay you to help them, to give them some relief, maybe that makes you a little more like the marcheuse.

I raise my eyebrows. I *am* there to help them, that's why they've come to me. But as an onlooker on the street I felt ashamed.

Well, maybe that's a reason to do something. Since you're not really helping anyone right now. Maybe instead of staying in your house all the time you can come out with us.

I will, I say, knowing it's a lie.

Alone after Clémentine leaves I stream a film called *La Marcheuse* on my computer, from a couple of years back. A young Chinese mother turns tricks during the daytime while her daughter is in school. In one scene she stands at her window while she takes a call from a potential client. How did you get my number? . . . I charge fifty euros . . . No I don't work at night . . . No I won't do it without a condom . . . OK, see you tomorrow. In the building across the way, a smarmy guy in a red silk jacket open to reveal his hairy chest takes a drag on his cigarette. He smiles a smarmy smile at the young woman. She quickly closes the curtains. Covertly, she watches him through the slit as he leaves his window and sits down on his couch, by his open laptop. I half-expect him to start masturbating, but the camera cuts away. The next day, the guy from the phone call picks her up in his car, takes her somewhere random to have her go down on him (he tries again to wheedle her into doing it without a condom) and then he leaves her in this random place, reneging on his promise to drive her home. She takes the métro back instead. We see her image reflected on the window of the train car.

Something Clem said has stuck with me for weeks now and I don't know what to do with it; something like whether psychoanalysis ought to be socially transformative to justify its existence. I'd always assumed it was its own justification, that its capacity for change was baked in. Isn't there necessarily potential for society if we work with people one at a time? The collective is comprised of individuals, after all. Or have I just been kidding myself, is it all just voyeurism?

I spend so much time looking out the window of my office, looking at the people in the building across the street, thinking about how they have no idea what everyone else is doing above and below and even right next door: the woman with the peppers has no idea about the little girl who dances to Taylor Swift, and in the upper left-hand corner someone watches TV and to the right someone else sits and reads the newspaper. There is a paradoxical kind of privacy in this kind of urban living; we observe without, for the most part, judging; we are observed but, one would hope, not judged. On the street it's different; we are not held by our buildings, our homes; on the street we knock into each other, and the fact that we are obligated to each other becomes visceral, becomes a woman standing very close to you, her voice shaking with anger, what, the fuck, are you looking at?

They've hung a drop cloth over the scaffolding and it's like seeing the world through a shroud. It has holes cut in the form of windows going down one side, so the men can poke their heads through and communicate with each other when they're on different floors, and so they can move buckets of things up and down without leaving their perch. I wonder why they have the sheet. They must not want detritus to fly out into the air or down on to the street. I get it. I guess I went through something like that, a change so dramatic that you send out harmful shards of yourself into the world. I wanted to drape myself that way after we lost the baby. Not to protect myself. To protect the world from me.

In Judaism, I've learned that when someone dies they cover the mirrors with sheets. They tear their clothes and sit on low stools. But it's the mirror-draping that resonates with me. It's not only so you can't see yourself, to ward off vanity. It's to keep the self you were before the tragedy inside the mirror. Not to displace that self, that more-or-less intact self, with this torn, suddenly decaying self.

Clémentine comes over and it feels like things are back to normal, or, I don't know, maybe something has shifted, I can't put my finger on what. We watch Éric Rohmer's *Conte d'hiver*, her first time, not mine. We watched *Conte d'automne* last month. This one's set in Belleville, it's one of my favourites. I hope she'll like it. She does, but she has opinions. I hate how dumb he makes her, she says, quoting the film. *Pascal? C'est un philosophe?*

I guess he's trying to show that she's instinctual, I say, that she's really not intellectualising anything that happens at all, unlike basically every single one of Rohmer's other characters. Clémentine shrugs. I like how it shows winter, she says, how it's like an enchantment falls over the land, even when the land is just Belleville. I love the holidays.

Not too much more time to wait now, I say. The weather's turning.

There's a knocking and it's not coming from the door but from the window. A guy in a hard-hat is standing on my balcony. He mimes drinking something. I open the French doors. Salut! he says. He has a nice smile. Could he possibly have a drink of water? And might I also have a hammer lying around? He can't find his. I am delighted to be able to participate, in some way, in this ravelling. I bring him a glass of water, a hammer.

Clémentine comes over and the flinting is so loud even at six p.m. that she brings me my coat and my shoes and says: we're going out.

She takes me to the cocktail bar down the block that opened not long ago. It's not the kind of place I'd have ever had the courage to visit on my own. They call it Combat, the official name for this quartier, itself named, David has told me, after the animal fights that used to take place here hundreds of years ago; I had thought maybe because so much of the Commune was fought here, but he says no, the name predates the Commune.

Combat the bar is a small space with a low ceiling, where they are burning pine-scented candles, not the pine scent they put in the floor cleaner but real pine, magicked into wax. She knows one of the bartenders there, a thin slip of a thing with tattoos and an undercut, and she greets a woman called Mouna who is sitting with friends in the corner, wearing a shiny green bomber jacket and sitting beside a small French bulldog. She's always in here, Clémentine says, she's a film director, a friend of a friend, she's going to be filming with Léa Seydoux. Daunted by all the ingredients I've never heard of in the cocktails, I order a glass of red wine, organic of course. Clémentine, who apparently does drink alcohol in cocktail form, gives me hers to taste, something medicinal and earthy that comes in a coupe. Santé, she says.

On the way home she laughs at the massive sign someone painted on the side of a building. IL FAUT SE MÉFIER DES MOTS. That's, like, your job in a nutshell, isn't it?

I have a November cold. I tell Esther how sick I've been and say my anal passages have been so clogged and I swear I see her crack a smile and I need a minute to recover.

Everyone has this cold. We have all been touching each other's fingers via the keypad at the supermarket and the ATM and the handrails on the métro, the whole city's holding hands and the whole city's sick. Productivity must be down, I'm sure the economy has slowed, there must be a dent in the GDP. My friend at the bakery wasn't there for a few days in a row, and then I stop going for my morning run because I feel too bad. Presenters on the news are absent, filled in for by substitutes who seem so happy to get on air until they, too, are struck down and substituted by still others. There must be a thick line of would-be newscasters behind them. Clémentine is sick as well. She comes over for tea and we take turns sneezing and blowing our noses. We watch a Kardashian marathon to drown them out and work our way through a box of tissues each. She and Jonathan were finally going to have their housewarming party but she's called it off because she felt so crap. When David asks why I'm still not seeing clients I tell him, well, I have this cold.

One day, when I think I've finally shaken it off, after a long day of flint flint flint flint and men's voices and suggestions of the world outside, I think: well it's enough of just sitting around the house. I text a friend and agree to come to a party she'd invited me to, likely more out of courtesy than expectation that I'd actually show up. I know that at the party I will see an American guy I used to sleep with, years ago. He doesn't know I'll be there, but I know he will, and the thought of seeing him again feels surprisingly nice. Even though he hurt me very badly back then, I no longer feel any angst at the idea of seeing him, the way I once did. Isn't that something.

It occurs to me that he's probably thought of me since then. He'd long since returned to the US; who knew but every time, or nearly every time, he'd heard of something French a hazy recollection of me didn't spring unbidden to mind, the way I sometimes think of him if I hear the band from his hometown that I like? And it doesn't mean anything, but it happens, my mind snags on him for a second. Even people we specifically eliminated from our lives are still there, lingering behind the curtain of the past. Some change in the air and the curtain lifts, exposes some memory, and resettles. I find this comforting. To think I'm still there, behind his curtains.

I'm all ready to go to the party. My clothes are good, my make-up is done, the shoes are on, keys in my purse. I open the fridge to have a sip of water before heading out. But at the mere sight of a jar of supermarket pesto I think: why am I going out? I would so much rather have a bowl of pasta than go to this party.

The shoes come off, the keys go back in the ashtray. Water on the boil, Netflix on the laptop. In for the night. The noise won't start till morning.

David comes the next weekend. It is my birthday. We go out for dinner and then we try to have sex for the first time in months. It goes OK. I feel hopeful. This lasts until

Monday morning, as the drills begin again promptly at 7:30. We're still in bed, even though he has to catch a Eurostar. The drills right on the other side of the wall, like they're going to pierce through our skulls.

It's like we're under siege, David says, how do you live like this? and in his voice I hear what he's not asking: why do you choose to live like this, instead of coming to live with me?

As I leave the house today I notice hanging down from our scaffolding is a light turquoise rope, like an offer of help, elegantly pooling on the sidewalk.

This morning my bakery friend is not there. But I see him on my way home, walking slightly ahead of me. I follow him up the hill for a little while, and he turns off on the rue de Tourtille. I do not go after him.

Nearing my building, I pass a woman with a dog. The dog is fascinated by something he found near a shop. He's not moving from there anytime soon, a man on the street jokes. Non c'est qu'il y a toujours des morceaux de poulet dans la rue de Belleville, il adore, she replies.

A mysterious crack appears in the face of my iPhone, and I do not remember dropping it.

By Wednesday, two days after David leaves, I can't take it any more. The flinting, the never-ending flinting. The drilling. The wallpaper in the kitchen. My therapist vaping. Hitting my head on the cabinets. The fucking owls. I can't find my balance. I'm always alone. I'm never alone. Knock down all the walls! As if summoned, the contractor calls. They finished their job, they can start Monday. I go online, book my Eurostar. The last-minute trains are expensive. I leave Monday at ten a.m. Later that afternoon, the guys will get the keys from the concierge and knock it all down.

But before that, it's Friday night, and it is time for Clémentine and Jonathan's long-overdue housewarming party. Someone I don't recognise lets me in; someone else I don't recognise takes the bottle of wine I've brought, a sparkling rosé procured up the road at the bougie natural wine bar, and I make my way in.

The living room is full of people talking loudly, and the music is some kind of bright indie groove. Someone is shouting to change it. *Put on Chick Corea!* There is a scramble to get to the record player. I'm perched on the arm of a leather chesterfield sofa, holding a glass of wine to my chest, and catch glimpses of the floorboards between the white sneakers belonging to Clémentine and Jonathan's friends. I envy their parquet in spite of the fact that I have a very nice one at home. Clémentine is arguing with someone about the government, Macron has just made a speech about safety, he goes on and on about it, and delinquents, and home invasion, and he says nothing about violence against women, they think it's a women's issue, it doesn't concern them, I *hate* these men and I hate the way they think. Her companion is nodding furiously and making sounds of agreement, bah ouais, bah ouais, bah, bah ouais quoi.

It is strange to be in Clémentine's space after these months of seeing her only in my own. It is a reminder of all the parts of her life that don't have anything to do with me, the place where she is herself when no one is watching. Clémentine, by the fireplace, is wearing a greyish-purple brushed-silk dress, and a pair of silver heels, the kind with the red sole that cost a thousand euros. Her hair floats above her shoulders; the mirror behind her shows a double view of her loveliness, her shoulder blades protruding and distinct beneath the thin silk, like folded wings. I feel oafish in my Converse. Should I go home and change? But Clémentine is coming towards me. I heave myself up off the couch, ready to be brought into the throng. Anna, you doll! You are so lovely! Come and meet my friends, Clémentine says, her hand on my back. I am embraced by several sets of cheeks, kiss, kiss name, kiss kiss name. Samira is an artist. Oscar is in PR. Gwennaëlle is studying cinema. Anna is a psy. Clémentine is her own charged atmosphere and we are all molecules obeying as she draws us in.

You're a shrink, oh tell me how much you charge, maybe you can give me a better deal than the one I go to, says Oscar with a grin, he's up for being social, he's ready to play the game. I'm so interested in psychoanalysis, Samira says, I'm working on this book at the moment, using some of Freud's dialogues, and then in counterpoint I've put all these pictures of mothers and children with black boxes over their mouths, you know, like men can talk, and talk, and women are silenced, and as she talks, the sound of the past depressurises the room, and the room becomes a tunnel, and through the tunnel comes Jonathan.

I look at Jonathan, and I look at Clémentine, and I say very calmly, but you're not Jewish.

And at that particular moment, whoever had wanted to turn off the indie bop does it, and the music cuts out, and the whole living room hears me, and you look at me for the first time in so many years, and your face wears the same expression that it did that time I passed you in the street, and now I know for sure you saw me, you had that same ironic supple twist to your mouth, that twist of discomfort, and concern, and am I dreaming, and am I mad, and desire.

II

Since I've been married, I find all women beautiful.

Their languid air, their purposeful movements, the turn of a bare arm as it reaches palm-up, the curve of a bare neck as the head tilts back and the blood rushes through. Any arm. Any neck. Even the old women. Oh the old ones! With the laugh lines round their eyes and the wink at the corner of their mouths, the amusement that could spill out bell-like from them at any moment. Even the chubby ones. Oh the chubby ones! Who know how to take their pleasure from this ancient world.

Since I've been married, I find all women beautiful.

Someone said that in a film, and my god, it's so true. Getting married is the surest way to turn every woman who crosses your path into Helen of Troy. They were always there, all around me. I just didn't notice.

And now it's too late. The gong has sounded. Ask not for whom the bell tolls. It tolls for my sex life.

I'm not that interested in cinema, personally; I prefer to stay home and read. But Florence loves it and she talks to me from time to time about Rohmer, Rivette, Varda. She took me to see Zeffirelli's *Romeo and Juliet*, and I didn't care for it, except for the fact that the actress in it looked just like Florence, dark hair, pale oval face, watchful expression. So I go with her to the movies, to make her happy. And we saw *Love in the Afternoon* and I thought my heart would explode.

She hasn't caught on. I'm not stupid enough to tell her.

She thinks I'm the same adorable husband who brings home the baguette in the evening and who goes to get the croissants in the morning, who can't get dressed by himself (she buys all my clothes, even my trousers, she has an impeccable eye), who writes her silly songs on the piano, who makes love to her with the utmost passion. We no longer fuck like we used to, but we give each other a good time. If we're too tired most nights, what does it matter? We're married. We have all the time in the world.

No, I'm not unhappy with Florence. Except –

Except –

Except that she's started talking about having a child.

A child! But you already have one (I tried to deflect her with a joke). She smiled that smile but insisted. I'm nearly twenty-five years old, she said. At my age my mother already had me, and my brother on the way!

Yes but what about me? I'm only twenty-seven, it's not time yet for a baby. I haven't yet achieved the material conditions I believe are necessary before I can begin to procreate.

When I talk like that with all the extra words I can tell I'm wearing on her nerves and she lets it go. But I live in fear that she'll start in again.

It's not like I don't have a good job. I am a paralegal. Should I have continued with my studies to become a lawyer, or a judge? Maybe. They make more money. They have more respect. But mine is an honest job, and in all honesty, I don't have what it takes to be a lawyer or a judge. I provide support. That's what I'm good at. It's what makes me a good husband, too. She's the brilliant one, my wife. She goes off to her seminars and I go to my office. She studies hard and dreams and I'm just glad when it's time to knock off work and I can grab a drink with my mates, happy the day is over, the work is done. I never bring anything home with me. There are brilliant paralegals who go on to law school and become lawyers or judges. I'm just not one of them.

I'm finally settling into my life; I finally have everything I need. I have my apartment, my dinners in restaurants, my evenings at the theatre. I have all that is owed to me, because I work very hard, and I pay my taxes, and I am a law-abiding citizen of the Republic. Just as the Republic grants me seven weeks of vacation, certain holidays, and a pension, the Republic will one day grant me a country house, a retirement with some rosebushes, and a dignified death. These are the kinds of things a good citizen may expect as his due.

But what would a child need? What would a child want? Who's to know what Florence would want once she had one?

God, I love women. I love their wrists. I love their short skirts, their long hair. When I was a child I forbade my mother to cut her hair. I wanted it to grow all the way down to her behind, so she could sit on it. She laughed at me and cut it anyway. It was the 1950s, and it wasn't very fashionable for women to grow their hair long. Not like now. Now women have abandoned themselves to the luxury of their hair. They all look like princesses. Blondes, brunettes, redheads . . .

Look at that one there, on the couch in the waiting room, her ankles crossed. She has beautiful ankles, exquisite tendons. I would love her as much for her fine tendons like the neck cords of a ballerina as I would for her mind, which I'm sure is sharp and worthy. I won't speak to her; she is in the middle of reading a book. That's all right. I'm perfectly happy just to look at her.

Since I've been married I find all women beautiful, and I find it more and more difficult to cope. The heart is a bachelor! I saw what happened to that guy and his wife in the Rohmer film. In the end she doesn't know if she can trust him any more. And he didn't even really do anything! I don't want that to happen to us. Florence is everything to me. I would never endanger what we have. It would be an unsurvivable loss.

Except. Except.

Except for Mélanie, the girl I loved before Florence. It's not that I still want to be with her, of course I don't. What concerns me is that Florence may have loved someone in her past the way I did. She says she didn't, that I was her first, that she was too busy practising piano and studying to be interested in boys. But she didn't seem inexperienced when we met, I think she must be keeping it from me. When I was kissing Mélanie, who was kissing her? When I was coming into Mélanie, who was coming into her? I can't think of it. I run to my memories as if in revenge. I focus on what it felt like to be with Mélanie. I summon the weight of her body on mine, her hair, the grain of her skin. If she showed up on my doorstep tomorrow like Chloé does in the film, we'd have a problem. Luckily that kind of thing only happens in the movies.

We moved into this apartment soon after we got married. We were stupidly happy to be setting up house together. We got ourselves some kittens, a sister and a brother, but they are an incestuous pair, always holding one another. Look at them lying like lovers, Florence said, bemusedly, their limbs all intertwined. Now it's something we say to one another, like saying I love you. Just one of those things.

The apartment belongs to Florence's grandmother, or, well, it belonged to her grandparents a long time ago, and then just to her grandmother, but since she retired to the country it has been rented out to a series of strangers. Now we're reclaiming it. It is in Belleville, near the intersection of four arrondissements, in what used to be a tiny village outside Paris where in the olden days people would come to get drunk before tumbling back down the hill to the city. It has a more dignified history as home to labourers and artisans, people who were driven out of Haussmann's Paris, and then as a place of welcome to immigrants from Eastern Europe, that is to say, to our people. To the north and east they're tearing down all the old buildings, Belleville looks like a massive worksite, I think now I understand what it was like to live in Haussmann's day. But what they're proposing is far from his harmonious unified boulevards: they've razed the once charming place des Fêtes to build these hideous towers, it's been completely disfigured, as if all the charm of the old world had to be obliterated to make way for the cruel mechanised modern one. Excuse me, I've suffered as much as anyone from the twentieth century, at least leave me my quartier, my cafés, my views. Et les guignettes, I heard an old woman saying to a friend one day, où sont passées les guignettes, les bal musettes? They've gone to make room for these cages à lapins!

La forme d'une ville change plus vite, hélas! que le cœur d'un mortel.

Everywhere you look they talk only of towers, machines for living that turn the people who live in them into machines in kind, or, as the old lady thought, helpless little creatures with no independence. This is what the twentieth century has done to the body. What about the people who were perfectly happy living there, who didn't ask for Modernity? Where did they move to? Well I know the answer to that. But the goyim who were left behind? They've gone to the banlieues, or they're squatting in the ruins of their old buildings, or those which are destined to be destroyed but haven't been yet. For some reason the bulldozers and city planners have spared our little shtetl, maybe because of all the shops and cinemas. This part of town is dirty, the people are poor, but they say it's on its way up. And so here we are, upwardly nesting.

We have to take down that wallpaper! Florence exclaimed when we moved in. I don't remember it being so hideous!

Oh, I don't know, I said, looking at the small blue flowers, faded where the sun hit them. I think it's pretty. Very English. Florence's grandmother was a lifelong Anglophile; it was a group of British soldiers who'd liberated her camp in '45.

We have to take it down, Florence said. Put up something more modern. I want it to be – I want it to be brown! she said with a flourish.

Why brown and orange paisley is more modern, I don't know, but Florence is the fashion plate around here. I know she needs to make this place her own, not only to live here but to inhabit this space that knows so much about her family's story, it's not surprising she would want to tear down any of the places where some of that sadness might cling. We moved in and up went the brown wallpaper. I don't know enough about interior design to know if she's a genius or quite possibly colour-blind. Luckily the apartment has enough intrinsic beauty – mouldings, original parquet, fireplaces in all the rooms, enormous age-spotted mirrors – that her collection of mud-coloured owl paintings is less offensive.

Florence's taste in music I like better. When she sits down to the piano I love to lie on the floor with the cats, curled up listening, watching her slippered feet as they work the pedals. The piano is enormous and takes up half the living room, so it's not like I have *much* of a choice. But she plays so beautifully I don't mind. She sits with her back straight and she doesn't do that swaying thing some pianists do. She simply plays. All the movement is in the music. Her hair falls over her shoulders, her eyes look straight ahead, she turns her own pages. Sometimes she moves her lips as if she's talking to herself.

She knows all sorts of things – Schumann, Bach, Chopin. She trained for years to enter the conservatoire, but her father made her go to university instead. Her father had a more intellectual path in mind for his daughter, which she has obediently followed. As she worked through a Bach fugue she paused to tell me Mozart had transcribed that one, because he thought it was so perfect. Why transcribe? I asked. Oh never mind. I guess you couldn't just buy sheet music, then, could you. Or maybe you could? But how did he listen to it enough to transcribe it? I asked, lolling beneath the piano with the cats.

He just heard it once and could write it down, she said. Imagine having that kind of capacity for attention, a mind so capable of closeness; he could lean so far into the music that it imprinted itself on his mind.

Her favourite piece is Satie's *Gnossiennes*, because they are played without time signatures or measures, in what Satie called *absolute time*. The pieces seem quite structured to me, but what do I know. Florence loves them. Unstructured structure. There's an order to the movements but it wasn't Satie who imposed it – they've been ordered this way by later musicians and academics. No beginning, middle, end. The variations aren't hierarchised. They come when they come. There's no resolution.

Florence takes this to mean she can play them in any order and as many times as she likes. Or she plays them through and then begins again with the first one she played. I tell her if Satie wanted to end with that one he would have included it as a coda to every movement. But she tells me she doesn't care what Satie wanted and she doesn't think Satie cared either about being obeyed. In concerts sometimes they play the piece everyone likes best again at the end as an encore. The one that sounds like a woman lifting her hair off the back of her neck, and delicately pinning it up.

She had a book about him lying around, and I picked it up out of curiosity, wanting to know more about the master of unstructured structure. Quite the eccentric. Lived in a one-room apartment in the southern suburbs of Paris for most of his life. Wore the same grey flannel suit every day. Saved his fingernail clippings, and, according to someone who may have been his enemy, his urine. Walked to and from his job in Montmartre. (I like to think of him composing as he went, the *Gnossiennes* as the sound of Paris, which can be moved through at the walker's own speed.) Gave his compositions odd titles like *Three Pieces in the Form of a Pear* and *Dried-Up Embryos*. Commanded the player not to play andante or adagio but to Ask!, to play Deep in Thought, to Make Demands on Yourself. To play With Great Benevolence, or Without Pride. At one point the musician – or the music? – is Quite Lost, and at the very end the instruction is to Bury the Sound.

No one really knows why the *Gnossiennes* are called the *Gnossiennes*. Some think he was referring to the Palace of Minos at Knossos, on Crete, to the myth of Theseus and the Minotaur. Others think it's a reference to Gnostic religion. It seems he was inspired to compose the first one during a visit to the 1889 World's Fair in Paris, the one where the Eiffel Tower was introduced to the world – it was built to provide an archway, or entryway, to the fairgrounds, like a pointier Arc de Triomphe.

Everybody was at the fair, from Annie Oakley and Buffalo Bill (hero of my childhood!) to Gauguin, Van Gogh and Debussy. But no one talks about Erik Satie, who was there too, and who went to hear the Romanian music. Thank goodness he did, or I wouldn't have these moments of bliss lying under the piano listening to my wife play the song cycle inspired by the Romanians, grasping for a through-line as she weaves a labyrinth of unmetred phrases. She gives me many threads. So many I don't know which one to trust to find my way out again. But at the centre there is no mythic creature to battle, only the flexing and unflexing of the cats' sharp talons as they test them on my trousers, sometimes sticking.

What does she think as she sits at the piano? Does she think of me? Is she still trying to impress me, like the first time she played Beethoven's 'Pathétique' in my presence and stopped halfway through because she wasn't sure she could finish it without making a mistake? (She didn't know yet I find her mistakes to be charming entrances into her psyche.) Or does she think of someone else? I stop myself from thinking about this any further.

In fidelity there are never two of you alone together.

And we sit at tables, and we lie in beds, and we dream our futures, and all the while, there are threads of other dreams woven in, a beach you visited with someone else, the name which you'd like for a girl but it happens to be the name of a girl from school she detested, the part of town you'd like to move to where years ago you kissed another girl at a party, you make all your plans and build all your projects but how many of them are yours, and how many of them are fragments of someone else's life?

Florence is in the kitchen, squinting at a cookbook. Florence is in the bathroom, weighing herself on the scale. Florence does her hair, Florence takes baths, Florence reads books, Florence plays the piano and chooses bad wallpaper, Florence belongs to me and it's bad enough to share her with her past, how can I share her with a child.

Florence, -rence, -rence
c'est moi qui ai toutes les chances
d'rester, rester, rester
par terre avec tes jolis pieds.

Florence, -rence, -rence
je donnerai toute la France
si un jour tu peux m'accorder
l'honneur de t'faire prendre le pied.

On my way to the métro this morning I pass a flier stuck on a lamp post. In this growing revolution of women, it says, we are finally gathering together. We alone can know our oppression, it's up to us to take charge of our liberation. Until now we have been separated, each of us shut up in our own family. WE MUST BREAK this isolation. We must talk together, sharing our experiences. Together, all of us women will set the agenda of this movement. I think about taking it with me, to add to my collection, my messages hidden in cupboards to surprise Henry with, but then I think: better to leave it up, as a beacon for other women. Someone else might need to see it today.

I think about the women in my group, as I wait for the train that will take me down to the university. We meet once a week out in Porte des Lilas, at the home of a young woman, a single mother, who works as a bank teller and lives with her own mother; on their shag rug we sit and talk about our jobs, our studies, our hopes, our frustrations, and, yes, complain about our husbands. It's saved more than one marriage and, I regret to say, broken up a few as well. We recently organised a walk-in clinic for women who need help, advice, therapeutic or legal, who might not know who to talk to, or have sisters around them to take them to our kind of group, some of them even ended up joining our group. We made fliers too. These are better.

Yet although it feels like my friends and I spend all our free time at our consciousness-raising meetings, we have lately been worshipping at the feet of a man who is more interested in the unconscious, a man who speaks in puns and riddles. Once a week we go to hear him, I sometimes see people from our '68 days in the amphitheatres sitting rapt like us, with their microphones out, capturing everything he says for posterity, they don't even laugh at his jokes, though he does. They walk out of the seminars and spill into the cafés debating his ideas, and I don't always understand the things they claim they've understood. I still feel that what he is telling us is useful, though I couldn't tell you how, only that I have the feeling that it is working on me at a level below language, just under my skin, and that it gives me courage to live in a new way. I call him the maestro.

On the quai there is a group of children with their teacher, each one holding a plastic bag containing a shoebox. What could be inside their little boxes? I can't imagine they would have gone en masse to buy shoes, it must be some kind of project. A couple of them wander over toward me, as I sit in my seat on the side of the tracks. Their small faces wear precise, concentrated expressions. And all of a sudden children seem to me the most adorable and desirable things in the world, something I don't want to miss out on: to have a child of my own who would have a concentrated little face. I want to know what they think about. I want to hold one of their little bodies against mine, to see what's in the boxes, the mystery of childhood revealed.

It's not easy for me to say that. I am ambitious and I have things I want to do. But I know it now. I want a baby and then a child and then a teenager, grandchildren, I want it all, the whole progression. I want my own child to adore, to bring up, to protect. I want it. There, I've said it. It's important to be able to say it without feeling the slightest doubt. I want a daughter, if I'm honest, a daughter I can talk to the way my mother never talked to me, or her mother her. Tell her things, teach her, help her be a girl in a world that hates them.

I have class at eleven a.m. most days. I can take my time getting ready in the morning, leave after Henry. There's no rush in the métro. In fact it's hardly ever busy at all at this hour. Sometimes when the train is detained in the station with the doors open it can be so perfectly quiet – quieter than the library where there is always breathing and rustling and whispering. Quieter than the sound of a concert hall in the split second when the pianist's hands hover above the keyboard, before they strike. Down here it's as if the city has swallowed our breath, and we're held for a moment, like a fermata. And then the horn sounds and the doors shudder closed and we're released.

It's strange to take the métro from Belleville, when I am so used to the Left Bank. I grew up on the rue des Lyonnais, in the 5th arrondissement, in a street where everyone I met knew at least one of my neighbours. If I said I lived in the rue des Lyonnais someone else would say to me, unfailingly, I know someone who lives in that street! Oh yes, I would say, the rue des Lyonnais is the best-known street in Paris that no one's ever heard of.

Now it's Belleville, a place everyone knows about but has never actually visited. We live in my grandparents' apartment, a place they bought in the 1920s, when my grandfather worked for the railway, which the concierge miraculously kept for them, installing her own family there so when my grandmother came back, it was waiting for her. She lived there until she retired to the Midi. When Henry and I got married, she made us a gift of the apartment. My brother will get her country house, he doesn't care for the city and honestly he probably is getting the better end of the deal; Belleville is notoriously insalubrious, so much so that they're tearing half of it down. I've seen the neighbourhood change since I was a girl, and there was Yiddish on all the signs, half the buildings were boarded up, people didn't have enough to eat. Then new Jews, Arab Jews, *les sef*; exotic Jews, we thought. And not only Arab Jews but Arab

Arabs, North Africans. I've loved it through all its transformations. There is something very frank here, people are honest about their needs, their desires, in a way that is covered up in the rest of Paris, prettified or disguised. I have always felt that part of me belonged here. It must be because this is where my grandparents felt so at home, immigrants in a neighbourhood of immigrants. They were always so happy in this apartment. Our house on the hill, my grandmother called it.

Only last night, in fact, I was setting the table for dinner, when in a flash I saw my grandmother setting the table for Shabbos when I was a girl, I swear I saw her there, in the flat, and as the moment wore on, I became small again, I was reliving the memory of seeing her reuse the same tablecloth we do, I had forgotten until then, but now I realise it's not just some lace tablecloth I found in the linen closet, from its fibres escaped the smell of the candles, and that of her guests, who smelled old, a smell that had nothing to do with my daily life.

I remembered strangers at the table, turning up one by one, in dark clothes, faces I'd never seen before, who didn't speak much French, only Yiddish or Polish, which I recognised but couldn't understand, they were put to work sewing in ateliers, or ironing, men and women alike, and their faces were tired in the candlelight. Some came weekly, others never came back. When I was older my parents told me that those were the people she'd been *there* with. She never talked about *there* with us, only with them. My own mother doesn't know much about what it was like *there*, only the couple of things my grandmother told her, and what she's pieced together herself, which isn't much. She escaped to the free zone with my father, and they lived as Christians in a small town in the south, but she never got over her guilt at leaving her parents behind. What could she do? They wouldn't go.

I found out when we moved in that before they were taken

they'd hidden a family in the small room next to our apartment. Just for a few nights, and they had to keep away from the window. Anyway that's what my mother said, who knows if it's true. She tends to exaggerate. The heroic concierge died years ago but her children have taken over as guardians now. Quite literally: we don't call them concierges any more but *gardiens*.

My brother's wife had a baby a few years ago and I go to see them whenever I can. Holding the body of a small person is not like anything I've ever experienced, I never played with dolls or babysat or cared about children; I was born an adult, I think. It was a surprise to feel a small body against my own for the first time. I was immediately addicted to the feeling. I had a terrible dream about my nephew one night, I almost can't think about it, they had caught us like they caught my grandparents, we were there, in that place, in one of those rooms, thrown in with hundreds of other people like us in that small space, and in my dream I was holding my little nephew in my arms as we both fought for breath, and I whispered in his ear that it was OK, that we could let go together, that I was here. I used to have night terrors when I was a child but they'd largely subsided, at least I thought they had, but that night I had to wake up Henry to be with me. I couldn't tell him what the dream was about, he has his own family ghosts, and I didn't want to disturb them. I wonder if he'll ever stop seeing us as dead or doomed.

We talked about dreams early on, me and Henry, I remember so vividly, it was soon after we'd met but not that soon, it was getting to be cold outside, I was staying at his old place over by République, the one with the wooden beams everywhere, and we woke up one particularly cold autumn morning and clung to each other under the covers, I was feeling funny because I'd had a strange dream, one I have from time to time, in the dream I am alone and there is nothing around me but white space, blindingly empty white space, and the edges are sharp and dangerous but also invisible, and I know that if I wanted to end my life I could go out to the edges where the sharp places are, and I know that it is a decision I am making not to test the chilly sharpness of the edges, and that's when I wake up, nothing else ever happens in the dream and it never gives way to another one. I remember feeling embarrassed to tell Henry about the dream because it's so odd and foreboding, and I don't want him to think I'm crazy, but, I remember thinking, I have to be able to tell him even my craziest dreams (they are always so far-out but precise), I can't hold anything of myself back from him, and so I tell him, but he's not disturbed by it at all, he says he doesn't recognise degrees of weirdness in dreams because, and this is when he astonishes me, he doesn't dream. At all? Ever? Ever, he says. You've never had a dream? I ask, my own dream melting off. I think I may have had some nightmares when I was a child, he says, but I don't remember them. All my life I've never been able to dream.

I'm disappointed, he said, your dreams sound so vivid, I wish I could visit them. Not this one you don't, I told him.

The strange thing about this dream is that I've been having it all my life, and when I told my mother about it, when I was much younger, still living at home, she froze. That dream, she said. It's almost word for word one your grandmother has been having since she came back.

How? How was it possible? Had she told me of this dream when I was a child, so long ago I didn't even remember being told?

That dream is what led me to psychoanalysis. I was interested not in dreams as the royal road to the unconscious, as Freud would have it, nor as wish fulfilment, but as the revisiting of a trauma that is impossible to face during the daytime. And in the case of my grandmother's, one so strong that it has perpetuated itself down the generations. How much further will it go? Can trauma, or a dream, pass through the blood? Will my own child still be dreaming this dream, this nightmare of what was done to his great-parents?

We went to my nephew's bris when he was born, Henry was so uncomfortable with the rituals, he couldn't stay in the room when they did it. He is not observant in the slightest, he is assimilated, secular, French. I was not raised by religious parents either but we had family who were and I remember them taking me to shul when I was little and having to sit up on the balcony, mutely watching while the men prayed. Thank you god for not making me a woman, one of their prayers goes. Thank you god for making me according to his will, the women are supposed to answer. The men debate and talk and think while women are supposed to run the house and raise children and gossip. We had so much in common when we met, Henry and I, similar back-grounds (Ashkenazi, family gone in the camps), similar enough politics (me: left; him: centre-left), both open-minded free-thinkers. But soon after our marriage it became apparent that we had different visions of what that might look like. Don't worry, I remember saying to Henry at the bris, we don't have to circumcise our son, if we have one. Who said we're having a baby at all? he said. The ring was fresh on my finger, but that was the moment it began to feel like it didn't quite fit.

While we eat dinner Florence wants to see the eight o'clock news. I watch her struggle to turn our ratty old television on, you have to turn the knob and lift it at the same time to keep it from turning off on you again, she never seems to get the hang of it and when I offer to buy us a new one she scowls and says she never wants to watch TV. But tonight, yes, there's big news in her world of feminist causes. We watch as a triumphant Gisèle Halimi guides her client out of the courthouse in Bobigny, the young woman shielding her face from the cameras. Halimi's eyes are glowing. On her face, a mix of pride and exhaustion. I feel a twinge of jealousy, that she gets to practise law as a true instrument of justice, instead of a question of paper-pushing and hair-splitting, bleeding people with money for ever more money.

You'll see, Florence says. They'll pass a law soon. We are becoming more and more free in this country. Florence is obsessed with the notion of freedom, especially for women. She is an optimist. She is forever going to meetings with other women where they sit around and talk about their freedom, or the ways in which it is checked and curtailed, usually by us husbands. (Everything is our fault.) She brings home fliers and pastes them up around the kitchen and sometimes even inside the cupboards. I opened one the other day to a mimeographed black and white image of a woman's bush and bits. UGH, I said, UGH! She tutted at me. That's *The Origin of the World*, she said. Courbet. The maestro owns it. They say he keeps it behind a sliding door. So I keep it in a cupboard.

The maestro again. He is all she talks about, when she isn't talking about women and freedom. So I can have a heart attack when I go to get a drinking glass? A thousand thank yous, my love. And thanks to the maestro as well.

She recently took it into her head that she wanted to become a psychoanalyst. The idea just came to her one morning, she said, looking out the window at Belleville, the people walking down the street, so many different kinds of people in this small neighborhood in Paris. It was as if Belleville, or the apartment itself, had inspired this desire in her. I just want to understand people, she told me. This was a shock; I had assumed she wouldn't work. When we met, on a beach in '67 (my god, her small tight ass with the bikini falling off!), she had recently graduated from the Sorbonne with a degree in literature. What else was she going to do with that, besides be a wife and mother? But in the years after she and her friends had graduated, they became progressively more political. They turned out to be a bunch of troublemakers, going back to the university they'd graduated from – mind you, they had *graduated* at this point – and filling up the amphitheatres talking about freedom and Mao, which, I'm sorry, if you ask me is a bit of a contradiction in terms. Next thing you know she's on the barricades, and throwing paving stones, and sympathising with the workers (Stalinists! I told her), reading Freud and all his children. But she was irritated with the men leading the movement, who were perfectly happy, she said, to make revolution by day and come home to a cooked dinner at night. And who cooks it? she asked. Their wives! Where is *their* liberation? When you were born, she likes to remind me, *women couldn't vote.* Your mother couldn't vote. My mother couldn't vote. She came home a few months ago and informed me she'd signed up for a masters at one of the new post-'68 universities. I told her she wouldn't be able to do that and be a mother, but she's convinced she'll make it work. I can take a break when the degree is over, she says, and when the baby is ready to start school I can go back and start my doctorate. She has it all figured out. But what about the second one? I ask. What second one? she says. But I know her. She'll want a second one.

She wants to integrate the maid's room, the one on the landing, into the flat, and turn it into a baby room. We haven't touched it since we moved in; it has some kind of importance to her and she didn't dare strip the wallpaper, or cover it over with her lurid greens and oranges the way she'd threatened. She hasn't said a word about the decor. Maybe she understands you can't give a baby a room like that. Babies need calm and soothing environments, you want them to sleep, not lie awake at night staring at busy patterns, we'd need to do it up in a soothing light blue, I could even stencil on some clouds, but what am I saying, I'm not stencilling anything for a baby we're not having!

I was happy enough for her to work, until this story about wanting to have a child. And now I'd almost rather she went back to the conservatoire to become a concert pianist. Because then of course she would have no chance of succeeding, and all that will happen is she will play the piano better and more often.

But if she actually does this training, I know her – she won't be able to stop herself. She'll go all the way and next thing you know there will be people traipsing through my living room to talk to her. And there she will sit, queen of her mad kingdom, drifting ever further from me and from these children she'll have stuck me with.

Morning. In the bathroom I go to take my pill, and then I don't, I drop it in the toilet. I have the right to take it, I think, and I have the right to throw it away.

Morning. Clinging blue sweater, the one I like. 'Il pleut des larmes' on the radio. Putting her coffee cup in the sink, a semi-circle of pink on the rim, it reminds me of last night, her soft mouth on my cock. Now her hair is pulled back and fastened in a small chignon at the nape of her long neck. Going off to her classes carrying her little briefcase.

Do I idolise her? Of course I do.

Working in the kitchen this evening I have the strangest feeling like I can see what Henry is doing on the other side of the wall, as if there were no wall. He is sitting on the sofa, by the end table, reading by the light of the lamp. Céline, Vian, Cendrars, or maybe some comic book. He slowly turns the pages. His legs are crossed and from time to time he uncrosses them. A curl falls in front of his face and he smooths it back. His crotch itches and he shifts around delicately, like the cats. He will not scratch it though I'm not there to see him. I have a keen sense of all of his movements. I feel this way sometimes while I am playing the piano. It is as if there were no walls in the apartment, as if we were utterly utterly knowable to one another. Sometimes this is wonderful, and I think, this, this is love, to know another person like this, and sometimes this is a problem, like I can't get any shelter from him.

I feel a swell of something I can't put words to when he comes in to help me make dinner, and awkwardly peels the potatoes with his long fingers, which are more accustomed to turning pages, or holding a pen, or a cigarette. Those fingers, I remember how I fell in love with them that summer, licking the salty taste off of them when we fell into bed after a day on the beach, enjoying the sensation of my tongue against their flat sides, along the ridges of the nails. He cut himself so often when we first got married. Have you never peeled a vegetable? I used to rib him. He's getting better, at least he no longer takes off half the flesh with the skin. Next I'll teach him to score and salt the duck fat, on our way to lessons in roasting a chicken. Honestly, you'd think he'd never given a thought to how the food got from the butcher to his plate. His mother did *everything* for him. Not to judge her, and she's had her share of hardship, but the only way to make a better world is to bring up our sons as feminists. We make all the people, we should be able to make better ones.

There seem always to be extra glasses in the sink to wash lately, Henry must be very thirsty. He might wash them himself sometime, I think, thankful we at least have a new dishwasher. He is a good husband, I think, picking up his abandoned cereal bowl from the kitchen table. A good husband, picking his briefs up from the floor of the bathroom. I left him because he left his dirty laundry *next* to the hamper, said a woman at my group the other night. That seemed a bit harsh. We have to find ways to accommodate each other, and be good to each other, no matter what, no matter —

And then I get this phone call that is so strange. It's from a guy I knew from Brittany, where we used to go in the summers till we had to sell our house there. The son of the family who owned the big house up the road. We got into a lot of scrapes together. But we lost touch when we went to university, and we only run into each other from time to time in Paris. (Paris, you small small town.) I didn't think he knew where I worked. But there's my secretary, buzzing to let me know that a Monsieur Jean-Baptiste de Lauzon is on the phone. It took a minute for the name to click. He always went by JB, which he perversely spelled Jibé.

Henry! How in god's name are you? he asks.

Can't complain, and you? I am so astonished I drop cigarette ash on the carpet.

I'm well, thanks, Claude is pregnant, so things are about to change around here, but I can't complain!

Claude, Claude, hang on, did I ever meet Claude?

Sure you did, she was with me when we ran into each other that time in the Bois. You were with that blonde girl. What was her name?

Mélanie. We split up ages ago. I'm married now, to a lovely girl called Florence.

Yes I know, Jibé's voice changes slightly. That's why I'm calling. Can you meet me in half an hour? He mentions the name of a café near my office.

Jibé looks healthy and tanned, in his red turtleneck sweater under a well-worn brown sport coat. He has already been served his coffee and is deep in conversation with the young lady at the next table. On my arrival, he gets up to pull out my chair. He seems genuinely pleased to see me, as if he weren't on some mysterious and possibly sinister errand that has something to do with my wife. He is hairy and unreadable.

Henry, it's good to see you. Square jaw, square handshake; he still has that little gap between his front teeth, that makes him look like an irascible child. You're looking well. Good cook, I guess, your wife. Anyway that's why I'm here. Your wife goes to school with mine.

That's a coincidence.

I know because she came over last week, and she has your peculiar last name, and I asked if she was related to you, and she said she was married to you. She didn't mention meeting me?

No, she didn't.

She was talking to Claude about someone just as I came in. Claude was calling her Jezebel, they were giggling. He drops a lump of sugar into my coffee. Plop. You still take one sugar in your coffee, or is it two now?

One's fine. Wait a minute, what do you mean? What was she saying?

Well I don't know exactly, he says. They were in the kitchen, and I came in to fix myself something to eat before dinner, and they went on talking for a bit until Claude realised Florence and I hadn't been introduced, and when I said I knew her husband, she seemed flustered. She blushed. She stammered.

Jibé, I say, you're such an asshole. I haven't seen you in how many years and this is how you make your re-entry?

I'm really hurt that you would say that, Jibé says, and he really does look hurt. This is something real that happened, in my house. What should I have done?

I need to think. Now that he has said it, could I wish it unsaid?

No, I want to know, and I want to know more. With more information I will be better able to manage the situation. A man wants to know what kind of woman he's married to. He can think she's one kind, and really, the whole time, really she's been another.

No, hang on, I don't want to know more, or if I do want to know I don't want it to be Jibé who tells me. With a feeling of unreality, as if I am no longer in my body, I stand up from the table and leave the café, leave Jibé holding his stupid small cup of espresso. What an asshole. I cross the street, I enter my office building, I start going up the stairs and then I go back down them. No one will think anything of it if I have stepped out for the afternoon. I am so efficient and so reliable as to be able to permit myself some inefficiency and unreliability once in a great while. I go walking, cross the river, walk further, still further, until my feet are throbbing, and still I keep walking. Florence and someone else? I have to admit, the thought had never crossed my mind that she might stray. We were too happy, and always together, and honestly, I didn't think she even had the time. It might be nothing. It was probably nothing.

But nothing gets into my feet and walks me all the way to her school. I find a conveniently large tree and wait outside the human sciences department for her to come out. It feels like I've seen something wrong, being here at this time of the day when I'm meant to be elsewhere. I stare at all the young people, who seem to be getting younger all the time. There are beautiful young women but I'm too upset to appreciate their beauty. I focus my attention on my tree instead. Oh, tree. Faithful tree. How many cuckolded husbands have you protected over the course of your long life?

After an hour or so she finally emerges, accompanied by a pregnant woman whom I recognise, yes, as Claude. (We had indeed met that time.) She kisses Claude on both cheeks, and then she descends the stairs to the métro. Florence is alone. I

don't

follow

her.

I go for a walk, try to clear my head. Head towards the river, back towards work. Stop at Gibert Jeune, have a browse through the bookstalls. Find an old book of photographs by Eugène Atget, my favourite. I love the pictures he took of the streets of Paris as the city transformed under Haussmann, but I love even more the pictures of interiors. They remind me of my grandmother's apartment on the rue Saint-Maur, not so far from where we're living now. She lived out her years in one small sitting room, densely furnished, dominated by an ornate wooden table, with a small kitchen in the corner, and a tiny bedroom. Her husband, my grandfather, died when I was small. He was a tailor. Something to do with the war, my father didn't like to talk about it and I never asked anyone for the details. As an adult I can guess that he was in the camps. She, miraculously, wasn't. The things she must have thought about sitting at that table. Jibé said something once when we were children, it's coming back to me now, it was a very cold day, the way only Brittany can be cold in summer, and his dad was building a fire in the hearth, and Jibé's asshole older brother made a joke about throwing me into it, and his father slapped him, and he skulked off. He doesn't know what he's talking about, Jibé said to me, with a hand on my shoulder, but I didn't know either what any of them were talking about, back then.

As I walk I try to think what I would do if what Jibé had told me were true. I would die if Florence left me. I would die and I would come back to haunt her, her and her new boyfriend, she'd never be rid of me. No matter what she did, I wouldn't leave her.

But what in god's name could she possibly be thinking?

I ran into an old friend today, I tell Florence at dinner that night. Jibé. We used to hang out in the summers in Brittany.

Mm? she says, between bites.

It turns out he's married to your friend Claude now.

Claude? she says, as if this were a name she hadn't heard before. Oh Claude! From school! she says. I thought you meant my high-school boyfriend Claude.

Why would my friend Jibé be married to your high-school boyfriend, I say, annoyed at the misdirection.

I don't know, she says, I just don't think of Claude from school as occupying the same plane as you.

But your high-school boyfriend does?

Darling, it's a lapsus, let it go. Tell me about your Jibé.

Oh I don't know what there is to say, he's kind of a dick, but a friendly one. She's pregnant.

Yes I know, she says. I see her most days at school. Lucky girl.

Why lucky? I feel myself becoming testy. Everything I have learned about Florence and marriage is telling me to cool it.

The baby, Henry, she's going to have a baby. I envy her.

But you have a baby, remember? I make my eyes wide, blink innocently. I feel a bit like JB as I do it. The idea occurs to me that I probably learned this mannerism from him, way back when, and forgot it was his to begin with.

It has the usual effect on her, to make her bristle, back away, like she's realised I'm no longer fully myself. She stands up, says she's going to play the piano. You can clean up for tonight, can't you, Henry?

So Henry knows something. Claude must have said something. How could she? But no; she couldn't have; she wouldn't. Could he just tell? A whiff of something clinging to my body, to my hair? I was with Max in his office after the seminar today. He came all over my chest, and afterward, as he mopped it up, gentleman-like, with a tissue, I said: oh. Now I understand why they call them seminars.

It's funny because it's my married name that made him notice me. The first day of class he asked us to share our names. After class he took me aside and said, that's an unusual name. Are your family Polish Jews? My husband, I said. Ah, he said. And you took his name? You could have kept your own. What was your maiden name? I told him. Interesting choice. You could have continued on in your life without marking yourself out this way. Interesting choice. The next class, when we took a break midway through class, he was there at the coffee machine getting a little goblet of vile oversweet coffee and he said it again, interesting choice.

His name is Weisz, like vice, and he is that, a wicked indulgence and something that grips me. I've never had such big hands on my body. We sit together in his office and he plays me his records and then he puts his hands on my body.

I am in love with him, I am in love with his shirt, with the way that it sits   just so   lightly on his torso, his collar that sits away   just so   from his neck. I've never actually wanted to rip someone's clothes off before. He has a wife at home so I have to be careful or she'll be wondering why all the buttons on his shirt popped off at the same time.

Desire makes us others to ourselves, the maestro says, and he is right, I am not myself when I desire Max, I am myself-with-Max, quite another person from myself when I'm without him.

I took Henry to see the Rohmer film about fidelity, and was surprised to find it's actually quite a feminist movie, while the main character is having an almost physical affair with Chloe and lusting after the female half of Paris his wife is very quietly and off-screen fucking her colleague. Good for her. But then it's not clear by the end of the film if their marriage can sustain it. That's Rohmer for you; Catholic. Moralist. It is one of his moral tales, anyway. I went to Max in a completely different spirit, one of openness and equality, the kind we've been demanding these past few years. For it not only to be the men who enjoy their bodies, and their desires.

I am sleeping with a man who is not my husband and I refuse to feel shamed for it. That's what we've been fighting for, love and sex and bodies without shame. And that's what I'm laying claim to.

But it is more than I reckoned on, more than I've experienced before, more than I can accommodate almost, to the point of it being nearly painful, no actually painful right there it's very painful don't stop right there don't stop oh god I can't wait to see him again to sit astride him again for him to move me again. I walk around the stone city with my pussy swollen and heavy, thinking of him. It's a big, big deal, a big deal in his office, on his couch, on his desk, on the floor, but it's not a big deal when I come home at night and there is Henry reading on the couch and waiting so patiently for me to start dinner. Henry has his daytime life at his own office with his colleagues and his walks and his lunches, and I have mine, and we have this evening life together, and that is what a marriage is.

Florence is practising the piano and I want to go out. I don't want to go out with her but I want to go out and if I want to go out I have to run it past her. It's an antisocial act, a marriage-betraying act, simply to leave. So I sit here behind her, watching her back, waiting for a pause.

When did I first notice that she really isn't any good? Her Satie. She plays it very badly. Her grace notes are graceless. Instead of adding a promising, mysterious touch of dissonance, of something happening of which we would have remained unaware without the visit of the note next door, the mystery vanishes. All these years I've listened, it's blurred together with the ideal performance of Satie, one I heard on the radio once, or at the beginning of a film. That must be why I found her interpretation beautiful: it wasn't hers alone I was hearing. Or perhaps it was a potential performance I loved, one I've never yet heard, the one she might give some day. The evening passes and I do not go out.

What is she thinking, as she lies there beside me, under the brown duvet we bought at the BHV because it had to be brown, does she think I am happy with the way my life is going, does she think it is all grace notes, no dissonance?

Henry is positively looming over me today, staring me down while I play, eyes boring into me from behind. I love it when he lolls on the floor listening to me, lazy as the cats, but when he sits behind me it makes me nervous. The apartment isn't big enough for the three of us, me, Henry, and the piano. There he sits, with his paper knife, slicing open the uncut pages of his books. I wish he would just go out.

Jibé turned up at my office today. When my secretary buzzed to let me know he was here I couldn't believe it. No word from this guy for a decade and then suddenly he's trying to see me twice in one week? He comes in, dressed in white shorts and polo shirt, a gym bag on his shoulder, along with a case shaped like a tennis racket, but smaller.

Henry, mon vieux, he says with all his teeth as white as his whites, I'm en route to the squash court, care to come along?

Jibé, mon vieux, it's the middle of the work day, and I don't have the clothes for it, or a racket.

They'll lend you all of it at the club. Come on, come with me.

And because I am curious, I go. Off with him in his flashy Renault Torino. The latest model, if you please.

We pull up at the racquet club in Saint-Cloud and the valet takes his keys. It's the kind of club rich people belong to in movies, everyone is svelte and no one seems to walk; they glide around and take part in bourgeois sports without breaking a sweat.

When did you join this place? I ask him.

Few years back. Good for business.

Which is what, exactly? I ask, but he doesn't seem to hear me. He's whisking me into the locker room, where from out of nowhere he conjures up a pair of shorts and a shirt. Size? he asks, gesturing at a pristine row of trainers in a closet.

On the court he dominates the ball, bashes me this way and that, my borrowed trainers screeching on the parquet floor.

Quite a few times I go flying, trying, failing, to return a shot. We play three games, and he wallops me in all of them. I stand no chance against him.

Afterward we shower and go for a drink in the bar. Pretty girls with tans in tennis skirts smile at him.

Are you taking me back to work? I ask.

You should make this your work, he says, gesturing around us. Get to know people here, you'll drum up business for your firm. Meet some new people. I can sponsor you for a membership. The girls are pretty too, he says, flashing a movie-star smile at a couple of women strolling by, I swear I can see his teeth gleam in the light.

Seriously, he says. If Florence is having a nice time on her own, why shouldn't you?

His eyes are kind even as his suggestion is insulting.

After class I go to Max's office. He isn't expecting me, I think I've come because I want to surprise him, maybe I'm jealous though I have no right to be and thought he'd be with someone else, some other student, maybe his wife. He's alone, feet up on the desk, the maestro's voice playing from a tape deck. *L'essence de la théorie psychanalytique*, he intones, sounding like someone reading the news on Radio Londres in the 1940s, a voice from another era, *est la fonction du discours, et très précisément en ceci, qui pourra vous sembler nouveau, à tout le moins paradoxal, que je le dis sans parole.* What's this? I ask, sitting on his desk, next to his feet in their tan suede Clarks. Have I not shown you my collection? he says, pointing at a shelf of tapes. My bootleg recordings. It's useful because he doesn't publish the seminars, they aren't written to be read, only experienced, but they're so dense you often need to listen to them a few times to follow his meaning, appreciate the wordplay as more than just linguistic showmanship. This is one from 1968. Oh, I say, is he talking about the protests? A little, he says, but this is from November, everyone had started to move on and think of other things by then. Here he's talking about language – he'd written on the board that the essence of psychoanalytic theory is a discourse without words. He's deeply suspicious of language, and the truth-value we assign to it. But the maestro being the maestro, he builds this argument by reference to mustard.

Mustard?

Mustard. He sits up, feet back on the floor, starts fast-forwarding the tape. There's this whole section where he talks about the mustard pot. He talks about condiments a lot, but he always says 'ce condiment'. As in – ce qu'on dit ment, what we say lies.

I think I know what he means, I say, settling into his lap, playing with his greying curls. There are some things that only make sense if I don't put them into words. You know? And the things we do try to articulate end up missing the mark, slipping this way and that, turning into inadvertent jokes. How does anyone ever tell anyone anything?

Jibé's question echoes in my head all night like Florence's Satie, different emphases each time. Why shouldn't *I*? Why *shouldn't* I?

Florence is reading Willa Cather. What is she thinking, as she lies there, what is she thinking. Florence on the couch, her eyes closed, her personality off. The way she looks lying there. Like at night, in the bed beside me. So tame, on her side, gently snoring. And then she turns over and she's suddenly in another key.

I will spend the rest of my life trying to know her.

At home, the cats lie like lovers, limbs intertwined. I lie on the couch and read Willa Cather. My perfume hangs in the air. I have started wearing Shalimar, like his wife, to bind him to me, and also so she won't catch on if he smells like me, because he'll smell like her. Henry noticed and says he loves it. He looks at me on the couch with that disconcerted look on his face. I close my eyes and imagine Max touching me and I lose myself in the Satie in my mind, the fifth *Gnossienne*, moderate, light, with just enough mystery in the turns of the keys. When I open my eyes Henry is still watching me.

I wait a week. I leave work early again. They come out of the building again. They do not see me. Feeling like a second-rate Columbo I tail them to the rue Linné, where they pause near the entrance of a café. I stand behind a tree, feeling like an idiot, a right piece of shit, a mistrustful husband, stupid paranoid until they are joined by a bearded man who puts his hands on their two lower backs, before guiding them into the café.

I can see them through the window. He lights Claude's cigarette but it's Florence he's looking at. The lighter disappears in his hand. Everything is small in his hands. The coffee cup. The pen he holds to write down what she says. Is her waist small in his hands? Her face? Her breasts? I can't think. Now she's taken the pen from him and is writing something on his hand, his enormous red hand, like a raw slab of tuna you find in the market, his red hand that will close on her small waist and pull her toward him and slide down her back, down her ass, down her crevice, down into my place, that cold, fatty tuna will slide into my place, I can read everything I need to know from the way she's smiling at him with her mouth open, as if he's just said something cheeky and she's deciding whether to be offended. The winter sun is making spots on the window, giant orbs of cool light, all the colours glaring at me, blinding. But still I can see, I know that face she's giving him. I know that face. I haven't seen it in years. The scene swims before me, as if it were that hot day on the beach. It is not a hot day. It is cold, and my lips are chapped, and I stand there watching them. She lowers her eyes and there is the secret look on her face that she had when we met. Claude is looking impatient. Claude is looking at her watch. Claude is trying to interrupt.

Florence is wearing her favourite dress. The one with the round collar. The headband I like. The one that makes her look about twelve. What is he, some kind of pervert? What is he offering her? What does he have to offer? I come out from behind my tree, I walk home a different way than she will go, I know all her ways, even her ways of betraying me. I know which panties she put on today.

I slip down the stairs to the métro, and glower at anyone who makes eye contact with me in the line 7. By the time I've changed to the line 11 I'm no longer quite sure what it was I observed. Maybe she's not fucking him, maybe they're just flirting. Maybe Jibé was wrong. Maybe I misunderstood what I saw in the café. Maybe I'm dreaming, hallucinating, maybe Jibé slipped something into my coffee, or someone I passed on the street painlessly shot me in the neck with a hallucinatory drug, just for fun.

She comes home about an hour after me. I watch her all night. She makes dinner, she slices courgettes, peppers, onions, garlic, so carefully, her pale thin fingers careful not to get in the way of the knife, every element so precisely chopped, so skilfully added together in the right order, the salt dissolves in the vinegar, she adds the mustard, she adds the oil, she adds the pepper, she whisks it all together, it sits there, separating, I sit there, watching, nearby the cats watch too, as they lie there like lovers, limbs intertwined. After dinner she washes the dishes and loads the dishwasher with the same look of careful concentration, while she listens to classical music on the radio. Then she goes and sits at the table reading, taking notes on a yellow legal pad stolen from my office. I watch her, looking for some clue on her face, in her posture, some undeniable physical charge that signifies I am sleeping with a man who is not my husband. I see nothing, and this is a relief. Love, writes Rilke, consists of this: two solitudes that protect and touch and greet each other. I do not want to know if Florence is cheating on me. When we go to bed I slip those panties off and fill her up to remind her that she's mine.

Café with Max and Claude today. There is something erotic about being with him in public, where we can be watched, witnessed; I like being dressed with him when we are so often undressed. I carry the feeling home with me, home to Henry, and there is enough leftover erotic charge that when he reaches for me, I respond to him, and with him enjoy the desire that was forestalled this afternoon. It seems to me that this is exactly how it should work, and exactly not how it is supposed to work. But why *shouldn't* I? I think as I lie beside him. Why shouldn't we all?

I didn't go in to work this morning, said I had a doctor's appointment, I'll go in later. Instead I went for a walk around the neighbourhood. It's been changing so much. This park they're building, it will have a view of Paris to rival Montmartre, but of course they'll fuck it up, we haven't done anything beautiful in this country since the turn of the century, all we've done is make the world more ugly, and this park, with so much promise, will be no exception. It looks like Belleville has been bombed. They capitulated during the war to spare Paris but of course they didn't want to spare our neighbourhood, it's full of reds and Jews, they've always been afraid of us, it's part of Parisian mythology that one day the barbarians will come gallivanting down the hill and loose themselves upon the beaux-quartiers. So before we could destroy them they sent us their wrecking balls, their excavators, their bulldozers and cranes, trying to finish the job left undone by the war. The people who lived here, who took care of the buildings, who renovated them as best they could, these cheap, badly built buildings, a legacy from the impoverished inhabitants of the previous century, the people who grew plants in the courtyards so the young people could have some green, understand how things grow, the tailors, the shoemakers, the leatherworkers, the metalworkers, the people who sent their children to schools, who eluded, or tried to elude, the dragnets cast out to entrap everyday people reconfigured as criminals, they're gone – deported, exterminated, or simply moved away. New people will come to live in these soulless new buildings, and what will they make of it, and will they think of the people who lived out their lives here, when the village was a village and not îlot insalubre numéro 7? What traces remain when we go?

Listen to me, I sound like a true Bellevillois, instead of a recent transplant; I have taken on their anger, their nostalgia, for a time and a place I had nothing to do with. Looking out at Paris in the autumn haze it is almost placid, I hear birds, the seashell roar of distant traffic, the occasional shouts of the men building the park. I stand looking out at the city, having my Rastignac moment, it's between you and me now, but I don't mean me and Paris, I mean me and Florence. À nous deux maintenant.

Max went with me to see the maestro today, at the faculté de droit. He spoke before, I don't know, a couple hundred people, mostly students training to be analysts, but also scholars in other fields, and even, I heard, some actors. He's a man of science who speaks like a mystic. Every word has its weight, as if he were dropping iron plumbs into a sea to anchor his thoughts. He delivers his speech like he's performing Molière at the Comédie-Française. It is often hard to follow. Today he talked about jouissance, and love, and the Other, and I stroked the inside of Max's wrist with my finger, afraid to outright hold his hand, and then the maestro said there is no woman, and that it is the instinct of the mother that prevails in her, not her own sexual pleasure, which turns around the phallus, and that man cannot enjoy woman's body because he is too busy enjoying his own enjoyment, and while I have known men like that, indeed sex with Henry has sometimes felt like that, it has not always been so, and I wrote it all down and put a question mark next to it and Max shrugged and I wanted to talk to him about it afterward but afterward he took me back to his office and I forgot all about the maestro and whether or not there are women with their own sexual desires because I was inside my desire, and soon Max was too.

At dinner Florence is full of chatter about her day at school. She has gone to see her messiah. They're holding his seminar at the faculté de droit this year, she says, your alma mater. Oh are they, I say. And so he was talking about jurists, she said, he was talking about jouissance and its origins in a legal vocabulary. Hmpf, I say, shovelling food into my mouth. To come and to own, to enjoy, she goes on, it's the same word, jouir. For Lacan, castration is a question of whether or not you have been cut off from your jouissance. I think for a minute about what this might mean, or what she might be trying to tell me.

He said jouissance is always phallic, Florence says. I don't think that's true, I say, do you? I don't know, says Florence, certainly it is in the legal sense, but in the sexual sense I don't see where it makes room for female pleasure. Perhaps it's a critique of phallic jouissance, she goes on. Either he is suggesting something really radical, and Jacques Lacan is a great feminist, or just the opposite.

The maestro got a look at Claude during one of his seminars and invited her to begin an analysis with him. I have to admit I was piqued that he'd singled her out and not me. Then she told me how he works. I was there in his office, she said, and I was talking, and barely fifteen minutes had gone by when he said: right. That's enough for today. And he shooed me out. Right in the middle of a thought!

What do you think that was about? I ask.

I don't know. I think it was very rude. I don't know if I will go back. How can I relax enough to free-associate if I'm constantly worried he's going to interrupt me and kick me out?

I ask Max about it later. Classic maestro, he says. She was probably spinning a pretty narrative about her psychic pain. He was trying to jolt her out of it. Did it to me once. Just hung up on me during one of our calls. Tell her not to take it personally. It's too easy to get into the rhythm of a story, to explain, to be in a state of accountability. Harder to stop in the middle of one and go back out into the world with your unconscious all jostled. But better for you, takes you closer to what's going on underneath it all. To the real, the thing we can't say in language.

I reported all of this back to Claude. Well it doesn't make any sense, she says; if our job as analysand is to put everything into language and his job as my analyst is to separate me from my language? How is this ever supposed to work?

I think we have to accept the paradox, is what Max is saying,

I tell her. We have to somehow accept having our stories broken before we can make sense of them. To stay alive in our subjectivity, instead of deadening ourselves into something we've overheard or intuited. We have to absorb what we're learning without passing it through language.

You sound like him now.

One cannot say everything and with good reason, the maestro says today, to explain why he is tracing this particular narrative for us, explaining things the way he does and not some other way. And no one could explain them as he does, his words slip and slide into other words, and as they do he uncovers the links holding it all together, little words hiding inside other words, implications we never could have teased out ourselves, a surprise around every corner. He is often incomprehensible but he seems to understand himself, and encourages us to take our own flights of fancy. Things slip away in language, he says, we can never say what we mean. If I were to say to Henry, for instance, I am sleeping with someone else, what would he understand me to be saying, what would I understand myself to be saying? There is the physical reality of what I have been doing and keeping from him, but there are other meanings too, things I can encode in language but can only ever point to; it would only ever be a gesture, and maybe one that was destined to fail. Language speaks à notre place, on our behalf. One cannot say everything, but in any case we are saying much more than we suppose ourselves to be saying. Language is a vast referential system, much like our loves.

I don't care that she's fucking him I don't care I love women, I love women, I love – that one. The one looking this way, the one in the orange turtleneck, the one with no bra on, I'll go with that one, where shall we go

Max, in class, lecturing us on female sexuality. On the different kinds of jouissance men and women can experience, or obtain for themselves. We can pretend to have the phallus or pretend to *be* the phallus, he says, but we cannot escape it. He's following Lacan to the letter, critiquing Freud's view of women as somehow secondary to men, passive where they are active; like Lacan he's trying to get away from the notion that the sexes must desire a certain way. But his critique still frames everything around difference, around the phallus. What about sameness? What about the clitoris? Just to be a pest, I put my hand up. Sir, I say. Have you not read Anne Koedt's incisive essay 'The Myth of the Vaginal Orgasm'? Max blushes. These men can talk about sex comfortably as long as the women they're having it with keep quiet. I know he is intimately familiar with the clitoral orgasm, having authored a few himself earlier this week. When I open my legs to his tongue, I feel I am making a real intervention into the history of psychoanalysis.

At home we watch the footage from outside the courthouse where the trial of Marie-Claire's mother and her colleagues has just taken place. We won't know the outcome for a couple of weeks. Some women outside are singing as the defendants come out of the courthouse.

> *Debout femmes esclaves*
> *et brisons nos entraves*
> *debout debout*
> *debout*

Apparently even Simone de Beauvoir testified today, alongside Delphine Seyrig and Françoise Fabian. It reminds me of the headiest days of 1968 but this time with women singing and chanting, calling for our rights, ours specifically. I feel a lump form in my throat.

I'm in the kitchen getting a beer from the fridge and she's out there playing Chopin too fast but I don't know, I don't mind. I want to resent her but she brings it a certain brio the tubercular Pole probably didn't have the breath for but that's her interpretation, her spirit. She wants to work against the grain. Look at this wallpaper. Designed to fly in the face of the world she grew up in, her grandmother's world of politeness and chintz, teacups and lace. A fake world, she said when we moved in, look what it emerged from, look what happened to it. I don't need to look, I said, I know perfectly well. She papered the walls in these flowers after she came back, if that's what she needed to reconstruct her life why be contemptuous of it? It's just not very honest, Florence said. It's more honest to make it ugly.

And your owls, I want to ask her now, are they more honest, are you living out your honesty with your owls, and your Lacan, and your boyfriend?

I always go too fast when I play the Waltz in C sharp minor. I spin out of control and hit the wrong notes all because it's more important to feel it than to play it exactly right.

With Satie there is no exactly right. You are outside of time stamps, outside of precision, it is all feeling.

Today at the faculté de droit it felt like the maestro was playing the Waltz in C sharp too quickly, enjoying his own enjoyment of language, I am not sure I recognise myself in his philosophy, I recognise only Henry, his fear of castration, of being swallowed up, his need to remain the master, in control of the body, of the narrative. He talks *so much*.

When I get home I put on the Joni Mitchell album Max bought me, and I am so happy listening to it, light up your something blue eyes I sing to my husband, and of course Henry immediately wants to know where the record came from, and why I'm listening to contemporary music. You never listen to anything contemporary, he says, and it's like an accusation. You just bury yourself in your classical music and your classes and your maestro.

And what about you, I whip right back at him, in your office every day stamping papers and filing them away, why don't you finish your law degree and go out and *help someone*. I've never faulted Henry for his lack of ambition before but now it's all I can see, he is an enormous blank space where some sense of justice should be.

Where once he would have defended himself to his very last breath, now he elects not to reply, just picks up a book and puts it in front of his face.

I went back to the club with Jibé today, I felt him actually trying to foist me on these women at the bar, have you no shame, Jibé, a married man like you, don't you know there are some fantasies that should stay in the mind only, that have to stay there, they must, and you with a baby on the way?

Before I shower, I take off the necklace Florence gave me when we got married, a small gold Star of David on a chain, and carefully tuck it away in my wallet.

I wake at four a.m. with a shudder, an orgasm in my sleep. I grasp at the particulars of the dream that brought it on before they can slip away. A piano lesson. Not mine, someone else's. The cats are there, entwined, as usual, but there is another girl playing the piano. And elsewhere in the room, me lying on a couch. The teacher, a blonde woman I've never seen before, inserts one of her long fingers inside of me and that's when I wake up.

And at the club, Jibé urging me to these women, there's a pair of them we've come to know, one of them he's fucking and the other is her friend, Marie-France. (Marie-fucking-France!) Marie-France, whose face is a question. She's old enough to know her way around, married, two kids, and yet that openness, the saucer eyes, so wide you can see the whites under the irises, blue irises, the crystal blue of certain Swiss lakes. Doubles, he says, meaningfully squeezing my arm.

I looked for Max in his office today at the usual time and he wasn't there. I saw him at Lacan and we sat apart and we didn't speak. He sat with another young woman, blonde hair, blue dress. Is he testing me? Lacan spoke about Plato, *The Symposium*, a text I'd heard about but never been taught, it seemed to hold an almost mystical significance for him, and for the other students. He was talking about the way that love serves as a border between two people, it is something they share, but also a delusion, and then he lost me. It made me wonder about Max, and about Henry. With Max we are forging something new, a new country, outside the bonds of a state-sanctioned relationship, but also engaged in something very old, the adulterous liaison, both of us escaping the official containers of our marriages, which are sometimes too small for all that we are, and feel ourselves to be. As for Henry, our love is the place where all the things we know about each other live, our histories, our common past, our hopes for ourselves, our shared projects. The border between us is composed of the stories we tell ourselves about what we are doing and hope to do. It is an illusion, not a delusion, and the container is as necessary as the overflow.

I go to see Max later on, much later, when I really should be getting home, and he sits at his desk innocently, as if everything were fine. The other young woman? He wasn't sitting with her, she was just sitting next to him. I have my doubts. I have no rights over this man and his body. What is it we want from one another, that we don't get at home? That he can't get from that blonde girl? What are we to each other? All I know is I am growing tired of being his student. I want to be his equal. I sit on his desk, and reach his height. He opens my legs. I want him there and I want Henry there. I want Henry. To open himself up to me. To let me move inside him. To spread himself open for me. To turn his mind over to me. To let me mouth his heart, lick his wounds, kiss his fingers one by one. Max moves inside me and I think of Mélanie, whose picture I once saw by accident, blonde hair blowing in the wind. Did she give him no schooling in opening up. I will do it. I will be the one. But Max is there, strong shoulders, clean scent of soap, soft facial hair on my neck, his mouth, I seek it out, our exchanges, I know things, he talks to me, tells me things he says he's told no one else, not even his wife, she doesn't know anything about his childhood, she wouldn't understand, he says, the arduous trip to Mexico, the hot sun and the stinging insects, the desert, the mystery of the Spanish language, the French school they sent him to, the priests, their hands and their robes, a local girl he loved, her parents who refused to let their daughter marry a Jew, his escape to Paris, the life he'd wanted to build here among books and intellectuals, the small chambre de bonne where he lived on eggs and ersatz coffee, the window through which he looked at Paris, his wife knows none of this, she is from here, good Catholic family, big family, wants kids, can't have them, she blames it on him, they fight, she doesn't know about the baby with the Mexican girl, the woman in the neighbourhood who took care of it, the girl's stomach pains, Valentina was her name, Valentina's blood, Valentina in the hospital, the guilt, Paris so soon after, he is talking in my ear now, he is telling me what he likes, he is calling me his little girl, I take his mane of hair in my hand, I hold his head back, away from me, I eye him down, I hold him there, I am in control, I am the one he talks to, I am the one—

Florence comes home today talking of Plato's *Symposium*. About how once upon a time humans were spherical creatures, with four arms and legs and two heads, and they were very strong and powerful and lacking in humility. Zeus had the bright idea that to take them down a notch, he would divide them in two, so that they would stay busy trying to find their lost other half. He gave them genitals which they liked to mash together which also kept them busy and made them happy, at least temporarily. I go to the shelf, and take down the copy I underlined in high school: *So ancient is the desire of one another which is implanted in us, reuniting our original nature, making one of two, and healing the state of man.*

I pause. She takes the book from me, and reads aloud.

And when one of them meets with his other half, the actual half of himself, whether he be a lover of youth or a lover of another sort, the pair are lost in an amazement of love and friendship and intimacy, and would not be out of the other's sight, as I may say, even for a moment: these are the people who pass their whole lives together; yet they could not explain what they desire of one another. For the intense yearning which each of them has towards the other does not appear to be the desire of lover's intercourse, but of something

Why is she reading me Plato what does she want from me don't you have a professor for that why don't you just go and get fucked by him let him fuck you like there's two of you or however you like it with him, I am yes I am lost in amazement at you, I want your friendship and your intimacy, I want what we had in the beginning when we talked for hours and I felt perfectly held by your gaze, who knows why you wanted to be with me, I have never known, I assumed it *else which the soul of either evidently desires and cannot tell, and of which she has only a dark and doubtful presentiment . . .*

was love, the very same love you're now parading in front of me, testing, challenging, it is you who is splitting us apart not Zeus

And the reason is that human nature was originally one and we were a whole, and the desire and pursuit of the whole is called love, she concludes.

Yes, she says. That's it. Do you think that's our kind of love? She sits down and looks me full in the face. Do you think we are lost in an amazement of love and friendship and intimacy?

I don't know how to answer her, now.

Yet they could not explain what they desire of one another.

They could not.

You can't.

Florence, it's been a long day, what do you want me to tell you? I love you.

You say that all the time but you don't tell me why you do, you don't even try to explain it.

Some things don't need to be explained, I say, feeling helpless, they just are.

Would you say that some things can't be explained?

Yes, I say, gratefully, I would. That's how I love you. Deeply and inexplicably.

She still looks doubtful. That's what they talked about today.

Who?

The maestro. And his respondent. I didn't get all of it, there was a lot of math and logic and wordplay and it was raining so hard on the roof you sometimes couldn't hear them. But the respondent was talking about how those primeval men became arrogant, because they lacked for nothing. They had everything they wanted.

What's wrong with having everything you want?

I don't believe anyone does, that's just it. It's that built-in, foundational lack that sends us out into the world trying to find people to help us become whole again, she says. And no one person will ever fill that role. It's unhealthy to deny it. Nevertheless we go out there searching every day, we do it over and over. That's what they wanted to talk about, repetition. That Zeus turned his new creations' faces forward so they would be able to see their navels, the places where they had been severed from their other half. But that meant they would go through life always looking forward, never looking back, and so they would be less aware of seriality, and patterns. Of their own repetitions. The encore, they called it. An index of the infinite.

So if I'm following you, you think I'm looking over and over for someone to get whole with?

Yes, she says, more or less, yes. So I wonder if you ever really loved me, or only went with this deep wordless feeling that you called love but that is actually a void that can never be filled. But then you lie about it and claim to have everything you want. It's dishonest.

With that she goes to the kitchen to clean up after dinner, and I am left to my own devices, trying to figure out what she has just told me, or asked me, and if I disagree, and what it all means. I have another look at the book. *I believe that if our loves were perfectly accomplished*, said Aristophanes, *and each one returning to his primeval nature had his original true love, then our race would be happy.*

But who is our original true love, I think. And how can we return to them. And would returning to them really cure us of our desire for other loves? And what about that singularity that the person we love seems to possess, that themness, that no-one-elseness? Surely we can't transfer it from person to person? When you have what you want there's nothing left to want. But how do you have what you have? Florence is in the kitchen doing the dishes, and the rain is pouring down the windows, and I settle into my place on the couch at Plato's long-ago banquet.

I get up in the middle of the night to have another look at Henry's old paperback Plato. I remember reading some of it in lycée, but without my copy to hand I can't remember what I thought of it. I reread the early bits, stuff he's underlined, put little tick marks in the margins, like little windows into his mind. How love is meant to be edifying, eros grasping at virtue. I do not recognise my experience of eros in this definition of it as necessarily tending towards the good and the beautiful; I suppose I have been mired in the muck of the female body, with no access to the clean, masculine soul; I think of one of Max's Joni Mitchell albums, the lyrics I just about understand, about love being like souls in physical contact with one another, that's not what I feel with Max, but it's what I think I might have felt with Henry, I try to remember, it's so long ago now. It was that day, at the beach; those friends; that child who spilled her juice on my towel, Henry who gave me his, striped yellow and white, in such good condition for a boy, I remember being impressed by how clean and fluffy his towel was, he was so gallant and handsome, that day, the friends, the sun cream he spread on my back, he didn't know I hadn't been with anyone yet, had barely been kissed, I was nineteen, I didn't know anything but when he put his hands on me, I thought I would do anything for him to keep them there.

In *The Symposium*, early on, Plato talks about how Apollodorus is attracted to Socrates because he sees how much he has to learn from him; he is so brilliant and that makes him beautiful;

Apollodorus saw in Socrates what he wanted for himself, and he loved him for it. The symposia, I read in a footnote, were places for eros and education; I think of the maestro's seminars like a kind of symposium, Max taking me there.

There was another passage the maestro referred to that I was looking for, the part in Diotima's explanation about how the man in love can only look forward, he can't look behind – he doesn't see the *encore*. That doesn't sound right, I remember thinking; look at Henry; he can only look backwards. He can't face the future knowing what he knows about his family's past.

Flipping through the book to find the passage I come upon a postcard of a statue, a reclining woman, her head covered by what looks like a beehive, a thousand bees massed around it, and down on to her chest. I turn it over and it's blank on the back. Where could Henry have found it? Maybe in the gift shop at one of the châteaux his mother used to drag him to, Fontainebleau, Chantilly. He's always had a bit of a fetish for French history, he's always been old-fashioned, nostalgic for a France he didn't know that probably never existed.

That didn't matter when we were first together. I remember how daring it felt to be with him, to sleep with this boy in the room he rented under the rooftops by République, to talk with him about all my ideas, and have him listen so attentively. We weren't feminists then, not yet, but when the May events happened I think we really started to realise that we had to build our own movement. I remember my friends and I brought roast chickens to the students occupying the Sorbonne, like little handmaidens, at a certain point it disgusted us. Where does all of this leave us as women, I remember asking Henry, and he thought there was nothing wrong with our condition as women, that the workers' struggle was a completely different question. But there is so much more to work for, I told him, our bodies aren't even our own. Now's the time to fight for them, you know? We can say so much more now than we could before, I said to him, no more hypocrisy, everything is opening up, and I assumed he was opening up with me. I suppose he wasn't, now that I think about it, I suppose the only things he was liberated to talk about were things he didn't want to talk about.

Reading *The Symposium* I see the passage the maestro mentioned is much more radical than he allowed: all humans are pregnant, Diotima says, and they want to be near beauty to give birth. From ugliness they recoil, and shrivel up. They cannot reproduce. They cannot create. I am not sure I entirely understand what I'm reading, but I understand enough, about why I want to give birth, and why Henry doesn't; he wants to be near beauty, but all he finds is ugliness, because that is all he expects to find.

I thought what I had with Henry was the sustaining love, and with Max just pleasure, self-abandon, time out of time. I was wrong on both counts. But everything I feel or have felt for both of them is this eros, this thing I want to make more of. More of it, more of us, all of us. This child that is the knowledge of beauty and of its shadows, to sustain us through the alienation of desire, the inevitable confrontation with danger and disease, and with the end.

I love you. What do we say, what do we hear, how far apart are we?

I saw her lover on the streets of Belleville this evening, there's no way he lives here he must be visiting her, he'd better not be coming from the flat, there will be bloodshed if he sets foot in this flat, and when I get home there is a copy of *Combat* on the kitchen counter. It's his, I know it's his. He had to have left it here. *What is this Stalinist trash doing in my kitchen?* I bellow into the other room. It's a well-respected newspaper, she says, mildly, as she walks in and picks it up. And it's not like I'm a subscriber. There's just an interesting article in it today. Do you have any idea what those men are really about? I say. They hate women. They hate Jews. They love repression. They don't! she says. It's a very nuanced newspaper with a nuanced editorial line and you don't know what you're talking about.

It's your lover's, isn't it, I say, and there it is, I've said it. It takes all my self-control not to say anything more, not to push her up against the wall, not to hurt her, I am standing so still, I think this is the moment, she finally has to acknowledge it, we'll get it all out into the open. I saw him in the street downstairs, I know he was here.

My – but what are you inventing, Henry, really. And she leaves the room. And I remain where I am, standing so still, summoning my stoicism, my self-control, willing myself not to throw something across the kitchen, a vase of flowers, a dirty mug, my dignity, throw it across the room and watch it shatter, and I don't, I breathe in, I breathe out, I think about all the things a kitchen has to contain, a vase, a dirty mug, my dignity, let it stay, let them all be, I move into the living room, see her squatting on the floor next to the television trying to get it to turn on, she is so inept when it comes to technology, and I think maybe after all there was nothing in the café that day, maybe I saw no one in the street, that this thing Jibé thinks he overheard her talking about, maybe it's just a crush, maybe it will all be fine, it is better to think this way, I feel calmer already, look how inept she is, she can't even turn on the television, how could she have an affair and keep it from me, and I go to help her.

We watch on TV as Gisèle Halimi comes out of the courtroom in Bobigny flanked by Marie-Claire and her mother. (What did Henry think he saw? He's next to me breathing heavily.) They've basically won. Her mother has to pay a fine, her colleagues have been found not guilty, the woman who performed the abortion condemned to a year in prison, but everyone is saying she won't serve it. (He can't have seen anyone, I've never brought Max to the house, who would be stupid enough to do that?) Halimi is a genius, not only did she defend these women but she went after the law, and she won. (I haven't forgotten the things Henry said about her when she defended Djamila Boupacha.) It really feels like things might be changing, like we might actually have a chance at changing the law. (The more he sits there, rigid, the angrier I get. It seems to me, with Henry sitting beside me, still angry that I dared to buy a paper he doesn't like, that it is men like him who might actually be the problem: officially supportive, but inwardly seething.) I also haven't forgotten the jokes he made about the three hundred and forty-three women who signed the manifesto saying they'd had abortions but no doubt about it if I got pregnant he'd waste no time finding out what we'd have to do to get rid of it. There is so much he shuts himself off to, because it threatens the way he understands the world; but even Max, who is worldly enough not to confuse ego and politics, is blinkered, doesn't understand what women are telling him, the body of work we are founding. He doesn't see that his revolution is incomplete as long as he and men like him are the ones writing it. (I brought this up at our meeting last week and we had to stay an hour later than usual, everyone had something to say about it. I came home late and Henry wouldn't speak to me, lord knows where he thought I was. Some of the girls were talking about joining Halimi's group Choisir, if I thought I could pay the dues without Henry finding out I would.)

I can't believe Florence would read that crap. A girl like Florence, with her family, with their story, aligning herself with these bullshit people, spouting the same kind of barely veiled anti-Semitic shit they were forty years ago, thirty years ago.

To think our families came here to escape poverty and persecution in Poland, only to find themselves impoverished, persecuted, and on a train back to Poland.

I have often wondered why my family came back here. Why they didn't go on to America, or Palestine, someplace that hadn't just enthusiastically deported them, delivering them into the hands of their would-be murderers. I wish I could ask them but there's no one left to ask, even the ones who survived didn't survive that long, turns out getting deported to a death camp then returning to the country that sent you there isn't great for longevity. By the time I was old enough to ask, they were gone. Some by their own hand. Some by disease. Others just stopped ticking. I've asked my mother, she knew my dad before he was taken, waited for him, was there when he came back, emaciated and sick. Sweet little French girl that she was, she didn't even stop to wonder why he came back there. Maybe you have to be a Jew to wonder. Maybe we just return to certain places like those cats you hear about making their way back when their family has moved to a new house, home is home, what can you do about it?

I've made myself in the image of the ideal Frenchman, perhaps to avenge them, except of course for my unpronounceable, unspellable last name, which I've kept also to avenge them, exactly as I inherited it from my father. That's my combat. See. You can be a Polish Jew with our name and also as French as they come. I am Henry son of Yitzhak and look at me now. Look at Marie-France as she runs her fingers over my forearm, as she moves a curl away from my forehead. Look at me at the club with Marie-fucking-France.

Claude is thinking of writing her final project on our consciousness-raising meetings. She says she's interested in the therapeutic dimension, in the way feminist groups have collectivised the clinical process. Talking not to one analyst, but to fifteen. It is there, at one of our meetings, that I surprise myself by describing my desire for a child to someone other than Henry. Claude, eight months gone herself, is delighted, doesn't see what the problem is. But my husband doesn't want one, I tell them all, and my lover does. He's been trying with his wife and they can't. The general assembly doesn't blink at my enumeration of husband on one side and lover on the other. The feminist current is urging. Have a baby, they say, have a baby. Take care of it on your own if you have to. Have yourself a little baby.

Someone has a copy of the full text of the Bobigny trial, which Gallimard has just published. It's called *Abortion: The Law on Trial*. I can't imagine having the courage to actually buy it in a bookshop. The girls are discussing, with great disdain, the total ignorance of the men judging the case. Can you believe he actually asked the abortionist if she inserted the speculum into Marie-Claire's mouth? *Debout, debout!* the girls sing. But have we really shed our shackles, someone else says, one of my friends went to get the pill at the pharmacy and someone behind her muttered *you slut*.

One of the girls takes me aside later, as we're putting our coats back on. Just don't lose track of us when you have your baby,

OK? Your friend too. Don't lose yourselves in your little lives and forget that you still have to fight. Her eyes are round, her eye make-up smudged. I don't remember her saying very much during the meeting. She's holding my hand.

I don't know whose idea it was, but we're in the métro on our way to Neuilly to have dinner at Claude and Jibé's place. They live in a modern building quite a ways from the station. You can tell this is the kind of place where everyone drives, I say drily. Not everyone, she says, Claude takes the métro. I am astonished. Jibé has that flashy car and he can't drive his pregnant wife to school? I think she probably wouldn't let him if he tried, Florence smiles. Claude is a very independent person. Sounds like someone else I know, I mutter, but she takes this as a compliment and squeezes my hand.

At the door we are greeted by a set of numbers like a typewriter. Hang on, she says, it's one of those new code things, Claude gave it to me. She roots around in her bag for her diary. It's in here somewhere . . . Ah there it is: 43B28. She types it in and the door opens.

Very modern, I say.

Very different to Belleville, she says. I grunt. Do you wish we lived in Neuilly? she asks me. No, do you? I ask her, surprised. No, she says. But with your job, and now that you've started going to that racquet club, I just – wondered if you didn't wish our lives were a little more—

Bourgeois? I ask.

No, she says, but yes.

Claude is hugely pregnant but waits on us at dinner anyway. How are you feeling, Claude? I ask. Fine, she says, eight and a half months along, the doctor says it could come any day! Jibé does nothing but make her life difficult. He complains about the lamb, complains about the wine, complains about the cheese, apologises to us when she's out of the room. Claude has been very busy with her schoolwork recently, he says. She doesn't keep the same eye on things she used to. It will be better when the baby comes and she can stop studying. You could be nicer to her, Jibé, I say. Ah, he says, she's a good little girl, she knows her place. Florence catches my eye across the table, and I wonder what things my wayward wife might know about Jibé's good little girl.

On the way home I think about my feelings of envy for Claude. I want a baby, but do I really want to be in her place? In her chic suburb with her asshole husband? Still, I do, I envy her. She's secure enough to do it, in spite of her asshole husband, she is her own supporting wall. That is what I envy. It's not that she has a perfect life or marriage, it's that she feels sufficient unto herself. She says she's going to keep studying, no matter what Jibé thinks, that even if it takes her longer she'll finish her degree, she'll do her internships, she'll be a therapist. She'll keep coming to our group. The answer is never the husband, she tells me, the group is the answer.

I think maybe I chose wrong, that I followed the heat of those early days into a marriage too quickly, without being sure we wanted the same things. Henry doesn't want a baby. He is still a baby himself, he says. And I know I can't argue with that. He goes off to the club with Jibé in Jibé's hot little two-seater, I know all about it, it's the source of much frustration for Claude, how are they supposed to get around with a baby when there's nowhere to put it? He just laughs at her and says he'll buy her a station wagon, and then she smacks him in the face, because he wants to turn her into a maman, in her unwieldy family vehicle, while he gets to zip around town, a single guy to all appearances, zip to work she says, zip to the club, unzip whatever it is he's unzipping, zip home again, zip zip zip. He is so *modern*.

221

True to the doctor's prediction, the baby does come early, and Claude quits school. I have other friends there but I feel her absence keenly. I go to see her at the American Hospital in Neuilly where she has given birth, she looks very small in her hospital bed, holding a creature that is infinitely smaller, that has black hair, and a tiny nose, that doesn't take its eyes off of her, not even to feed, and as it feeds I can't help but notice her enormous brown areola a halo above his head. Charles, she says. I take him from her and he's as light as an apple, as light as a book, as light as a shoe. Tiny and early. I brought you some books, I say, when the baby is in his little bed again, and she thanks me, and looks at them in the same unfocused way the baby looked at me. I move them to the bedside table. You can read them later, I say, when you've had some sleep. Her feet stick up under the blanket at the bottom of the bed, and she seems very fragile, and I suddenly feel very bad for her.

I've stopped taking the pill, Florence announces over breakfast. I look at her with incredulity. My wife is having sex with two different men and she chooses this moment to get pregnant? Isn't that a decision we should make together? I ask. It's my body, she says, and I can do what I like with it. All right, I say, but it's our life, and if you decide to have a baby with your body it affects me as well, doesn't it? Well, I am giving you fair warning, she says. You can take whatever steps you like to ensure I don't get pregnant. But I am ready to be a mother, whether or not you are there to do it with me.

Ultimatums from my beautiful Florence. I watch her as she stands up from the table, puts her cup in the sink, and goes off to pack her bag for the day.

I don't want a baby, Florence. I want to sit here and read. I want to go out for a drink. I want to listen to my hi-fi. I want to take the night train. I want to work as late as I want and spend my pay cheque on a sharkskin suit. I want to fuck you on the beach and take you to Australia, throw massive dinner parties and even do the dishes myself. I want to lie on the floor with the cats and listen to you play the piano and keep out of the way as your patients come through the door, I want to go to the theatre and the movies and out for lunch, and laugh at your jokes and your politics, and love you all the time. And you want to break all that, and you're not even giving me a choice in the matter, and you're pretending everything is fine. You say you want to build a new world but you just want to destroy the old one.

We meet in his office as usual but there are papers everywhere, he's wearing his reading glasses, everyone's going to be keeping their clothes on. I feel wrong-footed but he wants to talk about his work and frankly I'm flattered. Max is proposing a new article on desire and original loss, le fait de jouir n'étanche pas le désir original, he tells me, we go around spraying the world with our desire, but nothing we can do staunches the wound. It is loss that triggers desire. And that seems to me the saddest way to think of desire. As compensating some loss? I like the metaphor of spraying better, I say, not the wound but the idea of plenitude that we douse everyone around us with. But Max has those hooded eyes, and I can imagine what he keeps hidden there, an absence he can't name but can only gesture at in these articles, and with me.

And what if it was all the feminists' fault, I considered, on my walk today. Those stupid fucking meetings she attends, putting ideas about storytelling into her head, everyone has one she says, you just need to help them understand that it's worth something. Even the things they can't say speak, she says, that's why I want to do this job, of being a receiver of stories. She even wants me to tell her a story I don't even know myself. Would she be happy if I made one up, a sad little story of the Shoah, my mother's absolute incomprehension, my father's suicide, getting beaten up at school, everyone's favourite kike, Jibé's fucking brother and his jokes, would I make sense to her then? I stumble on some rubble left in the middle of the sidewalk and swear. What are they demolishing, you have to wonder, what kind of city are they making room for?

For New Year's Florence goes to her feminists, and I sit at home and drink. Happy fucking New Year.

My grandmother is very ill.

I dreamed about her last night. I walked into my parents' bed-room, and there she was, sitting on the edge of their bed. I thought: if she's there, she must have died. And my chest seized and I could barely move. The dream-panic set in.

Forcing myself awake, I thought: if I get a phone call in the morning I won't be able to bear the prescience of the dream.

There was no phone call in the morning, but it will come one of these mornings. All the people who have already gone – my other grandparents, aunts and uncles, schoolfriends – she will soon be one of them. The people I think about who aren't here any more, the people who surprise me in my sleep. Soon I will have another ghost.

And I am pregnant, now, as I wanted to be.

I bought myself a 1973 calendar to hang in the kitchen in cele-bration. Owls, one for every month. My baby will come in the eighth month of the year; it will be the first year that is entirely baby.

Henry is hosting his office poker game tonight, and they seem more than usually loud and swaggering, smoking around the table like something out of a movie. I hear Henry telling them about me as I walk out, hear him say *consciousness*, hear him say *raising*. How will I tell Henry my news, Henry who knows I have someone, and who is taking it exactly as I knew he would, like a little boy who has to be at the centre of everything, all the time, who wants to benefit from the liberations of the past few years without actually sacrificing anything for them, who likes to talk to his friends about his wife's feminism, feminism, what a dirty word, like a disease I caught, to laugh about it with them, I hear them as I'm at the piano and he thinks I'm too involved in the music to hear what they're saying, they're joking about my feminism, he doesn't understand it can liberate him, too.

When I came home from work today Florence told me her news. She showed me her calendar. I was enraged. To lay that kind of news on me, and then show me a fucking calendar full of owls, it was too much; I tore it from the wall, flung it away from me; she cried. Afterward we couldn't find it. I broke things. I broke our phone, picking it up to call Jibé and deciding as I dialled that it was a mistake to call him of all people, a fucking mistake a FUCK   ING   MIS   TAKE every syllable bashing the receiver into the cradle so the plastic cracked, a line right up it like someone wrote on it with a pencil. She didn't make me sleep on the couch, but I didn't sleep much anyway. Is it even my fucking baby? I wanted to ask, but couldn't, because I didn't want to know the truth, whether or not she actually is fucking that old man. I am trapped in this apartment with that bloody muddy wallpaper, like someone threw lumps of cow dung at it, with vaginas hiding in cupboards and slogans everywhere I look, and the ghost of Satie at the piano smirking at me, a cigarette hanging out of the side of his mouth and nestled inside the soundboard a jar of his fingernail clippings floating in urine.

Is it even my fucking baby? I ask her as she sleeps.

I take the train to the suburbs to go and see my mother. She lives with my stepfather in a modest house in Antony, a short walk from the train station. After raising me in Paris, they decided to move out there, where the air was cleaner, and they could have fruit trees in their back garden. Florence and I have talked many times about moving there too, but only in the abstract; we could never leave the city.

Their medium-sized pebble-dash house is behind a gate that gives an unearthly moan when you open it; every time I visit I offer to oil it and every time they say after you drink your tea, have some more tea, and after my tea I always forget and then I have to run to catch the train home. They don't fix it themselves, I am convinced, so I always come back to see them.

My mother is inside doing her crossword puzzle when I come through the moany gate. She's at the door before I can ring. Something must be apparent on my face because she calls me her kitten and brings me in for some milk. I stifle the urge to bury my face in her shoulder and cry. Maman, I say. Maman, Maman.

Claude has officially dropped out of school. There will be no final project on psychoanalysis and consciousness-raising meetings.

I tell Max about the baby. I think he should know. I've been offered a teaching job in London, he says. Just for a year. I think perhaps he hasn't heard me; I say it again. I heard you. Come to London with me. I'm not going to London. Is it mine? It could be mine. Come to London and have the baby there and it will be ours. I will take care of you and the baby. Begging, almost. I'm not going to London. And it could be Henry's. And what about your wife? Max makes a sound. She is with someone else now.

There's no time to think; there is too much else to consider. A new life in London, with Max, a baby, him all to myself. All to myself? Do I want all of him, all the time? Do I want to wake up with him every day? Listen to him chew his food every night? Fight with him about money? Raise this child with him? Something tells me he wouldn't even stick around for all of that. He is too generous with himself, with his time, his thoughts, generous in the sense of being unable to restrict himself to just one person. For all his faults, Henry would assume his responsibility.

I shake my head. You don't want me, not full-time. You only want me because I'm not entirely yours. Because I'm needed elsewhere.

That's not true, says Max. I want you all to myself. I need you here. Or, rather, in London. But he himself sounds unconvinced.

I'm sorry. I'm not going.

And that is how I know it will come to an end, when he leaves for London. But we still have time. And when the nausea is elsewhere, my pregnant body wants him so badly that I wonder if he is indeed the father, that my body has recognised him, or if this is simply my desire leading me astray, as usual.

I sit in the café on the corner of the avenue Simon Bolivar and the rue de Belleville, and think about what to do. What should I do? I think I will not stay. I think I can't be with a woman who has betrayed me as Florence has. But then, it might be mine. I can't leave her to raise my baby on her own. What will I do? I can't stay. Can I? I can't. And that is when I know that I won't. I don't know where I'll go, I can't fill in the immediate future. I think only: when I am old, I will return to this apartment, to my front door, to find out what I will have missed all those years with Florence. I know I have to leave, and I know I will have to return, and that I will find out about all those missed moments. There is something strange about a moment. We can't ever live inside of it. We live just after it. We live the moment better in trying to relive it, than in living it the first time around. Inhabiting the same space as the moment, we hear its echo, sounding louder. That is why I will come back. She will be waiting for me the way she was in the beginning. She will be with me as I wasn't with her at the end. She will have understood everything. I will have understood everything. Just like that. That's what it's like, to return.

Henry comes home with a resolved look on his face.

Look, Florence, he says.

I look.

The look changes.

Yes, Henry?

Look, he says, and looks out the window, where the night is beginning. Look.

In the morning his things are there, but he himself is gone.

There is a strange story about Henry's grandmother, Rose. I don't know if I believe it. She was living in an apartment with her family in a building in the 11th, not far from here, an elderly Polish lady who spoke maybe three words of French, who when she pronounced her three words revealed herself to be, quite obviously, a Jewish immigrant. They came for her family during the war. Some they caught, some they didn't; as luck would have it, some had left the house that morning. She was preparing her bag to go with the police when they stopped her. You're not on our list, they said. *Vas?* she replied. She wasn't on their list; they weren't going to take her. Through some bureaucratic fluke, the old Yiddish-speaking lady wasn't rounded up with the others. They say she walked out of Paris and hitch-hiked her way to the zone libre where she found some friends living under assumed names near the Swiss border.

Henry never told me this story. His mother did; she heard it from some cousin. Rose lost her daughter, her husband, her sister, other members of the family. Her son, Henry's dad, survived; though he didn't live a long life, he lived long enough to have a son, then he went too.

I never met Rose; she died long before Henry and I got together. But I admire her and I admire Henry through her. He has her willingness to submit to authority, but also her refusal to dissemble, to be other than she was. She was ready to accept the consequences of being herself.

I wish Henry would talk to me about all of this; I wish he felt that he could tell me things. There is an uncrossable distance between us. I think it's why I want to be an analyst; there are stories I think I need to hear, even if they don't belong to my husband; they will help me get ready for the day when he's ready to tell me his.

But I find myself increasingly thinking that day may never come. What lengths will he go to, to avoid being trapped?

I'm at the club, having dropped a load of cash at the car dealership for a brand-new Citroën SM, and Marie-France is there this afternoon, and she's rubbing my back as I cry into my drink, telling her I don't want to have a baby, how I don't want to reproduce all of this, you can't just paper over the past, but she's pregnant and there's nothing I can do about it, she won't even entertain the idea of going to see someone to sort her out, I'm not going to end up on television being defended by Gisèle Halimi, she said; I'm having this baby, she said.

Oh, Marie-France answers, her eyes wide. Oh.

Do you even know if it's mine, I want to ask her but I can't bring myself to, I can't confront Florence with this information, it's too important to leave what we have intact, even if it can't remain intact, it has to come apart for the right reasons not the sordid ones, not come apart in reproaches and betrayal but because we don't want the same things.

I take a breath, take a sip, she goes on rubbing my back.

That and because there will always be a doubt for me, when this baby is born. I will always be looking for that other man in my child. Every aspect of its appearance that doesn't resemble mine, I will wonder if it resembles his. Every aspect that does resemble me, I will doubt.

Marie-France of course knows several stories of similar things happening to friends of hers, in one instance the mother knew the baby wasn't her husband's, in fact she knew and he knew he couldn't have a baby at all, because of an accident, so he didn't mind very much when this baby turned up that he could call his own, he was willing to live with the lie to have a child. And in another case the mother left the one she knew was the father to have the baby with someone else. In several cases the mother had stayed to have the baby with someone she didn't love, just so she could have one. Don't ask how they are, she says, they're miserable, but at least they're mothers.

Do you know anyone who didn't want to have a baby and then did?

She thinks for a moment. No, she says, I don't know anyone who didn't want a baby.

Henry comes back tonight and throws a pair of keys on the table. What are those? I ask. The keys to my new car. I know I can't react, if I show him the anger I feel – the money I had been setting aside to knock down the wall into the baby room suddenly transformed into this car – I will be giving him exactly what he wants. And where have you parked this new car? I ask. On the street, he says. And do you think it will be there in the morning?

The way he threw those keys. The way they glinted in the light. There are things he wants to say to me, that he can't authorise himself to say except through these keys. All the locks he expects me to see to, so he doesn't have to. Without a word, I go to the kitchen to finish making dinner.

The car is there in the morning, and I drive it to work, and then I drive it to the club, and then I drive it to a hotel near the club, where I finally fuck Marie-France, and then I drive her home, and then I drive back to the hotel and sleep there till morning.

I always thought that Chopin was the poet of adultery. Maybe because of his thing with George Sand. That was just manner-ism, reverie. But now I know it's Satie. Satie was playing in the elevator of the hotel in Neuilly that we pressed ourselves into, in a hurry to get to the room, my hand already up her skirt, grabbing her pert little ass.

There came a period when I was very much not present, and Florence was going through the early days of her pregnancy more or less alone. I would leave her some ginger I'd picked up at the market for the nausea, or a note telling her to leave the washing-up. I was trying to be a good, if non-committal, hus-band to her. She wasn't home very often; we didn't cross paths; I don't know where she slept. I don't know much about those days, how she experienced them, how she was feeling in her changing body. Occasionally I'd leave her a note to say I loved her, and missed her. She never left one of her own.

There is so much we will never know about other people, no matter how much we love them, or how much time we spend with them. We can know all of their mannerisms, know inti-mately their bodily odours, the schedule they shit on, recognise the very scent of their wind. Some people think this takes all the mystery, all the magic, out of a life together, but there will remain inexorably something unreachable about them. Try as we may, we grasp and can't lay hold of their essence; there is always something that escapes. Take Marie-France, at whose edge I stand as before a body of water I am wading into. There is so much to know about her, though she seems like a limpid pool, knowable down to the bottom of her crystal-blue irises. Everyone is a mystery. I love you, Florence, my strong fragile beautiful one, my love like a paperweight, I love you, I love you, I think with every thrust into the depths of Marie-France's perfectly wet pink cunt. And I even love Marie-France. Her soul is the water, her soul is her body, tanned and blonde, her soul is all around me. In those moments I know she loves me more than her husband, who is not here after all, and I love her back, perfectly.

And yet the strangeness of her body, which is not Florence's. I wish for a moment there were a way to appreciate other people's bodies without fucking them. I wish I could talk to Florence about this problem, but if I did I would give myself away, not only Marie-France but Mélanie and all our other longings and histories; this is the unspeakable thing at the heart of a marriage, this problem of the other person's body, the places it has been, the things it has done. It's a problem of temporality: we allow them to stray this way as long as it was over and done with before we entered their lives. And in any case, Florence is not here to talk to, she is with Claude, or she is with her other man, or she is simply off somewhere by herself. The piano stands unplayed, and when I am home, I give the cats their food and empty their litter box.

We keep it clean at first, we keep things neat, fucking only at the hotel, but then we get a little messy and we fuck at her house until one afternoon her son comes home early from school and I have to get dressed right quick and pretend to be a salesman selling his mother something and then we go to my place when I know Florence won't be home, and then that is the ultimate betrayal, I know it as I'm doing it, as I lean over her on the couch, as I unbutton her blouse, and unzip my trousers, I know what I'm doing is wrong but I lower myself in anyway, and then it is all just ocean in my ears, a whooshing that is only feeling, and wetness, and the sound of wetness, and I fuck and I fuck and I am so lost in the moment that I do not hear the key turn in the lock, do not hear Florence's steps on the parquet, am not aware of her until she is leaning over us, as I fuck and fuck Marie-France on our couch. And do you know, once she is there, I have a moment where I think I should stop, and Marie-France catches my eye, and I see something there in those limpid blue pools that I want to lean into, something that reminds me of something from a long time ago, and so I don't stop, I fuck and fuck with desperation, with abandon, as my wife walks out the door.

III

There's no such thing as love at first sight.

What there is is a reaction.

Someone puts a hand on you from behind when you don't expect it and you jump, startled out of proportion to the touch.

When I first met Jonathan it was like – feathers brushed the wrong way. A disruption in the order of things.

And that's what it felt like again, seeing him, again.

Ça va, Anna, Jonathan says, as if there had been no break, no rupture in our narrative, and leans in for the conventional double kiss. Oh you two know each other, Clémentine claps her hands delightedly. A little, I say.

It would be too dramatic to leave, so I stay a while longer, just long enough for it not to be weird. I don't speak to him again, but I don't not speak to him, either. I speak to Sabine, and Sarra, and Serge. I speak to Gilles, and Denis, and Olympia. I wave to Clémentine from across the room as I slip out the door.

I go down the stairs, and out into the courtyard, and instead of climbing back up the stairs in my own building, I walk out the big bottle-green door, and on to the rue de Belleville, and I walk all the way down the street to the bottom of the hill, and I pause outside the café with the stellar young people and I think about drinking a beer alone. The yellow street lights are blurry. I am not wearing a coat and as I come back to myself I realise I am cold. I walk back up the hill to our building, and as I push open the front door, his eyes are in mine without my even meaning it.

Things are moving slow and strange. He has me by the elbow and he guides me to a back corner of the courtyard, by Madame Vasquez's window. He takes out a pack of cigarettes from his breast pocket and flips open his lighter. It's an expensive-looking silver one. I have an involuntary flashback to when he used to roll his own cigarettes. His hand is shaking. He doesn't say anything while he lights up, and exhales, looking up at the absurdly purple night sky.

Can I have one of those? I ask.

Every thought I've had about him all these years races through my mind, the missing him, his body, his voice on the phone, his hair in the wind, the sudden absence, the incomprehension, psychoanalysing in the void, the building with the scaffolding in the rue Monge, a flash of his naked leg on top of mine on a beach in Brittany, the setting sun turning it pink, seeing him on the boulevard de Courcelles, his suit, his navy suit, his dead mother, his shiksa stepmother, all his relatives dead in Auschwitz, the plaque at the elementary school in the 11th he showed me once, where his great-aunts and -uncles went to school before they were deported. All of it was why we weren't allowed to be together, not because his father cared, he didn't, with his shiksa wife, but maybe *because* his father didn't care, because Jonathan himself was trying so hard to reconcile his Frenchness with his Judaism, and because he felt right down deep, irretrievably, immutably, that someone without a similar background could not understand the depths of his hurt, and could not pass that hurt, that meaning, that sense of the world on to his children the way he needed it to be passed on. For your children to hurt like you hurt: what a mysterious ambition. Everything I have understood about parenthood from my patients would suggest just the opposite, that when he has children, if he has them, he will do everything in his power to protect them from his pain.

The irony is that David *is* Jewish, and he doesn't care that I'm not. The plaques around Paris are not nothing to him, but they're not his actual family members who were deported. His parents are from Tunisia. They've welcomed me into the family. They're lovely.

Months after we separated I would lie in bed at night, my body temperature elevated, electrified with the idea of him, feeling like if I concentrated hard enough he would feel me calling him. Then I would feel ridiculous for pining for this person who'd left me so casually, and fall asleep empty and with no way of projecting myself into the future.

So. You and Clémentine.

Me and Clémentine.

I didn't – she didn't tell me your last name.

She didn't?

No, she didn't. You don't think I knew, did you?

He studies my eyes, first one, then the other, like he can't decide which one to focus on. I don't know. It's kind of a co-incidence, don't you think?

Yes, I think it's a coincidence, I think it's a very weird coincidence.

We stand together without talking, alone in the dark. I get the feeling we'd both like not to be there; we both want to escape this new context but it's impossible to leave the court-yard, we are bound there by our history and who we used to be to one another. We stand by the window, smoking, held together by the energy of this coincidence, unsure what to make of it. I study the small neat stitching on the collar of his generic blue shirt, his hands that look the same after all this time, square hands, a rugged topography of veins on the back, the light brown colour of the loose skin where his thumb joins his palm. It seems absurd to know a pair of hands so well, and to be so estranged from their owner. His height puts me eye level with his jaw. I stare at the little black hairs as they push through his pores. He stares at the window. He is very close to me and I think is he going to kiss me, or embrace me, what is going to happen?

After a moment he takes his phone out of his pocket, looks at the time, and says he should be getting back to the party. He kisses me on both cheeks, and then he's gone again.

The next morning I wake up feeling like I've slept in an ashtray. The smoke is in my hair, in my pores, in my lungs, in my nasal cavities. I can't cough it up, it's inside me now.

We think that things come back, but in fact they were never gone.

David. I text David. I can't come to London on Monday. I have to stay here, get my shit together, start seeing patients again.

typing, WhatsApp informs me.

Then it switches to *online*.

Then *typing* again.

Then: *last seen today at 9:42 a.m.*

He finally texts back around noon. I'm disappointed, he says. But I understand. Do what you have to do.

Monday morning the guys come to put plastic drop cloths all over everything in the kitchen and in the living room, securing them to the floor with industrial grey tape. It takes an hour. I sit in my office while they work, staring out the window, trying to see my view of the city through the drop cloth on the scaffolding, wondering am I making a mistake, should I go to London, should I leave the wall up, and then they call to me. We're starting now, they say. Are you ready?

I give them the OK, and the sledgehammers begin.

The phone rings Wednesday morning. I have just come back from my run. I am dripping with sweat. There are men in my house, and dust everywhere. When I go to get some water from the kitchen I can see through to my living room. I don't recognise the number, but I answer anyway.

Come over, he says.

No, I answer.

Come over. Clémentine is out all day. I stayed home from work. I want to talk to you.

I don't think I want to talk to you, I say.

I think you do, he says.

I need to shower. I've just been out for a run.

Shower and come over.

He answers the door wearing trackpants and a faded T-shirt. He leads me into the bedroom and lies down on the bed. I sit on the edge of it, keep my feet on the floor. His and Clémentine's bed. Her taste, clearly. Light pink linen sheets. Worn from sleeping. A dent in her pillow. I recognise her scent in the air.

You look pretty much the same, he says, after a minute.

You look older, I say, glad of it. Do we have nothing else to say to each other besides these inanities? I feel the weight of missing him, all these years of wondering and missing, dissipate. He wasn't the love of my life, I think to myself. I didn't lose the love of my life.

But I don't leave. He is leaning against the pillows, his long legs stretched out in front of him. His T-shirt has hiked up on one side, and I glimpse his stomach. I put my hand to it, and feel the skin there, soft, so soft. I run my finger under the waistband of his trackpants. My hand slips under, straightens him out. The tip right under the waistband. I put my mouth there.

He is so familiar. The same taste as before, the same soft mouth, everything the same, fourteen years later.

I don't know what I'm doing. I think I should think it's wrong but I don't. Does he think it's wrong? Later on, will he feel ashamed? I don't want him to feel ashamed. Because as our bodies seek the old positions the one thing I don't feel is shame. I am removing Jonathan's clothing in Clémentine's bed and I don't feel ashamed, if anything it feels as if somehow she's invited me here. That what we are doing we are doing for all of us, so we can all be a little more free. That we are fucking something loose that is something valuable and beautiful. That this room was constructed for this kind of liberation. I don't avoid his eyes and he doesn't avoid mine. We aren't above the law, we are remaking it. We are passing our bodies back and forth across it, across whatever boundaries, walls, marriages, are meant to keep us apart. I don't have a final theory of eros, a politics of consent, a morality of fidelity, but whatever I do have is inside this room, moving across the thresholds that demarcate these kinds of beliefs, do this but not that, that but not this, across the borders of time and memory and what sustains us through all the things we do in a life.

The first time, my thighs tremble uncontrollably, and the second time as well.

He pushes until I break and mercury silvers out

Why aren't you at work? I ask, later, when we have been silent for a while. He doesn't answer. You have a tattoo, I say, noticing the inside of his wrist for the first time, where the letter V has appeared. I bring his wrist down to my face, smell the skin there, like leather and perfume. When did you get this? I suddenly remember being in bed with him years ago, when I had pointed to different places on my body, and asked him what I should write there, and there, and there, and he said he didn't want me to, he said he could never. Jews don't get tattoos, he'd said. A silence as we both thought of Jews who'd been tattooed.

A few years ago, he says.

Since that day at his apartment, we have found each other as often as we can. He comes over right from work, or in the middle of the night. The house is a mess, dust everywhere, the kitchen barely usable, we fuck in the ruins of what used to be my apartment, and then we get takeaway. Some days Clémentine comes and spends the evening with me, and goes home, and a little while later Jonathan turns up on my doorstep. Then he, too, is gone by morning. It's so absurd, I really should move in with *them*. One weekend he tells Clémentine he's going out of town, but he spends the entire weekend in my apartment. Miraculously, she doesn't drop in. That it is all very complicated doesn't dampen our desire. Obviously, obviously, it only builds up the need to see each other. I don't understand why it should be this way for him, he says so little about his own life, but I feel the urgency between us. It is like something we both need to go through, to reach the other side of. I know there will be a time after this, when I will again live in the after. But we aren't there yet. I hope, in having him again, to make the after more bearable, this time.

He is much the same as he was, still boyish, floppy curls, that smile, he wears the softest long-sleeved T-shirts with stripes and a boat neck that stands away   just so   from his beautiful neck and shoulders, soft jeans, black boots, mon beau marin urbain. He has the same weird sense of humour, a love for the off-beat, the what the fuck, random French rap from the 90s and obscure sci-fi films from the 60s. He still listens to jazz but he no longer reads Houellebecq. He is shyer than I remember but also somehow more himself. I still can't put my finger on what it is I love about him, loving him is like listening to a radio station in a country where I don't speak the language. I can't believe I'm looking at his skin again.

I don't change the sheets until just before David is meant to come home. I sleep in them as they are. His hair – his smell – his stains – our sweat – our effort – the memory of us together, trapped in fabric.

Smash, smash, smash, every day they smash a little more, until there is nothing left of the wall, standing in the kitchen looking at the living room it is as if the two rooms were superimposed on one another, it feels wrong, and also right, my will exerted on the walls of a building that stood for so many years before my birth, smashed to bits while I look on. The guys seem to enjoy it, smashing things. They put on the radio, go out to the balcony to smoke now and then, they kid around, they eat lunch, they smash some more. I joke with them about the smashing when they take their breaks, and learn a little of their stories. Maxime, the foreman, who's been smashing since he was a teenager; Ousmane who's just arrived from Mali where he was studying medicine and who's smashing until he can get settled and try to get into medical school here, his buddy Adama who is his cousin's boyfriend and who is going to start his own smashing company as soon as he can but it's so complicated in France, you have no idea, madame, I don't, I agree, the red tape, the barriers, the way people look at you. I bring them chouquettes in the morning and beer at the end of the day. They try to clean up before they go home but the dust gets everywhere, I continue to clean for an hour afterward, sometimes Clémentine helps me. I put up a sign of apology for the noise downstairs, but worry nevertheless about the neighbours, adding all this smashing to the already unbearable noise of the ravalement. What a time to redo your apartment, madame, I imagine the gardienne saying to me. It's my revenge for the ravalement, I imagine saying back.

How good it will feel to walk freely between rooms, and on the freshly laid floor.

At night, after the smashing, there is Jonathan. He is every-where, he finds every way in, I am all openings to him, and then I am left opened and wanting when he leaves.

Feel my skin. Do I have a fever?

One of these days, my bakery friend says as we're walking downhill with our bread, this is all going to cave in. In our recent meetings we've taken to walking downhill together, down the rue de Belleville, which, he said, gesturing at the Tour Eiffel visible in the distance, used to be called the rue de Paris. There's nothing beneath our feet, he says. The centuries hollowed out north-eastern Paris to build homes for workers here. But gypsum, what they were digging for, you know gypsum? They make plaster from it. But it becomes soluble when you mix it with water, and it crumbles. Many times the roads have caved in because of that. And then there's the water. I was reading in the newspaper, he says, they found cracks in the old aqueduct that runs beneath Belleville, there's this one guy, a volunteer, a retired guy, who every day walks the length of the old aqueducts checking they're OK, and he found a crack in one that was spreading upwards. The rue de Belleville could have collapsed!

Beneath our feet, he says, only water and air.

One day clearing out the rubble in the kitchen Ousmane brings me the Polaroid Clémentine and I took of ourselves. Our eyes are both closed as she kisses me. Ta copine? he asks, handing it to me. Not exactly, I say. I take it to my office, put it in a drawer.

They also find a calendar, from January 1973. Owls for every month. I bring that to my office too, hang it up, and prepare to live as if it were the year 1973, to enjoy the disjuncture.

This week they're ripping up the laminate floor. Beneath, damaged, decaying parquet, rip that up too, we're going down to the bottom layer, down to the struts. Are we going to bash right into my neighbour's apartment? I joke, not joking. No, madame, says Adama, solemn, they are safe. They carry the rubble out in blue plastic IKEA bags.

It feels like a chance to go back and get it right this time.

I want to see your face twist up. I want to see your face do that again.

They're going to start laying the tommettes I sourced online but they haven't turned up yet, though they were meant to be here by now; are they on the road from a village in Burgundy to Paris, are they sitting in a warehouse; the person I bought them from doesn't know and the shipping company says they need a few more days to locate them. Maxime, Ousmane and Adama are frustrated; they can't really work if there's no floor. I tell them to take a few days off, paid of course, and they shrug and say they'll check back in a few days, maybe they'll have shown up by then.

He's messing around with his fingers in my bra, he's making me want him, he asks if I want him, I say I do, he's tormenting me by holding back, and holding back, and holding back, until he gives in, finally, and relief comes through me in measured, military jerks, that have less to do with pleasure than with regulation

With the arrival of Jonathan comes the departure of my appetite. I stop going to the bakery because I more or less stop eating food. It's just as well because I have no kitchen. He still keeps nothing at my place, not so much as a toothbrush, though this time around it makes sense; his own toothbrush is just on the other side of the courtyard.

I don't know what he wants from me, what does he want from me? He has a twenty-four-year-old girlfriend with a perfect body, why isn't he home fucking her instead of me? What is he reliving through me?

I ask him one night about Clémentine. Is it serious, between you two? I don't know, he says, we don't talk about our relationship in those terms. It's like we live in an ongoing present. I don't know if we'll always be together. To tell you the truth, he says, I think she would be happier with a woman. Why do you say that? I ask. He shrugs. She says it herself. I think she doesn't know what she wants yet. And what about you? I ask. I couldn't tell you that either, he says. But I'm happy with Clémentine. I learn a lot from her. I like the way she sees the world. She makes me want to fight for something. I know what you mean, I say, and I genuinely do.

There is debris everywhere, in the kitchen, spilling into the living room, which became the staging ground for the tiles and wood and appliances and assorted other materials necessary to rebuild. The tommettes I bought – stacks of old, hexagonal terracotta tiles – have finally arrived and are in a corner. Adama and Ousmane spent a whole morning lugging them upstairs. Organic material, encrusted with someone else's past, brought by someone else's labour, into my house.

Will he come again tonight?

I come into the kitchen this morning to find a man I've never seen before standing over a tub of mortar, churning it up with a long stick, like butter.

Oh, I say. Good morning.

This is Mehdi, says Adama, walking in from the living room through a wall that no longer exists. He's the best guy for laying tommettes.

I am, Mehdi says, nodding but with humility. I lay tommettes all over Paris. Everyone loves tommettes! Even where there are already tommettes, people want me to lay new ones.

New old ones, he specifies.

What happens to the old old ones? I ask.

I take them home and sell them on eBay, he grins. Other people buy them to be their new old tommettes.

Like me.

Like you. You will have beautiful new old tommettes when I am done!

Later, when it is time, he smooths the mortar along the floor where the tommettes will be placed, making beautiful patterns, reminding me of land art, crop circles, mystical lines in the earth. It is too bad they will be ruined when he places the tommettes, and the mortar smears, dries, and strengthens. I am happy to have stayed home today to see the artistry happening in my kitchen, of which I otherwise would have been completely ignorant. I feel like I'm working with the ground, he says, when I ask him how he came to specialise in tommettes. My father was a gardener and this is a kind of gardening I can do in the middle of the city.

That's why I like them too, I say, as he begins to lay my garden.

He comes, every night. He doesn't text me during the day or give me any notice. I text him if it's not a good night. If David is in town. He always comes even if just to tell me he can't come, that Clémentine is staying home. Usually this is just after she has come over herself, so I already know, and he's come straight from work. I don't want to ask too many questions, about how this works for him, or for them, lest I should lean on it too heavily, and make it collapse. I try to remain open, open to whatever there is, in this strange parabola in my life, this pocket, in which so much is held.

He turns his phone off when he comes in the door, and so do I. It becomes a little ritual, to leave them on the table by the door.

Some nights we don't even sleep together, we just get drunk and talk for hours. He fills me in on his job, how he ended up where he is, his dissatisfactions and ambitions, we talk about everything that's happened in Paris, from terrorists to Nuit Debout to gilets jaunes, we talk about stupid things and important things, smartphones and the climate, home renovation and what I should do in the kitchen, the new electric trottinettes littering the sidewalks, rebooted television shows from childhood with actors we never thought we'd see again, Freud's early interest in the nervous systems of fish, the biodynamic wine we're drinking, bobos and whether we are included in that category. It's so good to drink with a girl again, he sighs, and I try to listen to what he's telling me, that he cannot relax with Clémentine, that there is some other level of consciousness they cannot access together. I take this to mean, as well, that the sex with her is not as good as with me, that with her he is never *gone*, as he often tells me he is after climaxing.

The other thing is that he doesn't use a condom, and I don't insist, though I am not on the pill. I talk to him about the miscarriage, my breakdown, not seeing patients; he knows I've been hoping for a baby; does he want one too? Is that another thing they don't agree on? It is another thing I leave unsaid, but every time he comes in me, I wonder, and I wonder, too, what kind of risky behaviour this is, the actions of a woman who wants out of her marriage, and into another one, or simply someone who has decided not to decide.

David comes to town to check on me, and the travaux. He inspects the tiles they are laying in the kitchen, he doesn't like the sink I ordered, he says the apartment stinks of bodies and I should air it out some more. He is not happy that I am still here, he wants to sell, make a new life over there, buy a house, make new friends, I refuse, I refuse, I refuse.

The day David leaves I meet Jonathan after work and he's traded his T-shirt for a suit, no tie, he looks sharp, like he's more of a killer than I took him for. For a minute I miss the student version of him, Jonathan at twenty-one, unruly dark curls, smoking pot in his bedroom, going to shows with his friends, the Jonathan who tended bar in Shepherd's Bush and ran away to Cameroon. We walk fingers entangled through obscure areas of wealthy Paris where no one knows us, through the Parc Monceau, down avenue Hoche, near the Salle Pleyel. Paris smells like wood fire and lapsang souchong, it is cold and our noses run and, despite the suit, he is remarkably shy like when we met, and I was so much older than him. He's a man now, we're both in our late thirties, he's caught up with me, he projects more of himself into the world, but he's still got that shyness, he's still hiding a little.

He was briefly angry when I told him David was coming. I have a flashback to his irrational fits of jealousy, his resistance to what is outside his control; I realise he hasn't changed very much at all.

His hand in mine again is like the closing of a gap in the floor-boards I've been stumbling over for years.

I work up the courage to ask him why he didn't email me back.

Email you back? When did you email me?

A couple of years ago. I thought I passed you on the street.

I'm sure I didn't get it. Maybe it went to spam? What email address did you use?

I pull out my laptop, type his name into the search box of my address book. He sinks to the floor, pulls my legs apart, eases my underwear aside with a finger, and puts his tongue inside of me. I tell him which email account I'd sent it to. He pauses for a moment, says he hasn't used that account in years, and I put the laptop aside.

One night I ask him about the Israeli girl he supposedly married.

Oh god, Vered, she was a psychopath.

I don't know what to make of this; when men call women psychopaths I am usually on my guard. Oh so she really did exist.

Yeah that was a mistake. I nearly moved to Tel Aviv. Don't know what I was thinking. I couldn't talk to my family for a while.

I decide to leave this where it is. There are some stories it isn't my job to solicit.

With Esther I talk about desire; she knows what's going on; she doesn't say anything, as usual, or she does but rarely. Mm, or mm? Little phonemes I can't read. Desire consummated but not slaked, I say, I know I am spewing banalities but they're all I have, I can never have all of him so I always want more, there is always a part of him in shadow, turned away from me. A machine for manufacturing more desire.

What's the machine? she says.

Sex outside of your relationship, I guess? Mine and his?

They're smashing the horrible owl-tiles off the walls. I think I would like to have a turn smashing things but don't ask. The satisfaction I get from seeing the tiles shatter and fall from the walls has to be enough.

Back in London, David is not there. He and some friends have gone on a weekend trip to Slovakia to get drunk as British men do, on cheap easyJet flights to European cities. I don't hear from him the whole time he's away.

A dream. Somewhere, in some waters, off what coast, getting overcome by the waves with my parents. I am small. I think all three of us will be swept out to sea. There is a strong undercurrent, and as we're pulled under, as the water is going up my nose and down my throat, they tell me it's unpleasant but we won't drown. They are convinced, I don't know how they convey this to me with the water taking them, too. I don't know if I can believe them. I don't like the open sea, I tell them, when the wave has withdrawn, I only swim in pools, when I swim at all.

Then there are the old insecurities. When we were together he could be distant and unreachable, non-committal. I had forgotten. But this time it mattered less. I was happy to be relinquished from the uncertainties of loving him.

I find myself, as he fucks me one night, idly thinking that he is probably still fucking Clémentine. I can't imagine where he finds the energy for two women in one night, but then, he's younger than me. As I ease him deeper, shift up to meet him, I am surprised to realise I am not jealous, but curious.

The banging. The banging. The banging. It was cathartic when they were smashing down the wall, tearing up the floor, it was very moving when they laid the tiles, but I don't even know what they're doing any more, it's just loud, every day is loud, inside and out. What was I thinking starting a home renovation at the same time as the ravalement. There is no escape now. I am reminded of a story of a woman I saw on one of those morning shows I watched so often, after the miscarriage, those early days that were all cling film, worse than cling film, cement days cementing me to the couch, anyway the episode was about women who had left their husbands and wanted them back. I just wanted to explode everything, to blow up my life, she said. I hated my job, I hated our house, I resented having to look after the kids, my husband did fuck all to help, and so I did it, I kicked him out, and quit my job, and now I have an even worse one, and I have to watch the kids by myself, and take care of this disgusting house, and I just really wish I could go backwards. I don't know what I was thinking, blowing up my life like that. Stories like hers are why, if I'm honest, on some level I was relieved that the baby wasn't going to come. Because nothing had to change. I didn't have to be responsible for anyone else. And I didn't have to be bound to David any more than I wanted to be.

I'm close.
   Open your eyes.
   I'm close.
   Open your eyes,
   I want you to see me.

Not long after Jonathan comes back into my life, I run into a friend from graduate school I haven't seen in a long time. I'm crossing the rue de Bretagne, doing errands in the neighbourhood, and there she is on the terrace at Le Progrès, wearing sunglasses, reading a book. Her hair neatly parted in the middle just like always. She greets me warmly.

I saw her a lot after Jonathan left. She went out drinking with me, I got so drunk in those days, and she was there that one night after we'd been drinking in the basement bar with the melting red candles, kissing random people, when I lay down on my side in the rue du Jour and puked. I don't tell her he's back, it would feel somehow like a betrayal of those days, like it had been for nothing.

Instead we talk about work, and real estate, and her book, and I leave feeling like we are all part of each other all the time even when we can't see one another, here in our cities, we are present even when we're not.

In the dark, with him, it's as if he's pushing and pushing at a wall inside of me that gives way as I shudder, only to reconstruct itself again for the next time.

David is still alive for me as an erotic object, sometimes I stare at him until he looks like a stranger to me, the way he was when we met. Early on I would look at him and ask myself is he really as beautiful as all that, and finding yes, yes he is, look at him there, I still want him, and I imagine I will go on wanting him well into my future.

But he is from a different tranche of life, he has nothing to do with this other earlier self, and she is the one in this room with this person who was there and was everything to her so long ago.

Being with Jonathan doesn't entirely feel like infidelity to David – in a way, it feels like fidelity to some younger version of myself. And yet I'm also meeting a new self in this infidelity, and she is the one I want. Far from feeling guilty or shameful I feel myself, I feel calm.

Esther says words like fantasy, and romantic narrative, and fragmentation of the subject; she says words like repetition, non-coherence, she says Freud and I refuse to be analysed, I resist the control that narrative imposes, because it's only one possible analysis. I nod and I give a good performance of thinking about trauma and repetition but it's just saying what she wants to hear and she knows it. You're telling me what you think you should say, she says, why don't we start talking about what you don't think you should say?

As they work in the kitchen they unleash all manner of foul odours. What is that, I ask, it smells like food rotting in a pipe for thirty years. Oh it's always like that when you tear out a kitchen, the guys tell me. It'll dissipate by tomorrow if you leave the windows open.

So we go to a hotel, and take advantage of this space that isn't mine and David's or his and Clémentine's but exists only for us and by us; to be not ourselves but entirely different people, strangers in a hotel, part of a long series of strangers who have slept in the same bed, whose faces we will never see. We come home from dinner drunk and ready to fuck again; we all but fall into the glass-box elevator in the old neoclassical mansion.

You're handsome.

Rooftops against the sky.

Push the button.

I like to think I'm considerate.

My skin is trying to tell us something. You have a rash, he says. Look.

I look down at my chest; it is red and splotchy, as if I'd had a hot-water bottle on my skin for too long.

What kind of symptom is this? Have you contaminated me? Is it showing on my skin how much I want to fuse mine with yours? Your skin as something to get past, to leave behind.

The ancient Greeks thought skin was the result of a congealing process, a cooling off of something having been heated from within, forming a protective layer like on the top of boiled milk.

In Levinas, being naked in front of the other is an ethics contained in the skin. How close can we come? Never close enough.

Skin is there to give cover; I want to flay you and get inside.

Clémentine. I can't tell if she knows something. Jonathan says he doesn't know either. Is there something defiant in her eye, challenging me, testing me, or am I projecting? It feels like a test of our relationship: to tell her what's happening would either be to go deeper and truer, or to end everything. I don't know her well enough yet to intuit the right choice. If one of us were to tell her she might see it as narcissism, a cheap confession. She talks about freedom, and Jonathan suspects she's been with other girls, and he doesn't mind, but he hasn't been with anyone besides her. I love her, he says, it didn't occur to me to be with anyone else.

I think back through our conversations, so many times we've talked about infidelity, but I can't remember what she said about Jonathan's freedom, I didn't know, yet, that she was talking about *my* Jonathan, that I would come to be implicated, personally, in that freedom and what he did with it. I do not want to be caught in this most banal of narratives. I want to be truthful with her. Jonathan says to give him time to sort out what to do, and I have to respect what he thinks is right. He's the one who lives with her, after all. But I live with her, too, in a way.

What would I want, if it were me? I don't know what David is doing in London and we haven't come to any kind of agreement about it; there is simply the expectation of monogamy. But I don't think we've said whether or not any detours from that principle should be mentioned. At the beginning of *Encore*, Lacan's twentieth seminar, which he gave in 1972–73, he says that if he has sometimes declined to publish his work, it's because he doesn't want to know anything about it, *je n'en veux rien savoir*. Moreover he says that among the mass of people who have gathered in the amphitheatre to listen to him is also a *je n'en veux rien savoir*. That what may be more important in psychoanalysis is what we don't articulate to ourselves – what continues to throb on, in the depths of our unconscious, that we instinctively know we can leave there, that it does better work there. Like Lacan's variable-length sessions, which he could end at any time, five minutes or five seconds in, often on the threshold of something important, enabling the analysand to go down the stairs and out into the world with that broken thought in mind. That what we do bring to the surface of our minds, what we introduce into speech, can create movements below the surface, disturb the silt, which then resettles, differently. This disinclination to know, this swerve away from knowledge, is more useful than knowing.

What is at stake in love? Lacan asks.

What is always at stake. Our very bodies. What we do with them, know of them, of each other. Encore, again. En-corps, in body.

The unconscious, he says, was invented to cope with the notion of love; to describe how we may feel a passion of which we are unaware but which drives us all the same, whose ravages become more apparent the closer you get. Love asks for love. It asks for it again and again. Again, he writes, is the name for this weak point, that place in the Other where the request for love originates. Lacan uses the word *faille*, the place where love starts like a geological fault. Everything in the culture tries to convince us that if we are truly in love with the right person, we will be as one with them. It isn't true. We are always each other's others.

Love is always narcissistic, he says, love is a recognition of ourselves in the Other, that is why we try to make ourselves into One, but this is impossible. Love, desire, the want we have for the Other is always a remainder, a trace, of what we have desired before.

A note under the door.

SATURDAY. MANIF. PLACE DE L'OPÉRA. PICK YOU UP AT ONE P.M. It's written on an article clipped from *Le Monde*, showing grieving parents holding up a picture of their daughter, Julie, killed in March. She's underlined a quote from the girl's father, *c'est vraiment un combat, on est obligés de surmonter notre peine, il faut que ça change.*

Saturday night, very late, Clémentine at the door, wearing her glasses. We missed you at the manif, she says, but at the same time it's probably good you didn't go. Here, she says, I bought you something. It's a small white paperback, poems by Robert Desnos.

I just saw it in a bookshop on my way home from the manif. I thought you'd like it.

Thank you! Why is it good I didn't go?

Oh it got really ugly, it was so fucked up. We were so peaceful! First we listened to some speeches and then we danced and while we were dancing the CRS came and started throwing tear-gas bombs. Can you believe it! One minute I had my arms around Lamia, it's all kind of dreamy, good vibes, and the next I'm blind and vomiting.

Oh my god, you poor thing! Are you OK? What the fuck!

What the fuck, seriously. I'm OK, I just, you know, can't wear my contacts for a while. The tear gas made all these loud bangs, a lot of people thought it was a terrorist attack, it was so aggressive, some of my friends had been at Le Carillon and were really upset, their PTSD was out of control. It is so fucked up. The government is holding a meeting on ending conjugal violence, we are not just a bunch of crazy dykes, how can they treat us like this?

She settles in on the couch and lights a cigarette. How did you get involved with all of this? I ask. Oh, she says, I was always going to manifs with my parents, and protesting in high school with my friends, but it was really MeToo that made me start thinking of myself as a feminist. I started listening to podcasts and going to events at bookstores and that's how I met Lamia, and she knew someone who knew someone, and . . . I ended up hooking up with those girls over the summer. They are fierce! We don't agree about everything, she says, like some of them have kind of a fucked-up idea of what feminism is, some of us are, let's say, more inclusive than others? Her eyes widen at the word *inclusive*, it is clearly important to her to include, she wants me to know this. I think that's always been a fundamental part of feminism, I say, hasn't it? Women coming together to talk and organise and, at moments of social crisis, take advantage of the disarray to push for their rights? In spite of our differences? Feminism can't accomplish much in isolation.

Says the woman who's isolated herself for months! Anyway what I meant wasn't just about coming together but about who we allow in, who we're fighting for and with. It feels like feminism has always been about extending freedom to the greatest number of people, but there are some women who seem to have forgotten that. They're saying they have the right to say these hateful things, these things in bad faith about what a woman is, they think they are speaking common sense, *we all know what a woman is.* They just make me really angry.

They're claiming freedom of speech?

They are, but their speech is hate speech and that *isn't* protected. You know what Jonathan is always saying. First they came for the trans women, and I wasn't a trans woman, etc. It just feels like the front-line fight against fascism.

Why don't you do something about it? I say. Work for a non-profit? Run for office or something? Something more than gluing letters to walls at night?

Because— she starts to say, then stops.

Actually I don't know why I don't.

My conversation with Clémentine makes me think of David's mother, so I finally reply to her messages, and we arrange to meet for coffee. She is a very well-coiffed woman in her sixties, young when she had her kids, and a human rights lawyer who always reminds me of Gisèle Halimi. She's also been on television a few times, in her robes and her gold hoop earrings. I think she's why David wanted to become a lawyer, though his field is so different from hers, much more academic, more about the finer points of interpretation than anything else. It might explain why he was so pleased to be tapped for the Brexit thing, he's used to working in a corner with no one noticing him, he's happy there, poring over legal texts in his glasses, his face lit up blue by the computer screen. I always worry about his eyes. Thalia doesn't mention my avoiding her, she's never liked to pry, she just likes to check in from time to time. We talk about the kitchen, the upcoming Christmas holidays, where she and David's father are going skiing, about David's brother, who is in love with someone new, about David's sister, who is looking for a new job, she wants to know if she can give me something to give to David next time he's in town, he never comes by to see us, she sighs, but you know David, always on the go, ever since he was a kid he's always been hard to pin down! Until he met you he was always running here and there. She had put her finger on exactly what I worried about, with David. Before we'd met, he made frequent trips abroad, or to the six corners of France, snowboarding or surfing or fishing, but my pace was slower, and so to be with me, his had slowed as well. Until this trip to

London. In the café with his mother, I worried again that this trip to London was a release of energy that had accrued from being in the same place for so long. His mother's words have what I'm sure is the desired effect; I want him there with me, back with me, I don't want him to go a-wandering. But in the long run, will a home together be enough for him?

Redo the kitchen, redo the bathroom, don't take his calls, show him how distance feels, make him jealous? Is that what this is about?

Clémentine takes me back to Combat, where we haven't been since that time she introduced me to Mouna and talked so reverentially about the actresses she works with. I have made fun of her, on occasion, because of it. Léa Say-who? Mouna is there as usual, as is the bartender with the undercut, all of us performing some kind of Belleville bohemia, some better than others. I am there and not there, drinking to take the edge off suddenly feeling unsure about David's reasons for going to London. Clémentine and Mouna fall into an intense conversation about a painter I've never heard of. The alcohol has its way with me, and when she puts her arm around me, I lay my head against hers. My gaze shifts out the window, where I see my bakery friend passing by. He smiles, lifts an imaginary bottle to his lips and drinks from it, and continues on his way. Turning back to me, Clémentine puts her hand on my hand, closes her fingers around my ring. Can I try this on? Um. Sure, I say, and slip it off. She slips it on to her ring finger. Now I'm married to David, she says with her giggle. Ha ha, I say, very funny. Can I have that back please? It's too big on you, it's going to fall off. Nope, she says, it's mine now. My finger feels conspicuous and bare, my thumb keeps worrying the spot. When we leave, she tucks it into the front pocket of my jeans. Better take good care of that now, she says.

One afternoon Clémentine invites me to a vernissage. It's for one of the painters I sit for, she says, she's ready to show some of the series we've done together. Of course I'll come, I say, and when I do I find myself – what, disappointed? – that she is wearing clothes in the paintings. You pervert, I think, you're fucking her boyfriend, what is your actual problem, how much more must you strip this girl back? I see her across the room, in oversized trousers and ugly sneakers, as if to counterbalance her beauty on the canvas.

The paintings are strange, I suppose they're surrealist, they feel very contemporary, Clémentine in a ballet leotard and tights, stretching, lying on a table with a plate of fruit on her head; on a sofa wearing a white silk jumpsuit I recognise with a sword down her front; from behind, holding a fork to her face. Sharp pain, sharp objects, but the paintings themselves have a softness to them. When I do come upon a nude Clémentine – wearing a bra and panties but one pulled up and one down, her nipples hardened and white in the daylight, inexplicably holding out a pair of tennis shoes, I find I have to look away. Elsewhere in the gallery, in front of a nude painting that isn't of her, she comes up behind me and circles my waist with her hands. It's always strange to have people you know see work like this, she says, but I'm happy you came.

You're not shy? I ask her. To be seen – *naked*, I want to say, but it seems like such a stupid thing to ask that I cut myself off.

Not exactly, she says. When I'm sitting for someone, and they're looking very hard at my body, so hard it's like they're not even seeing me as a person any more but as flesh in light, I feel like I've escaped from myself. But at the same time like I'm occupying myself fully, if that makes any sense?

In a way, I say.

So for people then to see this version of me, I don't know, I guess I feel held by the gaze, like of all the people I could be I am there, that body, this body. And then she is swept away by admirers, one of whom is Jonathan, who meets my eye, but only for a moment.

Before I leave, I return to the tennis-shoe painting and try to let myself look at it. I can't look away from the hipbone as the light catches it, it is such a true image of a hipbone, it is Clémentine's and it is also my own, and it is also Jonathan's, and it is also David's, every hipbone I've ever seen is there, it makes me want to touch everyone's hipbones, a place more intimate than anywhere else on the body, but especially hers.

No one is looking and I touch my thumb lightly to the canvas.

My bakery friend this morning. I saw you the other night at that bar!

Yes I saw you too! Strange to see you out of context.

Belleville is small, he says. Is that your wife I saw you with?

No, I say, because it is all too much to explain, someone else's.

Fair play, he says, and nods. You young people like to keep things open. I am impressed. We thought we were doing free love, he says, but we didn't know what we were doing.

We don't either, I say.

The news in the building is that the coughing guy has died.

When I visit Esther's office now the building is a worksite. They're redoing the staircase and all the landings. Coils drop down, wires track coloured paths across the ceiling, held in place by plastic ties, the kind they arrest people with, only smaller. The insides of the walls become visible, exposing craggy topographies of rock and plaster.

On the métro, everyone in identical black puffer jackets and a woman FaceTiming very loudly in Russian.

One of Lacan's most famous ideas is that the unconscious is structured like a language. Chains of associations form there, symptoms manifest as metaphors, it's intensely referential. His critics called this theory overly elegant and complained that it left no room for affect – for the explosions, the eruptions, what can't be contained in language or metaphor.

Lacan's answer to this is lack. The always already hurt; the perennial bruise. This is Lacan's affect.

But his critics are right about the disruptions. Lacan wants to contain them. He doesn't allow for how much they can hurt. Lacan is still in the Freudian realm of repression.

I have decided not to talk about Jonathan any more to Esther. I am cutting off the chain of associations, because if I try to account for what is happening, anywhere I start might take me further than I intended. And even if I invent a neat explanation for what happened, the part of me that loved him won't let me reduce it like that. Any summary of Jonathan will sound lifeless and exterior. I will sound like I don't know what I'm doing, worse, like I don't know what I know.

Is it a problem of telling? What should I tell? What can I tell? Who can I tell? What can be told? What account could I give that would stand up to it? What form could it take? What order could I give that wouldn't force it into disorder?

I have drinks with an old friend who used to live in Paris and moved to LA a while back. She tells me about the novel she's writing, which is a little bit about Coleridge, and she tells me how he wrote about soulmates by differentiating them from *yokemates*. Love and desire sometimes fall differently, she says. Sometimes we love the people with whom we share a house, and sometimes the people with whom we share a soul.

Maybe all the trouble starts when we try to make them coincide, she says. Anyway, that's what it's about.

Clémentine needs a night at home, she can't be out *every* night, she's exhausted, she needs a break, so Jonathan and I go and make out in the McDonald's at the top of the hill before we, too, decide to take a night off. Tongue-kissing in the back of McDo like teenagers. Corner of avenue Simon Bolivar and rue de Belleville, for all the world to see, except not, because we know Clémentine would never enter a McDonald's. We're not hiding from her, exactly.

Another day I see them walking ahead of me on the rue de Belleville, slightly uphill. They are so tall and capable, the two of them. He kisses her as they walk, he lingers.

Clémentine comes over one afternoon with a thick envelope in her arms, just delivered. Look! she says. If this is what I think it is, I want to show it to you. She rests it on the table in the entry-way and tears into it. Oh! she says. It is. She hands it to me, a thick coffee-table book about Remedios Varo. The surrealist? I say, looking through it. It's very beautiful.

She paints all these supernatural images, Clémentine says, of people who are there but aren't there but we can still see them, like – she turns to a painting called *Tailleur pour dames*, 1957, and shows me a woman sitting on an ornate bench waiting, one sup-poses, for her turn to see the tailor, and on either side of her are transparent figures which echo her clothing and her position, as if she were accompanied by two ghosts everywhere she went, but ghosts of herself. In the centre of the room a woman in a vulva-like enclosure of a dress balances on a tiny little wheel, holding herself steady with a very thin walking stick. The room is octagonal, and the parquet flooring like a spiderweb.

I think I'm going to propose a PhD on Varo, Clémentine says. I've always loved her work. But it's this one that I wanted to show you. She turns the page to an image called *Woman Leaving the Psychoanalyst*. Another spindly, elongated figure in a mysterious setting, this time holding a little basket of I'm not sure what in one hand and the shrunken head of a bearded man in the other. I laugh. Is that her shrink? I say. Has she beheaded him?

Varo, I think later, after Clémentine has gone, Vero, è vero, it's true, but also V for valid, V for vanity, V for velocity. V for the mark on my true love's skin.

Not my true love. Her true love.

Is he her true love? For a minute I am angry, displaced. I have often wondered what they see in each other. She doesn't want to be with a man, I don't think, she's not finished becoming herself, he is who she thinks she ought to be with. And Clémentine, for him? It isn't just about her tight young body, but it is also impossible without it. I find myself actually angry with her, and her body. He finds there whatever men find in younger women, I hear about it all the time from my male patients. They want to be looked up to. They want to be the teacher, the knower of things. This doesn't square with what I know of Jonathan. What I know of Jonathan, his past before me, his past after me, his present, is a series of slippages.

I had lunch with my father today, he says, late one Sunday night, lying in my bed. I went over to see him. He'd forgotten I was coming. I found him elbow-deep in Lacan, revising his edition of the talks he gave outside of his seminars .

How is your father? I ask.

OK. He seemed in more of a hurry than usual, Jonathan says, like he was bogged down in all this busywork and couldn't stand it. He's been working on this edition for years.

It takes the time it takes I guess, I say.

I don't know why he can't finish it. It's not like I see him slacking off. He works so hard.

Maybe he doesn't want to finish, I say.

Maybe, says Jonathan. I worry about him. He has a research assistant but the assistant doesn't seem to do very much. He looks as if the papers are getting the better of him.

Maybe he's being thorough, I say. Wants to have his own eyes on every piece of paper he includes. It's not enough for someone else to look at them, he has to do it himself.

You and my dad always did get along, Jonathan says.

He got me into Lacan, I say. I wouldn't have had the courage to dive in if he hadn't helped me.

I remember you arguing with him, Jonathan says.

That doesn't mean I agreed with him, or Lacan, all the time.

You argued with him about desire, I remember that so well, I was embarrassed.

You were young.

I was young and here was this older woman I was obviously fucking *talking* about fucking with my father at Sunday lunch, Jonathan says. I felt so exposed. Like I was sitting there playing with my erection.

Honestly he can be a bit of a prude, a moraliser.

My father?

Lacan.

How?

When it comes to the ethical ramifications of desire, Lacan thinks: no. You don't give in. You'll just want something else later, so why indulge something that could prove harmful to other people? But I think it's reinforcing an imprisoning structure to phrase it in terms of giving in or not giving in. You're only creating more desire by making something forbidden. We need desire to live, but there are different kinds, and it's the forbidden kind Lacan worried about, without realising it was his own moralising that was feeding it.

Yeah. That's what I remember you saying. Basically telling my father, with me right there, that you don't believe in monogamy.

But I do. I did. It's just that I see it as something you practise, rather than some kind of law, which you can violate, and for which you should be punished.

But you're not practising it now.

I'm not.

Quiet as I stroke his arm, his shoulder, his back.

Oh god, Jonathan says.

What?

I – oh, fuck.

What?

I just realised I'm, like, living out his book.

Which one?

The Unavailable.

Oh that one, I say. I love that book.

I hate that book.

You never told me that! Why do you hate it?

My father, Jonathan says, is a womanising bastard. I love him but it's true, he's a bastard. He doesn't see it that way, *he* says he loves easily and well, but he's a serial cheater. He cheated on my mother, he cheated on my stepmother, he cheated on his first wife, and he invented a whole intellectual framework to justify it. He's slept with his students his whole career. He's completely unethical.

I let this sink in. But I'm not sure that what I'm doing – what we're doing – is unethical. My instinct is that it isn't. That something about living ethically together is bound up in not judging our desires, or controlling and punishing them. But maybe that's just me justifying it.

So you think it has to be justified.

I'm not sure. Do you?

I'm not sure either.

Is it possible that infidelity isn't something you commit but something that creeps up, a series of inoffensive doors you open, so by the time you find yourself in front of the one that counts, the one that matters, that changes everything, you are too far gone? You are so deep in it but you got so deep in a kind of innocence. I think for a moment. Maybe the problem is the word. Infidelity. I never noticed before but it makes you an infidel, believing in the wrong god. But really it's another kind of fidelity – to yourself, to your dream of yourself, to the other people you love. I get out my phone and look up the etymology. See? it's an Old French word, that has to do with a lack of faith. But I have so much faith. I am full of faith.

Our conversation sends me back to Max's book again. Tous les désirs visent la jouissance, he writes, all desire desires its expression, and I thought, for the first time since we'd bought the flat, about jouissance in the real-estate sense, meaning to enjoy the property one has acquired, the right to jouissance is one conferred on the owner, I remember feeling like only a man could have come up with this idea, could have crowned the fulfilment of desire with something as cramped and claustrophobic as ownership, and I tried to explain it to David but, lawyer that he is, he saw only the pragmatic side, of course they had to come up with a word to theorise ownership, to talk about the state of ownership of a property, imagine someone else came along and started squatting in the place you'd paid all this money to acquire? The law needed a concept to express what your money has bought you the right to do there, and to describe what he does not have the right to do there. Well I just about disagree with everything you've said, I said.

In my session with Esther this morning, she suggests that in rebuilding the kitchen, in remaking this apartment, I have been trying to reconstruct my own pleasure, to reaffirm my jouissance.

Well fuck, I say, surely there are less expensive ways of doing that? You think I'm getting off on redoing my kitchen?

In a manner of speaking, she says.

In a residence hall in Ménilmontant, largely populated by students at the architecture school, there are quite a few women hard at work, pouring black paint into receptacles, painting letters on to sheets of paper with medium-sized brushes. Others collect them and clip them to clothes lines to dry; still others gather the ones that have already dried to lay them out on the floor. Loads of people are milling about, of every gender, though they are mostly young, Clem's age if I had to guess. Clémentine kisses two of her friends hello. Who are they all, I ask, do you know them? There are more and more of us, one of her friends says, leaning in to introduce herself. Isa, she says, kissing my cheeks. Last week we were ten. This week twenty. The only people who can't come out with us are cis men. The girls laugh. But as you can see they're more than welcome to help us with logistics! And indeed there are a couple of guys walking around trying to be helpful, telegraphing humility. Clémentine and her friends are all so pretty and committed, like militant fairies. I feel as out of place among them as the boys must, but also inspired by them, and protective. And envious. And a little ashamed of myself, for sitting at home all those nights when I could have been out here, doing something.

Why do it at night, I ask, it must be more dangerous.

It's illegal, Clem points out, and I feel like an idiot, of course it is. We scope out our locations during the day but we paste at night, Clem says.

Anyway we like to do it at night, her other friend says, dark hair, neck tattoo. Amina, she introduces herself, we met at Clémentine's party, do you remember? It's a way of occupying space at a time when the city doesn't belong to us.

It's a simple principle, says Amina. We want everyone to hear us but we don't say a word. People passing in the street. People on the bus. People coming home from a long night out. We want people to stop, think, take a picture, show it to their friends.

We want to make it public – make it so people can't ignore it, can't absorb it and forget about it as they go about their day. We want to defamiliarise the streets, says Isa. The same but slightly different.

It's our way of leaving a trace in the city, Clémentine says.

Like street art, says Isa. But less macho.

I'll never forget the first one I saw, I tell them. Tu n'es pas seule. I felt like you were talking right to me. But I loved that you were also talking to everyone.

Je te crois, says Clémentine, that's the first one I saw.

OK, les filles, au boulot! says Amina, and we start gathering up the letters we're going to paste up tonight. We head out into the darkness with our buckets of glue, our chunky thick brushes, our carefully painted letters. We peel off in pairs, and Clem and I go off to our assigned spot, on a blank wall next to a school on the rue des Panoyaux. Clem licks her finger, peels off the top letter. We begin. L. The walls are bumpy, I like the grain of them under my hand as I smooth out the paper, before I add the final layer of glue. E. There's an ambient feeling of urgency and threat in the air. S. E. X. We have to act quickly so we don't get caught, says Clem, the police are understanding but they do give out fines. I. S. M. E. Sometimes a group of guys will come along and give us trouble, the more people hear about us the more trouble they give. E. S. T. Some guy drove into a group of colleues in Montpellier. It's pathetic. P. Have you ever been sexually assaulted? she asks, casually. A. A few times, mostly in the street, I say. Once in the rue d'Ulm in broad daylight a guy came up behind me and put his hand up my skirt into my under-pants. R. Did you tell anyone? T. No, I say, I hit him with my bag of books and he laughed. O. It's very exciting to be out like this, I say, the adrenaline high, the street lights yellow, the air blue, but I feel very old. U. And guilty, we didn't do things like this when I was your age. T. We went to manifs, we protested, we signed petitions, but nothing like this, it's like activism skipped our generation. N. I mean some people my age are activists but . . . O. I feel like I wouldn't have known where to start if I'd wanted to join them. U. Things are probably more outwardly fucked up now than they were back then, Clem says. My grandmother even came out one night. S. She was a big feminist in the 70s, went to consciousness-raising meetings and everything, she was a member of Choisir, you know, Gisèle Halimi's activist group. Anyway said she thought the days of being militant feminists were past but now it's clear that they're not. A woman is killed in France every two days.

A
U
S
S
I

We stand back to admire our work. *Sexism is everywhere. So are we.*

She turns me to face her, looks at me for a long time, so long I think she might kiss me. Or I might kiss her. What would she do, if I did?

Come on, Clem says, let's go find the others, and the moment is gone.

It is joyful, this communion with all these women, these ideal-ists, the ballet of painting on the glue, placing the letter, smoothing it down, recovering it with glue, moving on to the next. Passers-by stop and talk with us, they ask what we're doing, we tell them, they sympathise, or they argue. I saw a bunch of those torn down the other week, one woman says. You're clearly ruffling some feathers. We're not afraid of ruf-fling feathers, one of the girls says, men come up to me while I'm out here and I feel like I'm ten feet tall, I tell them to fuck off, it's amazing. I've grown balls. One of the others snorts. You mean you've grown a clit! There is, briefly, an argument about essentialism, and I detect some dissent within the group, remem-bering my conversation with Clémentine.

And then it dissipates as we head off to the bars en masse. We go dancing on the rue Oberkampf, the music is good, the beer is cold, we dance, we drink, we goof, and Clémentine is there watching me dance with her friends, and soon she is dancing with me, her body against mine, her face turned away, her body ever closer and her hands, her hands, are smooth on my skin. Next time you come out, she says in my ear, we're writing on your body.

What? The music is loud, I'm not sure I've heard her correctly.

We're getting you a tattoo. Next time. Here. Her hand on my waist, her thumb strokes my ribcage. Think about what you want.

I can't take the métro to see Esther, there is a strike, the train workers are protesting the new point-based retirement system and I don't blame them at all. I walk the distance from Belleville to Bastille.

TU NE MARCHES
PLUS SEULE

> PAYS DES DROITS DE
> L'HOMME A-T-IL PEUR
> DES DROITS DES FEMMES?

NOS JUPES SONT
COURTES, PAS NOS
IDÉES

> GUÉRRILLÈRES

ON PARLERA

In some of them, I hear Clémentine's voice.

BRAVO
TU AS UNE
BITE!

RÉVOLUTION
QUEER

LA RÉVOLUTION
SERA
FÉMINISTE

Anna, she's saying.

Anna, she's saying.

I don't remember what else she said because lately I sit through these sessions with her in a fugue state, I am somewhere swimming, I have always thought of my patients as swimming when it's flowing and they aren't interrupting themselves or judging what they say, they are as if underwater and they only need to come up from time to time to inhale deeply and then back under the surface they go.

I just remember Esther saying my name, calling me back up.

Have I been talking all this time? I ask.

You've been sitting silently for forty minutes, she says.

Then it is the holidays, and David comes in from London, and we go to his family first, then my family near Orléans. We eat and talk easily and it's like we haven't been apart. My mom wants to know when I'll be going back to work and my dad wants to talk about the new virus in China. In his televised holiday address, the president pays tribute to the hundred and forty-nine women killed by their partner or their ex over the past year. It is strange to be with my family, after this long period of solitude, and then with Clémentine and Jonathan. David doesn't know anything, and I'm not going to tell him, it would be an act of selfishness. But do I want him to guess, do I want to be found out, do I want to scare him? These are the things I would suspect of a client. But of myself? Am I hiding from myself? I look back through my journals, I see anxiety, strange dream imagery, I can't self-read, it all goes sideways. Journal, Esther would say. I journal. Am I trying to escape my own fear that David will leave me by leaving him? Am I thwarting him, Lacan, my own father, patriarchy? What is it exactly all this is tending toward? The way we accept certain ways of being with people in the world and can't accept others. About trying to break the bounds that society has woven between sex and ethics. About desire, trying to understand it and live it out, rejecting the ways in which it is monitored and moralised and contained. Asking what happens if we dive in to it, knowing that it will always leave us wanting more. How can we live with each other, and enjoy our bodies, and each other's bodies, when we know that desire is part of an endless chain? And that it is being in this chain that makes us alive? How do we live out our desire without hurting other people? What do other people need to know about our desire?

Where we run into trouble is the idea of futurity. As long as it's one day after the next, a perennial present, all is well, but when it comes to looking down the road a little bit, there things fray.

I don't want to talk to Jonathan about anything like a future. I don't want to introduce the thing that transforms the atmosphere, a chemical introduced into an environment, that slowly absorbs all the oxygen.

I really, really don't want to break anything, not for him and not for me, not for Clem and not for David.

I have made my life. He's made his. No one wants to disrupt that.

I don't have any answers.

Perhaps this period in my life is a study, a series of impressions, to store away for later.

But then when we all come back from the holidays I find myself, anyway, asking. I don't know why. C'est plus fort que moi. We are out in Belleville, and the city gives me confidence.

It won't work, Anna. We already tried, remember?

But that was when you cared about religion. Clémentine isn't Jewish.

(I am embarrassing myself, going on like this. They've hung the paper lanterns up for Chinese New Year. They stuck them right on top of the Christmas decorations stretching across the street.)

It's not about that, and it wasn't really about that then, Jonathan says.

Explain it to me, I say.

He says husband. He says complicated. He says it isn't right.

Right according to whom, to what? I ask. He doesn't answer.

(I know things are over between us. They never began again, really; by sleeping together we were reliving the past, doing it all over again with our adult bodies, our adult lives.)

You're not going to leave him for this.

You're right. I'm not.

I won't break up your marriage.

I'm not asking you to.

(But I am, I am, I'm asking you again to break something, and again, you're imposing a structure on us that has nothing to do with us, that needn't exist at all. I am holding on to you and you are slipping away, again.)

What else can I do? I book my train to London. In the taxi to the Gare du Nord we have to stop because the dragon is out and people are dancing in the streets, beating drums and chanting.

Epiphanies are momentary when they're not false.

The sun glints on the steel cage of a pseudo-station we're sitting in, contained, paused, on the way into the Channel Tunnel. We're about to dive underwater, away from you.

And here we go.

I'm reading an issue of *Le Parisien* someone handed me on the way to the Gare du Nord. It's only the 6th of January and they're reporting that there have been four femicides in France so far this year.

Outside: trees like spikes, like the spires of the churches dotting the landscape.

Missing Jonathan already. Loving what we were doing together. How to be without you now, again. Starting to lose consciousness and panic. Underwater. My heart is racing. Think about something else. There's a tightening sensation in my chest and my lower abdomen feels like jelly.

When I head for the bathroom I walk in on a man peeing on the floor. He doesn't notice me as I back away. I walk through the car, find another one, with a clean floor. There are grains of rice in the sink. Or fingernail clippings.

Walking back to my seat a wave of tall people comes at me and I feel like a child.

I've brought the Robert Desnos book Clémentine gave me, but he's no consolation either. Just as lovelorn as I am. *The one I love is not listening to me. The one I love does not hear me.*

I close the book, play some music on my headphones, Christine and the Queens, 'Safe and Holy' opens up like an electric cathedral. French singer singing in English. Another in-betweener, the ass on two seats as they say. I love the way she distorts her vowels, safe and hawley, safe and hawley. Then the song 'Jonathan' comes on and I have to listen again when I realise what she's singing.

I'm so in love with you I'm exhausted from it.

David is glad I'm in London. It's cold here, colder than Paris. Cosy, though. Blood oranges are in season and they cut through the dark and damp. He makes eggs for breakfast, like a real Englishman. I am liberated from my Brita. We drink craft beer in pubs that play The Cure and early Radiohead and I feel like I've found some of my old joy again, I think I can move here, have a new life, away from my old grey city. David is right. London is turned towards the future.

He is a different version of himself here, jolly somehow. One morning as he makes me breakfast he tells a joke. It isn't very funny but I laugh like it is.

When he looks at me like that I want to be everything he wants me to be, I want to laugh enough to make him feel funny and happy and safe.

The slow rhythmic swilling as he coaxes the eggs to scramble. Maybe I don't have a home. Maybe he is my home.

Clémentine WhatsApps me every couple of days.

'allo 'allo 'allo!

ma chérie I want to buy these trousers what do you think are they good or 💩

ça va ma biche je pense à toi je t'envoie des bizzzzzz

kiss the queen for me

Jonathan does not.

I have a dream that I've been invited to the Queen's lesbian wedding. I'm not sure what's happened to her husband but she's getting hitched again, this time to a nice American woman, very unpretentious and lovely, and for some reason I've been invited to the wedding, and because it's a queer wedding no one has to curtsey to her. She wears Vivienne Westwood tartan.

In London I ride a lot of buses, trying to get my bearings by staying aboveground. I haven't been in a decade; it's changed a lot. The Shard looks ridiculous from a distance, unfinished. Every vacant industrial space has been transformed into a café serving sour coffee and aggressively artisanal bread. I wear black pepper and cade for Clémentine and the coat I know Jonathan likes, and I watch the families like toadstools clump together misshapen at the Tate Modern. It is cold and new and I love it all.

At the same time there is a pressure on my temples of which, in time, with the new rhythm of daily life, I become more aware. It is like the weather here, foggy and heavy; it makes it difficult to see. This weathery place. I come to understand that it is a form of mourning which has taken up residence inside my skull. A familiar feeling of something precious having been abandoned, trapped in the weave of the past. I try to find a place for my own agency, my will, inside this feeling. Every day I try a little harder. This place seems to have been made for mourning, built by people in grief for some foreign thing whose existence I never imagined, still can't conjure. There is an abyss at the centre of every culture. In Paris I was aware of skirting along its edges; I knew where the pit was and could contemplate it without falling in. But here in an unfamiliar place with its unknown history I have no spatial awareness; or I have to build it up, slowly, for myself. Those are the moments when I most resist London.

I take the bus from East London to the Freud Museum, a place I have wanted to visit since I was in grad school. I gasp at the entry fee, £14, but remind myself it's important to support the institution, and its attempt to keep Freud relevant. The till is run by two women my mother's age, one of whom has a high-lighted copy of *Moses and Monotheism* open in front of her.

Entering the great man's book-lined study, I catch my breath. There's a charge in here I've only felt in churches, the air itself feels heavy but solemnly so. The musty smell of books and leather and lilies are trapped in it, preserved, like my grandmother's silk scarves held her perfume. If you had put me in this room without telling me whose it was, I would have thought perhaps someone had died here. No sooner does this thought cross my mind than I remember that Freud had indeed died in this room, in a special hospital bed installed during his final weeks. He loved this room because of its view on to the garden; however his sickbed was kept in the centre of the room, away from the win-dows, for fear of bombings. His death from mouth cancer was slow and painful; his body was rotting while he was still alive, and when it began to give off a powerful smell it kept his devoted dog from his side, and attracted flies. His sister-in-law noted that a lesser man might have put an end to his life well before this point. In his last days, he read Balzac's *La Peau de chagrin*.

I look to the shelves: is his copy up there somewhere, or tucked away in some climate-controlled vault? Each leather-bound book seems saturated with energy, as if his dying gaze had rested on each one, bestowing it with a fragment of his spirit as it left his body; each ancient clay figurine in a glass cabinet emits a signal from antiquity. Perhaps one of them contained the sheet of animal skin that was endowed with the power to grant its holder's every desire, as in Balzac's novel. I film the wall of books with my phone, and jump when I see myself reflected in the vitrine. Near the entrance is an ancient Roman bas-relief of Gradiva, or *the woman who walks*, who was the subject of an essay Freud wrote about a novella called *Gradiva* by the German writer Wilhelm Jensen, published in 1902. The relief on Freud's wall, the caption-card informs me, is a copy of the one that inspired Jensen's story.

'Gradiva' was Freud's first essay about a work of literature; he reasoned that if he could write on dreams, he could also write on works of imagination, for what else is literature but the dream of the writer? (At times I have wondered if some of my patients are making it all up, if all their stories are dreams.) Jensen's book is about an archaeologist and his obsession with this image of Gradiva, of which he is able to acquire a plaster cast: it depicts a woman walking along with a particularly charming gait; he imagines a whole identity for her, a back story, a personality, bringing all of his training as an archaeologist to bear on the mystery of the woman. Soon after, he dreams that he is in Pompeii the day of the eruption of Mount Vesuvius. In his dream, he encounters Gradiva and cries out to warn her of the danger, but though she sees him, she calmly walks to the steps of a temple and stretches out on them, laying her cheek to the marble step to sleep, becoming as if marble herself, before ash rains down on her body, burying her. Upon awaking he cannot shake the dream, it begins to obsess him, and drives him to travel himself to Pompeii where at the 'hot and holy' midday hour, the 'hour of ghosts', according to the ancients, he encounters a young woman who is unmistakably Gradiva herself. She both indulges his fantasies and insists on her own uniqueness; her name is Zoe, and she speaks contemporary German. In Freud's reading, if she colludes to some extent in his delusion, it is to free him of it. Freud read it as a study of repression, cured through transference, Zoe a double for the figure of the analyst who allows Jensen's archaeologist to break the spell the figure had cast over him by transferring his desire on to her, that is, on to the analyst, where it could be safely expressed, and then dispelled. 'The process of cure is accomplished by a relapse into love,' Freud comments; we have to re-live earlier obsessions, in his view, for them to lose their power over us.

Pompeii provides the perfect metaphor for repression, being a place where something could be both preserved and inaccessible. It struck me that Freud's study in Hampstead played the same function, and I wondered what it is we're trying to perpetuate when we maintain these spaces where important things were written, or said. I suppose they're places to visit those we never had a chance to meet; I suppose if we are open to them, they will suggest all manner of dreams, and give us what we could not otherwise give to ourselves.

Walking back towards the Overground from the Freud Museum, I notice, here and there, the very English names that appear on the small blue plaques on the sides of buildings. It would seem the English have not yet come to commemorate people who don't have names like John George Duncan Oliver Bernard Shaw Smith Keynes. I remember Jonathan once received a letter from someone whose name he could not pronounce, Suzanne, can you read this for me, Wa—, I cannot get my mouth to do it, English is an impossible language, Susan Wainwright I said, who is she? She says she knew my mother, and was sad to hear she'd died, she'd only just found out from a mutual friend whom she hadn't seen in years, and she has some stories about her from Oxford. I'd entirely forgotten that Jonathan's mother had been English, that she had been at Oxford, that there were people here in London who would still know who she was, there most surely were, she was from the northern part of the city where the prosperous Jews lived, leafy and red-brick and hilly. I hadn't yet made the connection that in coming to London I was perhaps reminding Jonathan of his mother. I could have passed her family in the street.

I remember the passage in *Encore* I came across last summer, where Lacan writes that the reason he hates History is that it was invented to make us think it has some kind of meaning. It's like my patients who come in heartbroken, they've been abandoned, rejected, dejected, and they talk about what was meant to be, or should have been meant to be, and I tell them I have always taken great comfort in the chaos of the universe, that nothing is meant to be and History means nothing but what we decide on its behalf, that people can't use our Histories against us, that we can rewrite them ourselves. It was Jonathan who helped me understand this, though he didn't agree when I explained it back to him. History exists, he insisted, it has inherent meaning, what are you talking about, looking back he must have thought only a shiksa could say such things. I so exasperated him in my student days when I was exploring all these heady ideas, taking it upon myself to renounce History because Lacan told me I could, when he saw himself as so much the product of History that he could never, not via Lacan or his girlfriend, find his way to rewriting it. We met each other at the wrong time, but that time and this one, too, were both part of our own History which we are continuing to write.

Lying in bed next to David as he sleeps, I think: you can see the child they were in the person that you love. When they sleep, of course, they are innocent, relaxed. But when they're awake there's something in the involuntary wrinkling of the nose when they talk, the bend and tilt of the eyes, and most of all – most of all – in the supplication of the eyebrows. Most people when they talk are just children asking for what they want, using their children's wiles to try to get it, appealing to their interlocutor's love or sense of pity. It takes love to see that child again. It takes a certain wilfulness to consider their needs as seriously as you would those of a child.

I've been living out a mad love, seizing the Other and incorporating him into myself. But the only liveable love has to maintain a certain distance. It seems more radical to accept your lover's alterity, and with that, their essential freedom and autonomy.

I remember a day, soon after we met. We were in the forest, on an early springtime hike. It was getting dark. David said he knew where we were going but I felt panic rise in my chest like a bird, caught there, flapping maniacally. The path was narrow, and he, the more experienced hiker, walked slightly in front of me. Watching his strong legs, I fixated, to control my breathing, on the sight of the tendons behind his knees as they flexed and straightened. They were very sexy tendons. Or ligaments.

Whatever they were I loved them, and they brought me, no kidding, out of the woods.

David is new and different every day. He is not the limits of the known world. He is the enigma of other people. He meets my eye when he laughs. He has arms and a torso that are solid and made for my hands, and knees like you wouldn't believe.

Clémentine comes to London to see me. We go out for curry, we walk on the Heath, we go to the National Gallery and see Hans Holbein's *The Ambassadors*, a painting I have read about in Lacan and she has read about in John Berger but neither of us has ever seen in person. Berger, she tells me, writes about the conflict between the realism of the ostensible subject of the painting – these two clearly very important men, but also everything else, down to the most minute detail on the mosaic floor, the men's furs, the intricate work of goldsmiths and jewellers – it's a material history of a certain class in 1533. And then there's this insane wonky skull.

If he had rendered it in the same naturalist vein as the rest of the painting, Clémentine says, it would have lost all its meaning. I mean it still would have been a memento mori in the classical sense, a vanitas, but it wouldn't have disoriented us the way it does, the way the thought of death *has* to, for the memento mori to work. So it's not just like something we take for granted along with the rubies and the lute, like, oh yeah, death too, but like – here she puts a dramatic hand against her forehead and pretends to swoon – *oh my god, death!*

OK, she says, that's my *Ambassadors*, or Berger's *Ambassadors* anyway; now you do yours.

OK I'll try. Let me see. First of all, only the guy on the right is an ambassador; the other one is a bishop. But I don't think Lacan says that, I just remember being struck by the fact that they're two French guys in England and that is apparently enough to elevate them both to the role of ambassadors? But Lacan. He's struck by the fact that at this particular moment in history when the concept of the individual is emerging, as well as a new theory of perspective, Holbein gives us this distortion, this piège à regard. He goes so far as to call it castrating, meaning that it cuts across our vision, it interrupts our sense of reality. Everything in the painting is there for a reason, to show something – all the scientific instruments, the globe, the books – but the skull doesn't *show* anything. The meaning of the painting is the experience of looking at it. Its meaning is constructed temporally, through the process of looking at it. Just as for Lacan the subject is always in a state of construction, the subject itself is a process. Things are always changing, we are always changing. Your experience of the painting is incomplete until you realise what that weird image is at the bottom, the skull. For Lacan, this incompletion is the source of all desire. The basic, constitutive lack. We are all lacking and it will never be any different.

But now we know what the painting is of, she says. We've figured it out, we've completed it.

Only for a moment. When we return to the painting we may not remember it. It will never not be distorted. Our gaze is always partial.

I always remember it, she says.

Later, back at home, Clémentine is making dinner for us, chopping vegetables for a stir-fry, she has her back to me, her spine long beneath her T-shirt, and I think how sad we were, these two intelligent women in a museum, trading the insights of great men, letting their vision stand in for our own. What were we trying to prove? At dinner she charms David, because of course she does.

That night I dream about being back in the National Gallery, which is also, somehow, the Louvre, and I am at once myself at this age, and also very young, as when my parents first took me there. But as I walk through the museum, both alone and with my parents, I realise there is a passageway that leads to my apartment, and that I'm about to be back in that dream where I find another part of the apartment I didn't know existed, that I will be able to fill up and make my own.

I've come to see these dreams as a delicate balance between fulfilment and lack, the only point at which we can stand to live. Maybe we want more space in our homes when they are new to us and their interiority is a mystery. But when we have lived in them for years we know all their nooks and crannies, we think we have exhausted the space they offer, and worn down the floorboards.

We keep dreaming of new wings, of more space, but these dreams are more about the wish to live more profoundly in the ones we have, than a desire to sell up, move out, resettle.

On Clémentine's last night we go to see a French band we both like play at a little venue near Old Street, dark with people smoking the occasional illicit cigarette, the kind of place where the owners don't care, and everyone misses the days before the ban, when we couldn't see each other clearly through the smoke, but perhaps we felt things more intensely as a result. It is a sit-down-and-listen kind of place, and we grab a table not too far from the front and drink our beers in the close, companionable heat. The lead singer has a voice like a woodwind, a warmly timbred alto, and when the band begins to play a Cowboy Junkies cover of a Velvet Underground song I dissolve into some liquid version of myself mixed with world, with the warm bentwood chair I'm sitting in, with the scuffed mosaic floor, with the French singer who is slightly out of place in London, dépaysée, with the husky insistent bass guitar, with Clémentine, who slips an arm around the back of my chair. Her arm isn't touching me, but I am encircled by her, by the music.

By the time the singer reaches that heart-healing end of the song, as the guitarist slides through the never not surprising chords of the bridge, notes of bright acidity in the otherwise warm liquid of the music, I have, quite simply, arrived elsewhere, gone further than Old Street, been transported back to a place I haven't been in a very long time, felt feelings of safety and origin I thought had escaped me forever. Or maybe, in fact, I am somewhere I have never, ever been.

In the early morning when it is not quite light I slip into the guest bedroom and climb into bed with Clémentine. David sleeping in the other room, we touch one another in ways we couldn't in Paris. The shock of being with a woman, the feel of her under my hand, soft hair, slick sex, all depth, sinew, opening, soon gives way to the uncanny feeling from my dream, finding new spaces, new places to be, to dwell, as if her body were a place I was visiting, at once unfamiliar and utterly known to me. When our eyes meet the feeling vanishes, she takes her body back from me, even as she unfolds it to me; her eyes take me in and keep me out.

By the time we wake up, David has gone to work. He will be wondering where I went in the early hours. Will he have seen my bag still there, my keys in their place, will he have deduced that I am with Clémentine?

I make some coffee, and we sit at the table. I don't know what to do with my body besides press it to hers, but she is on the other side of the table, and it seems she wants to talk.

So, she says.

So, I say.

You left Paris in a hurry.

I did, I say.

Jonathan and I talked before I came here, she says. He told me you two were involved again. And he told me you weren't involved any more.

And you came anyway?

I came anyway.

Why did he tell you, if it was over?

He said he felt dishonest keeping it from me.

You're not angry? Or jealous.

I don't own him. He can do what he likes. We're not married, she says.

You think being married makes a difference?

It might. It places a relationship within a certain moral framework, let's say, that it doesn't otherwise have to occupy. She sips her coffee. She is as always preternaturally calm. But the vulnerability is there in the way her hand shakes, in the way her eyes don't quite meet mine. I want to know what Clémentine wants, what she really wants, not the story she's telling herself, or me, or Jonathan, and I can't find a way to ask her. I realise I don't know where I stand with Clémentine, where I've ever stood with her. We have taken our relationship to another level, and she's acting like nothing has changed. Or, perhaps, like it had been on that level all along.

I don't know what you're telling me, I say.

I'm not telling you anything. Don't worry about it. I just didn't want you to think you couldn't be open and honest with me about how you're feeling, about Jonathan, about David, about what we did this morning.

She takes a deep breath. I have to tell you something. She sounds so serious that I grip the table. I feel oddly light, like none of this is real, like I might float away back into my real life.

When we were unpacking our boxes, I came across some of Jonathan's papers.

His papers?

His . . . papers. You know what I mean, like old cards, stuff from high school, pictures of his mom.

OK, and?

And in his papers there was a picture of you.

I freeze.

It's clearly from a really long time ago, you're on vacation somewhere, your hair is blowing in the wind, right across his face.

It was a long time ago, I say. I didn't realise he had a copy of that picture.

It was on printer paper. He printed it out.

Were you angry? I ask, feeling oddly disconnected, as if I were speaking with a patient.

Well I didn't realise it was you, at first, I just thought it was a picture of an ex-girlfriend. I had only just met you. But when I went back to your place to give you the Janet Malcolm, I thought, Anna looks very familiar to me and I don't know why, I felt like I knew you already. It wasn't until you came to the party, and you and Jonathan recognised each other, that I realised you were the girl in the picture. *Then* I was angry. Absolutely incensed. I felt like you'd both known the whole time we were getting to know each other, I felt like you were plotting behind my back, I tore up the picture and left the pieces on the counter and went out. When I got home he'd cleaned them up. We never talked about it.

But you didn't say anything to me.

I felt caught, she says, my principles dictated that I leave the two of you alone to live out whatever story you needed to, it didn't concern me. But I also felt like it *did* concern me, like I was directly implicated, some kind of bridge between you. I wanted you both, and you both wanted me, don't interrupt me please, I know you did even if you didn't know it yet, and it felt wrong, somehow, I felt left out. She wipes the back of her hand across her eyes, a smudge of last night's eyeliner drawing a line across her cheek. I feel a crushing sense of responsibility but I don't know for what.

I think, she says, I think you should come back to Paris. I think there's nothing for you here except David's job. Your work is there, your patients are there, everything that makes you who you are is there. Come home and finish your kitchen. David will be back soon enough and you can see what's what when you're in the same place, a familiar one, not here, where it's so different and foreign that you don't have your bearings and you might make the wrong decision.

I don't know, I tell her, trying to be honest. I don't know if I can come back, knowing you're living with him, sleeping with him, making plans for the future.

You don't care about Jonathan, she says. You only think you do. He's just something you can't let go of. Clémentine has the lightest, barest snot shaving sticking out of her perfect small nostril. It moves as she breathes in and out, like a flag. It undermines everything she is saying, makes it all slightly ridiculous. She strikes me as an eminently rational child, old before her time, as if her very nature were against her nature. She has an uncanny ability to see through the stories we tell about ourselves and each other, yet she seems unaware that she, too, is bound up in these stories. I don't think she's right, on this last point, but I am impressed by her belief in her own rationality. She reminds me, for a moment, of Esther.

Clémentine leaves that afternoon, and I listen to a France Culture podcast while I tidy up the flat, an interview with the great Lacanian analyst and philosopher Colette Soler. I strip Clémentine's bed as she says something like there are moments in our lives when we are faced with choices, irreversible choices. She is talking about Lacan and desire, and what he said about giving in to it. For Lacan, she says, to give in to desire is to cede who we are, on an intimate level. Then a snippet from Lacan himself, speaking in his peculiar old-fashioned voice. *Deranged desires, disorganised, deregulated desires.* We are made of desire, he says, made of what we don't have.

As I load up the washing machine, I think, he's not wrong, but it also isn't the great tragedy or moral infraction he thinks it is. Giving in to desire is *part* of who we are, we have desires, we identify them, we follow them, we live in them, we can't keep them at a distance.

Moving back into the living room I clear up a pair of David's shoes which have been sitting under the coffee table for a week, put them in the closet. Then I think maybe I should put them back: if he wants to wear them, he will not think to look in the closet. But he must, I have decided, learn to look in the official places for things instead of leaving them all over the house. His nail scissors, his lens case, his socks. On some level, I am not made for co-domesticity. Why do I stay with David, then, instead of leaving him, freeing us both to pursue whatever desires might arise? Why do I continue to love David, to put away his shoes, his socks? I don't understand why the love keeps going with some people when with others it so often simply goes? Or carries on underground, ready to be tapped into? We don't have a child to keep us together, so why? I put his lens case back in the bathroom, I wipe down the counter, I fill a glass from the tap, as I drink the unfiltered water I miss, momentarily, my Brita.

When I leave for Paris, I tell David I love him, and that we're getting through this.

I walk in the front door, expecting my half-destroyed apartment, and instead I find my new kitchen, the hammering and smashing and debris neatly folded into this clean, admittedly not very original space, with its metro tiles and butcher-block counters. Our open shelving, our nothing to hide. Beautiful tommettes, new and old at once. I make a mental note to text Mehdi my thanks. The dishwasher is so new I don't know how to use it. It doesn't have a basket for silverware, just a top shelf with little nodes in it which I assume is for the silverware but I have no idea how it might fit. Googling *how to load silverware in dishwasher* I come across a meme that says that in every household there is a person who loads their dishwashers like a Swedish architect and a person who loads it like a racoon on meth. I have gone from architect to racoon.

The scaffolding is still up outside, we're still a building enshrouded, but inside there is new life. I am very pleased to meet my new old kitchen that doesn't know me at all. I feel a twinge of regret as I remember the owls – they were friendly, after all, and without them, there is nothing directly linking me to whoever hung them. There are no more ghosts here, the faint chemical odour that hovers in the air has surely cleared them out, and for a moment I feel lonely.

I order in some food, put my feet up, fall asleep in front of my laptop.

But before that I send a couple of emails to some patients.

In the morning the sound of the ravalling is gentle. Just a quiet scuffing as they put the final touches on the building.

I think if I closed my eyes, and listened only to the sounds and smelled the smells, I would know I was in Belleville without being told. But then, if I closed my eyes, I wouldn't see the Eiffel Tower, like our own very toy, down in the wealthy city below.

Running feels good, as I inhale the sharp cold air, as it oxygenates my body, as I keep my rhythm around and down the hills. At the bakery, my friend greets me warmly. Hello! he says, and where have you been? Have you been time-travelling? No, I say, just travelling. I've been in London. Though now that you mention it, it was like visiting the twenty-first century, or even the twenty-second. Bah, he says, in spite of it all I'd rather stay in the twentieth. The long twentieth century, I say. Very long. There are twentieth-century people I'd really rather not leave behind. Do you know the music of Erik Satie? he asks. I do a bit, why? He refused time. The time signatures other composers use, he says, he didn't like their constraints, their regularity. Instead he wrote in what he called *absolute time*. I like the sound of that, I say.

At my office window, I watch the family across the way sit down to lunch. The daughter looks like a doll, playing with a doll. The mother disappears as she moves across the room, visible only when she walks in front of the windows. I refocus on the windows themselves, the peeling paint around the frame and above the gutters, the places on the façade where pollution has darkened the cream colour of the building, the dead plants in the window boxes of their upstairs neighbour, the family probably thinks they know their building so well, when in fact there is so much of it that escapes their view. A few leaves are still clinging on, living in absolute time.

Clémentine at the door tonight, though I hoped it would be Jonathan, or why not both of them together, I don't know, honestly, which of them I want more now. She looks shaken. Welcome back, she says, weakly. Someone broke in to our flat.

Oh my god. Are you OK?

We're fine, we weren't home. They took our computers. Not much else to take.

Did you have your writing backed up?

Yes, she says, thank goodness, it's up there, she makes a gesture towards the ceiling, in the Cloud. My writing is all around us. But they busted up the lock and now we can't close the door. Jonathan is there now dealing with the locksmith.

Even now hearing his name in her mouth makes me feel a strange combination of elation and distress. He's there, he's dealing with the locksmith, he's hers, I can't be with him, I don't want him anyway, I wish he would leave me alone, he is leaving me alone, he's with the locksmith.

The police came, too, she says, we had to file a report in order to make an insurance claim. Is it OK if I stay here a bit? She doesn't wait for an answer, slips in the door, takes me to bed, and I think: this is all I want, her body, her taste, but also her need to be protected from incursions, from people who would take things from her, in which category I obviously don't classify myself, because what could I take from her that she is not giving. Look at the way she's looking at me now.

Your kitchen! she says in the morning, getting herself a glass of water. And are you happy now?

Clémentine comes over every day, and some days we sleep together, and some days we try not to but end up fucking anyway. It has happened; we need each other now. I need her, I am able to say, but I don't understand this need, I have never been with a girl before, never knew I wanted a girl, until I wanted her, her body in her mesh bra, her mesh panties, my fingers on her, in her, learning what to do, afraid of being wrong, letting myself be led, it feels right, we keep going. Her hipbone in the morning light. Her body contracting under mine. My body one muscle that contracts and releases and contracts again, under her tongue, her fingers, her thighs. I think fleetingly of Jonathan, wonder is this a way to be close to him again, or was it always about Clémentine, this whole time? I try to turn my questions off. No what does this mean. It means in and of itself; alone it has meaning.

We don't say things like I am yours and you are mine, we don't make plans beyond the following weekend, where we'll eat, where we'll walk. We are each pinned in our situations; we couldn't afford to run away together and we know it without discussing it. All her radical politics, her Deleuzian critique of psychoanalysis, can't spring us free.

The robbery has left a deep impression on her. She keeps talking about seeing her clothing and jewellery strewn all over the apartment, the violation of it. There are new, stronger locks on their doors, but she says she doesn't feel safe. It must have been someone in the building who buzzed them in, she says, or maybe they learned the code, it's not hard. I remember when we were apartment-hunting for this place, we saw a flat further down the hill, and while we were standing outside waiting for the agent to let us in to see it, a marcheuse walked past us. She called out the code to us, over her shoulder. Suffice it to say, we didn't take the flat.

Clémentine talks about the robbery every day, going over it again, and I listen. As time goes on the idea occurs to her that they could move. Some days she cries. When she turns up at the door I don't know who I'm letting in, my ex-lover's girlfriend, my own lover, a patient, a friend. I adore her in all her roles but necessarily have to stand in different places with relation to her, depending on which one it is today; there are different levels of distance that are allowable and necessary, and other times impossible to overcome. When I put my mouth to her mouth, I have to be sure I'm not crossing a line; she wants me, but is it right for her to want me? I tell myself that in the end, she bears her own responsibility for turning to me in this way, and that she is gathering information about the kind of life she wants.

And what kind of information am I gathering?

It is confusing, for me, to be with another woman; the script isn't pre-written, as with a man, where they have the upper hand by default, and I have to fight with them for it, but equality is not always given with a woman. I want her, and she wants me, but is that enough? What are the ethics here? What does this mean?

I don't know where our boundaries lie now and I make the mistake of asking her about Jonathan. This is, apparently, the one area I'm not allowed into, the place where her calm rationality breaks down. It happened because she was leaving to go home, and I was feeling particularly needy, I wanted her to stay with me, or I wanted Jonathan to come, or I was just so fucking completely fed up with David being in London I couldn't stand myself for a minute longer, or life, the unassuageable yawning gulf in the centre of my being that demands to be filled with sex and love and food and buying things and kitchens and kittens on the internet or all of these things at once, made me say, as she was putting her shoes on, all your radical politics and he's the person you go home to?

She shrugs. The heart wants what it wants.

It does, sure, but it's our responsibility to think about what we want and why we want it, we can't just close our eyes to our desires.

Yes, we can, she says, and I think you should try it sometime, she says, bristling. Why do you have to explain everything to yourself? Or demand that other people do the same thing? Why can't something just be?

The compulsion to repeat, I begin, it has a hold on us that we can try to break—

Oh fuck off with your Freud, Anna, seriously, she says. I'm not your fucking student. Just fuck off for once.

She starts to leave, and turns back, and puts her arms around me.

Maybe I like the way it holds me, she says.

Jonathan comes to see me, and we have the same conversation I have recently had with Clémentine, in reverse. He sits on the coffee table. I sit nearby, on the couch, and wait.

So. You and Clémentine.

I'm starting to think we need to sit down all three of us. Don't – don't make that joke.

And it's just a little adventure for you, right? Because you're not going to leave your husband and become a lesbian or anything.

I honestly don't know, Jonathan, I don't think so, but I would prefer not to think about it at the moment. He's not here, and you're not here, and she is.

But you know I wanted to be here, it's just – circumstances. He finds a rubber band beside him on the table, picks it up and plays with it, stretching it, wrapping it around a finger, watching the blood gather. The conversation feels similarly blocked and pointless. I can't square what he's saying with what he said, out on the rue de Belleville, the day before I left for London. I can't figure out what it is he wants from me. What do you want from me? I ask finally. He shoots the rubber band into a corner of the room.

You know, he says finally, it all reminds me of something that happened right when we got together. The first time.

What exactly?

We met through friends at that bar, but you had been there the week before and met other friends of mine.

That sounds vaguely familiar.

It came out that you had been kissing one of those guys the previous week. And I got really angry, because it made me feel like you just went to that bar and kissed a new guy there every week.

Ah. I do remember that. I remember liking that it made you jealous.

Well it never sat right with me. It made me feel, from the get-go, like you might be someone I couldn't quite trust.

But I didn't even know you the previous week. Weren't you out hooking up with girls too?

I wasn't, he said.

So you were judging me, from the outset. And now you're judging me again, this is confirming something you've always thought about me.

I'm trying to understand devotion, he says, and for the first time I hear Clémentine in his voice. Devotion, and the way it can move. Like with my father and my stepmother. I don't think the fact that he married her means he loved my mother any less, though I did think that for a long time. Are you happy now? I'm finally talking to you about my father.

Go on, I say.

He gets up and walks over to the window, turns his back on me, speaks as if to the city. I think I worried that even if my mom were alive, he'd still have gone off with Sylvie. He was married to someone else before my mother, I know that, and he left her for my mom, when he met her in London.

All this desire slipping around, it must have made you very uneasy.

I didn't know what it all meant, how if you loved someone enough to marry them you could then go and love someone else. It makes me not understand devotion. Or it makes me suspicious of it.

I think, I say, I thought we understood one another because

we were both by nature jealous people, but maybe not, maybe jealousy keeps you isolated somehow, it's not something that can join you to another person. Jealousy doesn't see or understand anything but itself.

He turns back to face me. You're fucking with Clémentine's transference, he says, changing the subject. I was helping her.

OK you've lost me now.

Do you know why she was in the hospital? Did she ever tell you that?

She didn't, I say, I didn't want to pry. And I'm not sure you should tell me either. It should come from her.

It was because of that guy, he says. Her girlfriend's dad. He did a number on her. Annihilated her self-esteem. Drove her into an eating disorder. Her parents think he groomed her for years.

You've discussed this with her parents? Jesus, Jonathan, it's not like she's a minor.

They brought it up with me. I think they were concerned about her going to live with another older man. They worried it was a pattern. I told them they could trust me to take care of her. In the kitchen now, leaning with his back against the new butcher's block countertop. When will I get used to there no longer being a partition between these two rooms. That he can just walk, like that, so freely between them. It is still so odd.

You don't need me to tell you that that's not a reason for her to stay with you, I say. You know that's ridiculous even as you're sitting here telling me. And honestly, she hasn't told me these things and it feels like a violation of her trust, somehow, for you to tell me.

Why shouldn't I give you important information about the person you're sleeping with? I see a fury that has rarely emerged in the years I've known him. He wants to tell me, fine, he's telling me, he has to be the bearer of knowledge, the layer-down of the law. To assign everyone to their places, so he can experiment with different viewpoints, see how they feel, the lover, the father, the protector, the interloper, so that he might, perhaps, finally, find his own. He doesn't realise that a place is only ever temporary at best, a device for containment and not an enduring identity.

His phone vibrates, and he pulls it from his pocket. It's Clémentine. I have to go.

I'm sorry to have made you so angry, I say, walking him to the door. I honestly thought—

If it's any consolation, it was only you I meant to want.

Towards the end of the day there is Clémentine at the door. Anna! she says, rummaging in her tote bag. Lamia gave me this book and it's incredible and I wanted to tell you about it right away. It's about this woman – fuck that's not it – she's in love with this guy and so much so – ah *there* it is, and she pulls out a copy of Chris Kraus's *I Love Dick* – so much so that she is willing to debase herself by writing him all these letters! And so it isn't really about him at all, it's really about desire and daring to make art, and the importance, for a woman artist, of being blatantly narcissist in order to actually become who she is. But! she says, flipping through the dog-eared pages, this is what I wanted to tell you about. She finds the passage, reads aloud in her accented English. *Desire isn't lack, it's surplus energy – a claustrophobia inside your skin.*

That's it, she says. That's why I can't get on with Lacan. I don't see my desire as a lack of something. Not a phallus, not some substitute for it, but like – it's like some people plant this seed of energy in you, that loads of other people don't. And as it takes root I feel like I'm shimmering with excitement, and need to get physically close to them, to share it, to feel *their* shimmer. Do you know what I mean? And I think I know what she means, I think I have been trying to share Clémentine's shimmer this whole time, and I pull her closer, and then she says something that makes me wonder what exactly we've been doing this whole time.

I really think you need to rethink your theory of desire, Anna. I think if you weren't so often *wanting* but *sharing* you'd be so much happier with your lovers. She throws her arms around me and gives me a squeeze, then kisses my cheek. It's my birthday next week and Jonathan and I are going out of town for a bit. We might be moving soon, she says, I don't know, we've talked about it. We'll stay in touch, yeah?

And then she's gone.

I have to go for a walk after that. In a second she has gone from being someone I love, or think I could love, to someone who's playing a role, and watching herself do it. I love Clémentine's shimmer but it seems to me for the first time constructed, not natural; willed, not produced. She read the giddy parts of *I Love Dick* without the heavy stuff, the feelings of shame and failure, the marital estrangement. She missed the parts about what it takes to live with other people, the unsolvable problem of alienation between the self and the other, the constraints they place on you, the small spaces you have to occupy together. Kraus calls desire a *claustrophobia* inside your own skin – a need to get out of the body house, to jump inside someone else's for a change. How does she account for *that*? She didn't, she left that part out. There was still so much to talk about. I was left frustrated, as if there were soap left on my skin and the hot water had gone.

What she said sounded like a wish for how sex and desire could work, not an insight into them. Where was the unconscious, where was trouble, where despair? I am jolted into my own body by a bright late-afternoon sun as I open the front door of the building and step out on to the street. Belleville looks completely different, since I've been back from London. Maybe it hasn't changed at all, I'm just seeing it with new eyes. I walk downhill a bit, make a left. Since when is there a crêperie on the rue de Tourtille? And a hipster coffee shop? Across from which an atelier with an African mask in one window and a Keith Haring in the other, but if it were really a Keith Haring you'd think the place would look a little more spiffy and less random, there are hand-painted paterae hung above the vitrines, I like them better than the fake Haring. I look at my Google Maps to figure out what kind of place it is but it isn't on the map. It doesn't have a virtual presence, only a real one, how strange that these days we can only understand what things are in a realm other than that of bricks and mortar, flesh and blood, perhaps that's always been the case, what can we know by looking with our eyes, anyway. I think of all the artisans who used to live and work here, the shoemakers, the glass-blowers, the printers, mechanics, now replaced by potters and weavers and 'makers' of all sorts, I guess it doesn't matter, as long as they're making something. It's all so bougie now it's hard to believe this was once an îlot insalubre. Still. I miss people who were just people and did everyday things and didn't prendre la tête about where they ate and where they went out. Bobo Paris, new Paris, stripping away my soul. À N O S S Œ U R S. The signs are all over the city, Clémentine and Lamia and all their friends have been busy. E L L E LE Q U I T T E I L LA T U E. It occurs to me for the first time that she was actually upset about what happened with me and Jona-than, and that her reading of *I Love Dick* was a way of telling me I had been wrong, that I had misunderstood love, that he had chosen her in the end, and she had chosen him. For now, I add, she's with him for now, but it's clear she wants to be with a woman, she just doesn't know how to authorise herself to not be with a man, a man like Jonathan, so correct, good-looking and smart and trying so hard to resolve the unresolvable contradictions of being French, Jewish, male, human, being a body and feeling its desires, making those desires socially acceptable, circuiting desire into appropriate relationships, and, above all, holding people responsible for their mistakes. I don't remember him being so paternalistic. I make a right on to the rue Ramponeau, where the famous Marxist writer lives, where there are tiled buildings and postmodern architecture that I don't understand but David tells me is significant. By choosing to walk some places I am choosing not to walk others, byways not taken as paths of thought left unexplored, the city as unconscious, by refusing a destination I am opening myself to its possibilities, denying the morality of direction. I think about the opposite of the city, about small rooms, or maybe they're the essence of it, the essential cells of it, I think about claustrophobia, about desire as a place we inhabit that is possibly not big enough for two people, much less three, or four. The city as a place where we have to live together with our ghosts, that's what we're all trying to accept. More signs from the colleuses here. I remember a conversation I had with one of them, I asked her why she does it, what she hopes to get out of it, and she said she didn't know, she really didn't know what would come of it, but look, she said, you and I, we have certain rights now that our mothers didn't have, that our grandmothers didn't have, and that's because someone fought for them and didn't know how it was going to turn out, so the way I see it I'm part of this chain of women doing things and hoping it will have an impact, we're all just trying to move forward in whatever way we can. I think: walk up to the park, or down to the city? Down to the city. Past the place with the cheap beers on the boulevard, a right towards the métro, towards the place where the young woman in *Conte d'hiver* works in a hair salon, not one I've ever been able to locate. Left on the rue du Faubourg du Temple, I pass a group of young people wearing woollen hats and trench coats down to their ankles and the season's white sneakers. They are smoking, and one has a red kiss mark on his cheek which wrinkles as he takes a drag. I think unexpectedly of a pair of friends I once lost, when one of them had cancer and the other encouraged me to stop by the hospital to visit, but I didn't know them well enough, and I worried it would be awkward for all of us to have me show up in such an enclosed, ritualised, intimate space. It's only years later that I can understand it would have been a form of

embrace, another knot in the bonds of friendship, to enter that space with them; through my absence I severed whatever links had grown between us. He lived, but I never heard from them again. Further down by Goncourt is the place where I saw that woman trying on clothes in the street, a big heap of them on the ground, spilling out of the garbage bins, she was wriggling into a pair of black leggings like she was in the changing room at a dance studio. Fluctuat nec mergitur mural by the canal, he is rocked by the waves but never drowns, followed by another, paradis pour les uns pas un radis pour les autres. I see men fishing and wonder what on earth they could possibly find that would be alive and worth fishing for. They drained it a couple of years back, and everyone went to see what they would find in the bottom, twisted in the mud. Shopping carts, Vélibs, toilets, blown-out tyres, bottles. Trash. What the city of Paris accidentally lost or wanted to forget about. But if they really wanted to forget, I thought, they'd have thrown it into the Seine, not into a canal that is dredged every fifteen years. These were things people wanted to find again. I think about stopping to talk to the fishermen, but I am too shy, and continue on my way. Place de la République, kids skating, every which way, remembering the memorials here, a few years ago, running into a friend I hadn't seen in a while as we both contemplated the flowers, the candles, the pictures, the scraps of things people had left in their grief, the pens, oh right the pens. Clémentine would have been in her first or second year of university. How it all must have scared her. Was that the missing year, the one we never talked about? Was that when she went to her girlfriend's father? Down rue du Temple, past the Monoprix where I once bought an umbrella in a downpour that stopped the moment I got outside, the rue Dupetit-Thouars with the art bookshop where Clémentine bought a tote bag, the square with its playground where I once went with a friend as her toddler dug in the sandpit. Oh they've been here too.
JEANNINE FUSILLÉE PAR SON MARI 18.03.2010

ELLE NOUS MANQUE. These horrifying stories summed up in all caps and pasted to a wall, the city is screaming and no one is listening, I hope Clémentine will start a non-profit or a lobbying group, or something like that, if there's anyone who has the necessary confidence it's her. We need heroines. The government holds meeting after meeting and nothing ever comes of it, how can it, it's women trapped in their houses with dangerous men, it's all of masculinity that has to be looked at head on, confronted, rethought. Maybe that's why she keeps loving men, maybe that's what she's trying to do. Soon it's the Marais, the place Renée Vivien, the galleries, the expensive clothing shops that weren't here when I was a student, I walk for a long time among the tourists and the teenagers, and take a right on the rue Rambuteau to pass Beaubourg, and I suddenly remember that it was at the cinema across the street that Jonathan and I saw that Wong Kar-wai film years ago when we were young, I try to remember the name of it, I can't. I wind my way through the narrow streets of Les Halles. There is much construction happening in this neighbourhood lately, widening streets and renovating the old houses, and of course the new canopée over what used to be the food market, the belly of Paris. Suddenly remember from the book Clémentine gave me that Robert Desnos's father was a poultry dealer here. Some of the houses are covered with scaffolding, and on one of them I notice a construction worker in a woollen ski cap sitting up high, shielded from the street by the netting. His feet dangle off toward the ground; he watches the crowd below with what looks, from here, like curiosity. I see him noticing me noticing him, and I look away, embarrassed. Down the boulevard de Sébastopol. I can't believe she and Jonathan would move out, just like that. I wonder yet again what she sees in him. I know what I see in him, but she is so young, her life still open, not determined; she doesn't want him, I know he isn't what she wants. But I can see he numbs some lack for her. She is contenting herself with him, but behind him there is only more wanting. Does she realise that? There are so many things I want to explain to Clémentine, but no sooner does the thought cross my mind than I hear the condescension in it. Is she more at ease with ambiguity than I am? Or is it just arrogance? Fucking Jonathan, I wish he hadn't said anything about her girlfriend's dad to me. But at the same time, I'm glad he did; I see her confidence in a different way, now; if she was inviolable then she can't have been violated. A memory of her mouth and I stumble. I recognise the Tour Saint-Jacques a little ahead. When I was in grad school, in my early years alone in Paris, I was preoccupied by it, by the fact that it had been in a state of restoration for many years, I was in a hurry for them to finish up, I wanted to see it, I studied it obsessively, and for so many years, as it stood there under the scaffolding, I idealised it, waiting for the day this medieval tower would be revealed to us, if only they would hurry up, and I imagined what it would look like, and scrutinised the photograph Brassaï took that Breton uses in *Nadja*, *à Paris la tour Saint-Jacques chancelante*, the unsteady Tour St Jacques, half under scaffold. As it was peeled back the tower began to reveal itself, a little bit at a time, and what turned out to have been underneath was something of a let-down, so clean and flat and nothing like what the medieval builders had in mind, newer than new even, and I realised I loved it better with the scaffolding, when we didn't know what was taking shape beneath. Actually come to think of it it reminded me of a painting Clémentine showed me, one day when she was giving me a mini-lecture on female surrealists, called *Tomorrow is Never* by the American artist Kay Sage, what a funny name, when Clem said her name I thought she was saying *que sais-je*, or *what do I know*, the painter's name a marker for everything we're unaware of, maybe that's why this piece stayed in my memory, it shows these marble sculptures surrounded by scaffolding standing in a misty surrealist cloudscape; the bars of the scaffolding obscure the structures they're supposedly shoring up, but is any work happening on them? Difficult to say. They seem to be, like the tower, in a permanent state of being remade; their essence can only ever be glimpsed over time rather than established in one go. Like the tower itself they are dream structures. It wasn't the tower I loved so much as that exoskeleton – that testament to work, to remaking, to the possibility of transformation. I can't wait for it to get dirty again but by the time they re-reface it we'll all be dead, and maybe my grandchildren will tell their grandchildren how I used to tell them about the beautiful exoskeleton, and they'll love the construction more than the monument, too. Crossing the river, on the Pont au Change, I look to my right, as I always do, in the direction of the Eiffel Tower, no longer a little light-up toy as from the top of the Belleville hill, but something immense and legendary. And what century is it here, on the bridge? The Pont au Change has always held a particular interest for me. I read a poem in the Desnos book. Je suis le veilleur du Pont-au-Change, veillant au cœur de Paris. It's a resistance poem, written in the 40s during the Nazi occupation. One of the only times, I think, you'll read the name *Hitler* in a poem. Desnos – who would himself die in a Nazi death camp – writes that as war thunders nearby he keeps watch over Paris while it sleeps, but also, also, over the whole war-torn world. He salutes those who sleep after a long day of travail clandestin, printers, message bearers, distributers of tracts. I salute you, all of you who resist. Walking across towards the turrets of the Conciergerie, the old prison that once held Marie Antoinette, I salute all those who would have resisted, but couldn't. Those who had to stay home, who couldn't take risks, who were taken instead of fighting, those who were imprisoned, including Desnos himself; crossing the Pont au Change I salute Robert Desnos, beautiful bespectacled surrealist who wrote poetry in his sleep. *The one I love is not listening to me. The one I love does not hear me.* As I reach the Palais de Justice, the sidewalks are eerily absent, no one about, no one queuing for Sainte-Chapelle at this hour, the blue hour, I think of something Clémentine once said, during one of our talks, before everything that was going to happen had happened. Marriage is a kind of boundary, she said, it's a border protecting a country of two, and I'm against borders. Clémentine's version of intimacy, I thought, was radically open. For a while I had lived there too, in her borderless realm. With her gone will the checkpoints go back up? I cross the next bridge toward Saint-Michel, and as I look to the right to Pont Neuf I see there is attached to it a team of green men, suspended on a piece of moving scaffolding in between the bridge and the river. They appear to be cleaning the side of it. I didn't know they cleaned the bridges. I assume they're in a hurry, it's getting dark, it gets dark so early, but the days are growing longer, it's still winter but you can feel the darkness lifting, a bit more light getting in; we're on the right side of the solstice now. There are a few tourists around taking selfies, remember the selfie sticks, you never see those much any more, or maybe I don't see tourists much any more. I allow myself to look to the left. I haven't seen Notre-Dame since the fire, I never come down here. I make a left on the quai Saint-Michel and walk closer. That night we watched people sing 'Ave Maria' in the squares of Paris and I cried when the spire fell. *La flèche s'est effon-drée!* people were yelling in the streets, the way they would have centuries ago when there was no internet yet to spread the news, no TV, no radio, just word of mouth to mouth. The day after it burned, we started trying for a baby. I read that just the week before they had taken out some irreplaceable medieval statues of apostles for restoration. Lucky statues! to have been decaying at precisely the right time to be noticed, and saved. They said there were parts of the altar that were completely untouched by the roof's collapse; they said the firefighters had tears streaming down their faces; they said it was a miracle. Enough to make you a believer, someone said on TV. They say Macron wants the cathedral rebuilt within five years; he is determined for this only to be a temporary setback in the life of the ancient structure. It seems incredible that I hadn't known Clémentine then, it wasn't even a year ago. As I get closer to Notre-Dame I see more and more people. The air is getting chilly and I tighten my coat around my body, wishing I'd brought a scarf. Someone's lit a wood fire. It's probably time to head back to Belleville. I put on my headphones, search in my phone for the music I want. Joni Mitchell's guitar, finding its way through the chords of 'Night in the City', something joyful in her overlapping yodels, her voice overtaking itself in waves. The people are thronging outside the cathedral's hoardings, blocking off the parvis and the work of restoration from view. I dive into the crowd, and give myself over from thinking to feeling, and the music moves me through my city, back across the Right Bank, back up the hill, back home.

The scaffolding is down. Taking it apart made as much noise as the refacing. Lots of clattering and banging, the sound of metal scraping on the sidewalk. When I walked out this morning I saw them there, passing the rods down to one another, level by level. The inside of the building is still the same. The flaking paint on the walls, the dust gathered at the corners and joints of the stairs, the missing bits of moulding. Outside the building looks innocent, as if it had always been clean. It's good to see it again.

I go back to Esther's office soon after I return to Paris. We spoke by phone once or twice while I was in London, but now, in front of her, I feel a renewed commitment to what it is we're trying to figure out in this room together, and so much gratitude that she makes the time to do it, even if I'm paying her, even if it's her job, it doesn't diminish the fact that she is invested, she knows my story, she watches the way my thoughts go, she sees connections where I don't.

I keep going back to the first time I saw Clémentine, I say, with those plastic bags in the crook of her arm, it seems so unlike her, she does her shopping with tote bags, she never uses plastic bags or plastic wrap or anything like that, she's so good.

Why does that make her good?

Because she's thinking about the environment, she's doing her part.

And yet that day she wasn't doing her part.

No. I assume the move was hectic and she couldn't be good all the time.

So it's OK not to be good all the time?

If you're mostly good, yes I think it's OK.

And by you not doing your part, are you bad?

I will very occasionally ask for a plastic bag, I say. If I'm caught without a tote bag. If I need to save some food I'll use a freezer bag. But Clem just seems to manage, somehow, without them. She just thinks about things more than I do.

I know you to be someone who thinks about things.

I think about things but I don't do anything about it. Clémentine goes out at night and pastes up feminist signs.

Oh is that Clémentine. They're very good.

Clémentine and a bunch of other women who don't just sit at home feeling bad about themselves.

You don't usually sit at home either, Esther says. She asks how I'm feeling about work. If I'd like to get back to it yet. I tell her I've written to some patients. I don't know if I can carry their grief, their fear. Like if I come into contact with it it will infiltrate me. I can't bring it into the house. I want my office for myself.

You can't because you won't let yourself.

You think I need to figure out a way to receive their stories without letting them affect me.

I think after all this time you know how to protect yourself at work.

I don't answer. I'm not thinking about my work, but about Clémentine.

It's a lie, I say. I don't believe her story about surplus. It seems cut off from any sense of history, of mourning, of melancholy. It's a performance of liberation.

And yet, says Esther, she seems – liberated, doesn't she?

It is good to see the building again. The things we've lost we're always happy to find. No matter what we may think of them. When we find them it is like the first time we saw them, and wanted them. *The finding of an object is the refinding of it.* Everything goes on as it does; there is no form to life except maybe that of a circle. We keep playing the same song. The scaffolding is down, but it will go up again. There is no resolution.

Clémentine and Jonathan moved out not long after the *I Love Dick* day. David never knew about Jonathan, only about Clem. He doesn't talk about it, I don't know what he makes of it, I don't know if he realises there will always be some part of who I am he can't encompass, and likewise for him as well, some part of us both that doesn't even have anything to do with having sex with men or women, that is a symptom of being embodied and desiring. So much happened so quickly, we got distracted and I didn't try to talk to him about it again. I do believe this is for the best; let the silt settle. He came back to Paris when it looked like a lockdown was imminent, France closing a week before the UK, and he finished the Brexit project remotely. I think being shut up in the apartment together was exactly what we needed. Within the year we had a baby and she took over my office; I met with my patients on zoom. Sometimes when I sit in the chair and feed her, I look out over Paris, and wonder where Clémentine and Jonathan went next, and if I'll ever see them again, and what will happen then. I will never not want Jonathan. I will never not want Clémentine. I will never not want David.

And now, I will never not want my baby, it's a form of need just as physical as the others, another kind of desire.

I look at her face as she feeds, and wonder who or what will haunt her. What will she know of her past, of our loves? Where do they live? In the blood, in the heart, in these walls?

Motherhood is a new form of repetition that is also an inexorable progression forward. Every morning I take her to the childminder. Then I go for my run. And back to get the bread, where I sometimes see my friend. I often think of Clémentine, and wonder what she would say about this new institution I am now a part of, and in my three a.m. moments, when the baby's woken me repeatedly throughout the night, when I don't know how I'll ever get back to any version of the Anna who knew Clémentine, I wish she were still here to help me figure out who I am when I'm not a mother, or who else I can be when I am. There was a new sign up on the rue de Belleville the other day, right by Combat, and I like to think it was Clémentine who put it up.

TU TROUVERAS
TOUJOURS
NOTRE
SOUTIEN
SUR
LES
MURS

That morning, the morning of the scaffolding finally being gone, I ran into my friend at the threshold of the bakery. He opened the door for me. The scaffolding is down, he said. But it will go up again.

I drew closer, and fastened a kiss on his cheek, like closing the latch on a door.

2007–2023

3 rue des Lyonnais, Paris 5ᵉ;
19 rue de la Mare, Paris 20ᵉ;
51 rue de Belleville, Paris 19ᵉ;
61 boulevard de Magenta, Paris 10ᵉ;
London NW3;

finished in the writers' studio at Shakespeare & Company,
38 rue de la Bûcherie, Paris 5ᵉ.

Author's note

The signs posted by the colleuses are real; I have taken liberties with where and when they were posted but the words themselves are those of the women in the movement, to whom I give all thanks and recognition here, especially those who appeared in the documentary *Riposte féministe* (2022), directed by Marie Perennès and Simon Depardon.

In English, in order of appearance:

YOU ARE NOT ALONE

DADDY KILLED MOMMY

WE ARE ALL HEROINES

WHAT GOOD IS IT
TO BE ALIVE
IF WE HAVE TO
LIVE ON OUR KNEES?

SHE LEAVES
HIM HE
KILLS HER

STOP FEMICIDE

WE ARE
THE VOICE OF
THOSE WHO ARE NOW VOICELESS

CÉLINE
THROWN FROM A WINDOW
BY HER HUSBAND
19TH FEMICIDE

MY UTERUS
MY CHOICE

NO MEANS NO

WE WILL STOP GLUING WHEN
YOU STOP RAPING

SEXISM IS EVERYWHERE
SO ARE WE

YOU NO LONGER
WALK ALONE

IS THE COUNTRY OF THE RIGHTS
OF MEN
AFRAID OF WOMEN'S RIGHTS?

OUR SKIRTS ARE SHORT,
NOT OUR IDEAS

WARRIORS

WE WILL TALK

WELL DONE
YOU HAVE A PENIS!

QUEER REVOLUTION

THE REVOLUTION WILL BE
FEMINIST

TO OUR SISTERS

JEANNINE SHOT BY HER
HUSBAND 18.03.2010 WE MISS HER

YOU WILL ALWAYS FIND OUR
SUPPORT ON THE WALLS

Acknowledgements

For information on Erik Satie, I am indebted to Murray Baylor's edition of *Trois Gymnopédies & Trois Gnossiennes* (Alfred Music Publishing, 2007).

Other indispensable references were (of course) the work of Jacques Lacan, as well as that of Elizabeth Bowen, Éric Rohmer, Élisabeth Roudinesco, Bruce Fink, Darian Leader, Jamieson Webster and Nathalie Zajde.

'Desire can only exist by virtue of its alienation' is a line from Juliet Mitchell's introduction to *Feminine Sexuality*, ed. Juliet Mitchell and Jacqueline Rose (London: Macmillan, 1982). 'I don't want to know anything about it' is taken from Lacan's twentieth seminar, *Encore* (ed. Jacques-Alain Miller; Paris: Éditions du Seuil, 1975).

I discovered the Lacanian epigraph while reading through Cormac Gallagher's translation of *Encore*, in which he worked from unedited French transcripts, a 'pirated' version of the seminar. It's heroic work and I thank Gallagher for making it freely available online.

'Qui a déporté nos parents? – Des Français. Qui conduisait les autobus? – Des Français. Qui conduisait les trains? – Des

Français. Qui gardait les camps à Drancy, à Beaune-la-Rolande, à Pithiviers, à Gurs? – Des gendarmes français. – Qui sont venus arrêter nos parents à l'aube? – La police du 20e arrondissement.' – from *Belleville, Belleville: visages d'une planète* (ed. Françoise Morier; Paris: Créaphis, 2003), p. 70.

'Depuis que je suis marié je trouve toutes les femmes jolies' is a line from Éric Rohmer's film *L'amour l'après-midi* (1972).

The English translation of Plato's *Symposium* is the edition by Benjamin Jowett (New York: The Liberal Arts Press, 1956).

Some of the imagery in the novel was inspired by the paintings in Shannon Cartier Lucy's 2020 show *Home is a Crossword Puzzle I Can't Solve* at the Lubov Gallery in New York, notably the image of the woman cling-filmed to the bed. The tennis-shoe painting is called *Offering* (2018).

The meme about the dishwasher on p. 357 comes from a tweet by @ColeyTangerina, 23 February 2023.

Thank you to everyone at Shakespeare & Company for your hospitality and generosity, it makes me so happy to know I might have moved across the Channel but I still have a home in Paris.

Thank you Antoine and Alexandra Flochel for your hospitality and generosity, as well as Can Cab class of June '23 for camaraderie and support as I put the final touches on this manuscript!

Thank you Alba, Sarah, Emma, Sam, and everyone at Wylie.

Enormous thanks to Kaiya, Clara, Jessie, Graeme, SJ, and everyone at Chatto, and to Jenna and Lianna at Farrar, Straus and Giroux.

Thank you to Dr Amy Cohen.

Love and thanks to Amanda, Deborah F, Deborah L, Elisabeth, Harriet, Jayne, Joanna, Natasha, Rob, Rosa, Sandeep, Seb, Shannon, Stelios, Stephanie, Susan, and Sylvia.

Thank you Orkia Sumareh Touray, for looking after the most precious thing in my life – thereby allowing me to write these books.

To my family – Elkins, Eisners, and Hackbarths – I hold you all very close.

And thank you to Ben and Julien, most wondrous beings. You are home.

A Note About the Author

Lauren Elkin is the author of *Art Monsters* and *Flâneuse*, a *New York Times Book Review* notable book and a finalist for the PEN/Diamonstein-Spielvogel Award for the Art of the Essay. Her essays have appeared in *The New York Times*, *Le Monde*, *Frieze*, and *The Times Literary Supplement*, among other publications. A native New Yorker, Elkin lived in Paris for twenty years and now resides in London.

Made in the USA
Columbia, SC
23 December 2019